LEGENDARY COMICS YA

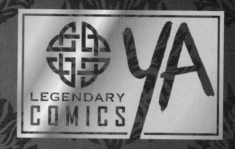

Presents

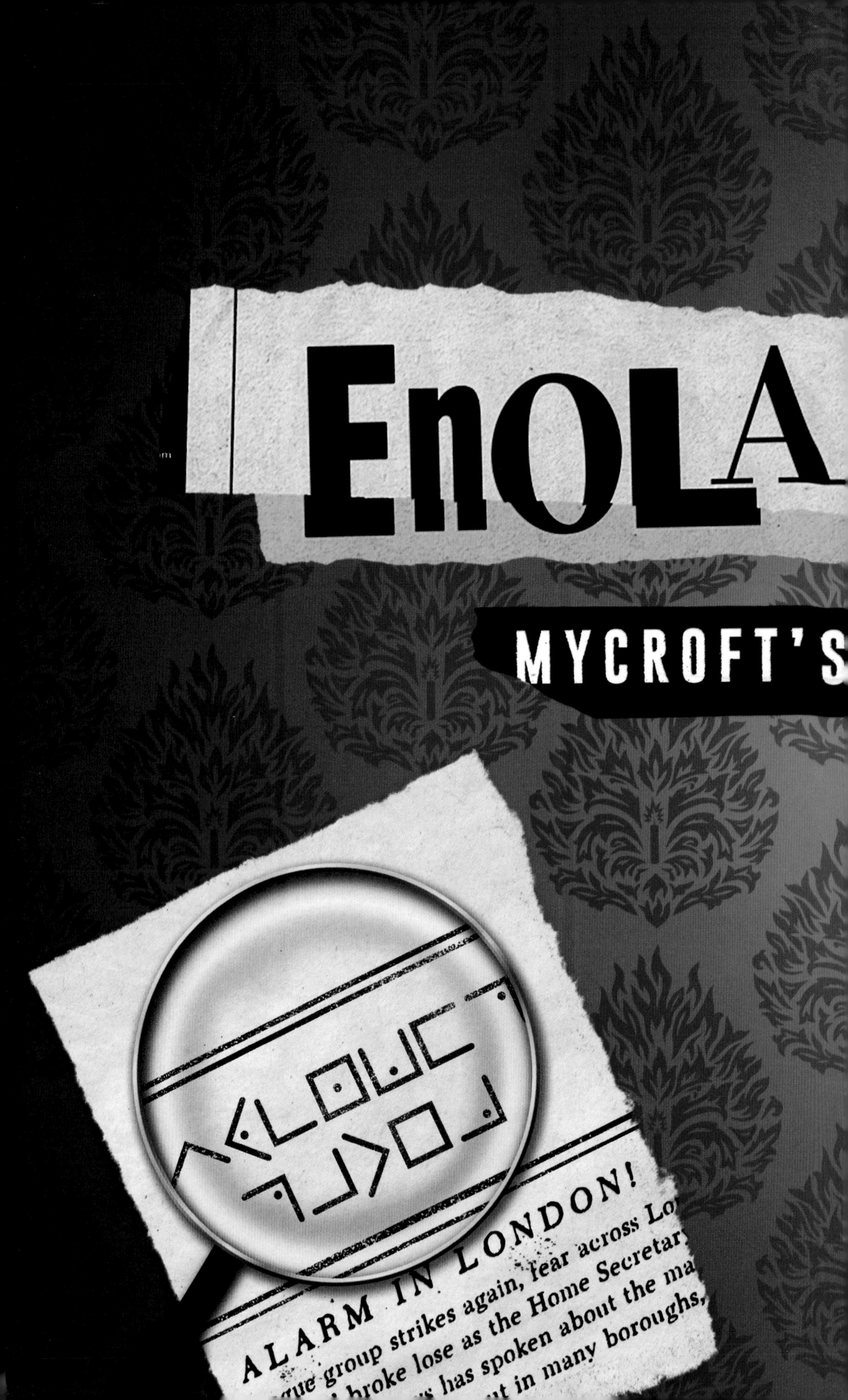
EnOLA
MYCROFT'S
ALARM IN LONDON!
group strikes again, fear across Lo
broke lose as the Home Secretar
has spoken about the ma
in many boroughs,

HOLMES

DANGEROUS GAME

ENOLA HOLMES
MYCROFT'S DANGEROUS GAME

STORY BY:
Nancy Springer

Written by:
MICKEY GEORGE

Interior Art by:
GIORGIA SPOSITO

Colors by:
ENRICA EREN ANGIOLINI

Lettering by:
HALEY ROSE-LYON

Design and Production by:
EMMA PRICE

Flats by:
SABRINA DEL GROSSO
PAULO F. CROCOMO

Cover Art by:
CAT STAGGS

Cover Design by:
TYLER SMITH
OF COMICRAFT

Logo by:
KATIE AGUILAR

Edited by:
NIKITA KANNEKANTI

Special Thanks:
ALI MENDES, ALEX GARCIA, ZAK KLINE, SARAH JARVIS,
LEGENDARY MARKETING

LEGENDARY

JOSHUA GRODE
Chief Executive
Officer

MARY PARENT
Vice Chairman of
Worldwide Production

CHRIS ALBRECHT
Managing Director,
Legendary Television

RONALD HOHAUSER
Chief Financial Officer

BARNABY LEGG
SVP, Creative Strategy

MIKE ROSS
EVP, Business & Legal Affairs

KRISTINA HOLLIMAN
SVP, Business & Legal Affairs

REBECCA RUSH
Director, Business & Legal Affairs

BAYAN LAIRD
SVP, Business & Legal Affairs

LEGENDARY COMICS

ROBERT NAPTON
Senior Vice President and Publisher

NIKITA KANNEKANTI
Senior Editor

SARA HASKELL
Director, Publishing Marketing & Sales

[Chapter One]

Bicycle
noun [c] (informal bike)

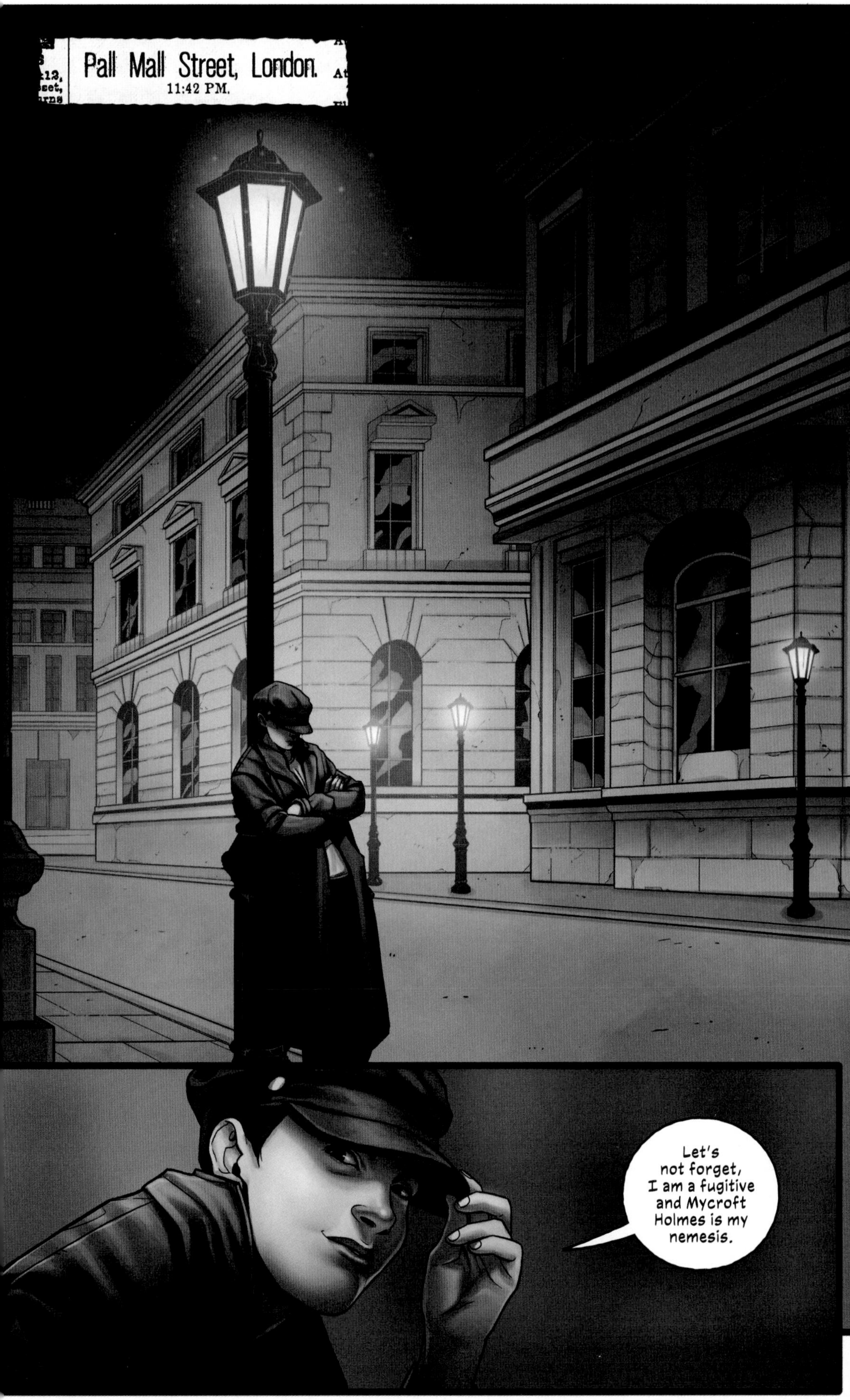
Pall Mall Street, London.
11:42 PM.
Let's not forget, I am a fugitive and Mycroft Holmes is my nemesis.

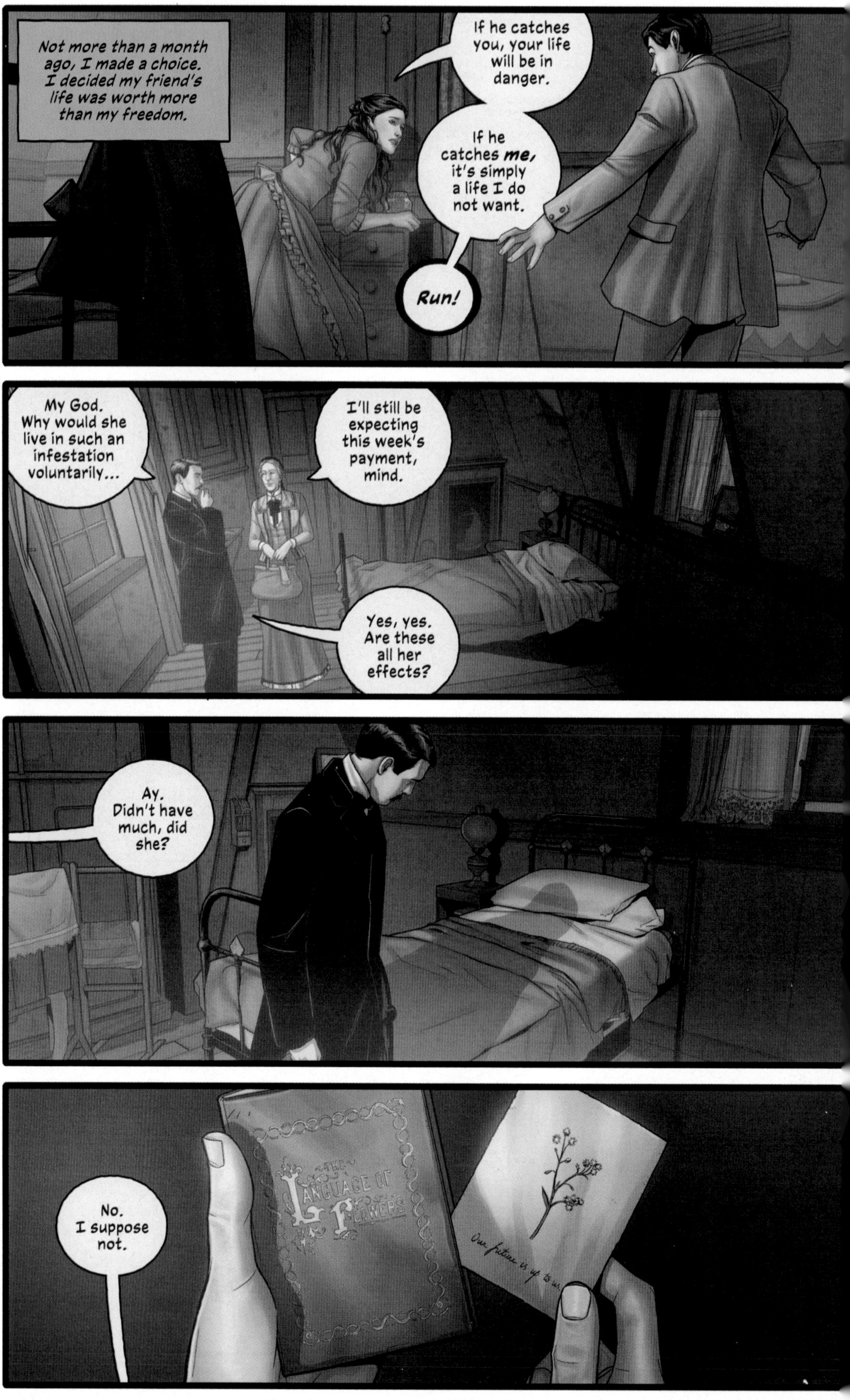

Not more than a month ago, I made a choice. I decided my friend's life was worth more than my freedom.
If he catches you, your life will be in danger.
If he catches *me*, it's simply a life I do not want.
Run!
My God. Why would she live in such an infestation voluntarily...
I'll still be expecting this week's payment, mind.
Yes, yes. Are these all her effects?
Ay. Didn't have much, did she?
The Language of Flowers
Our future is up to us.
No. I suppose not.

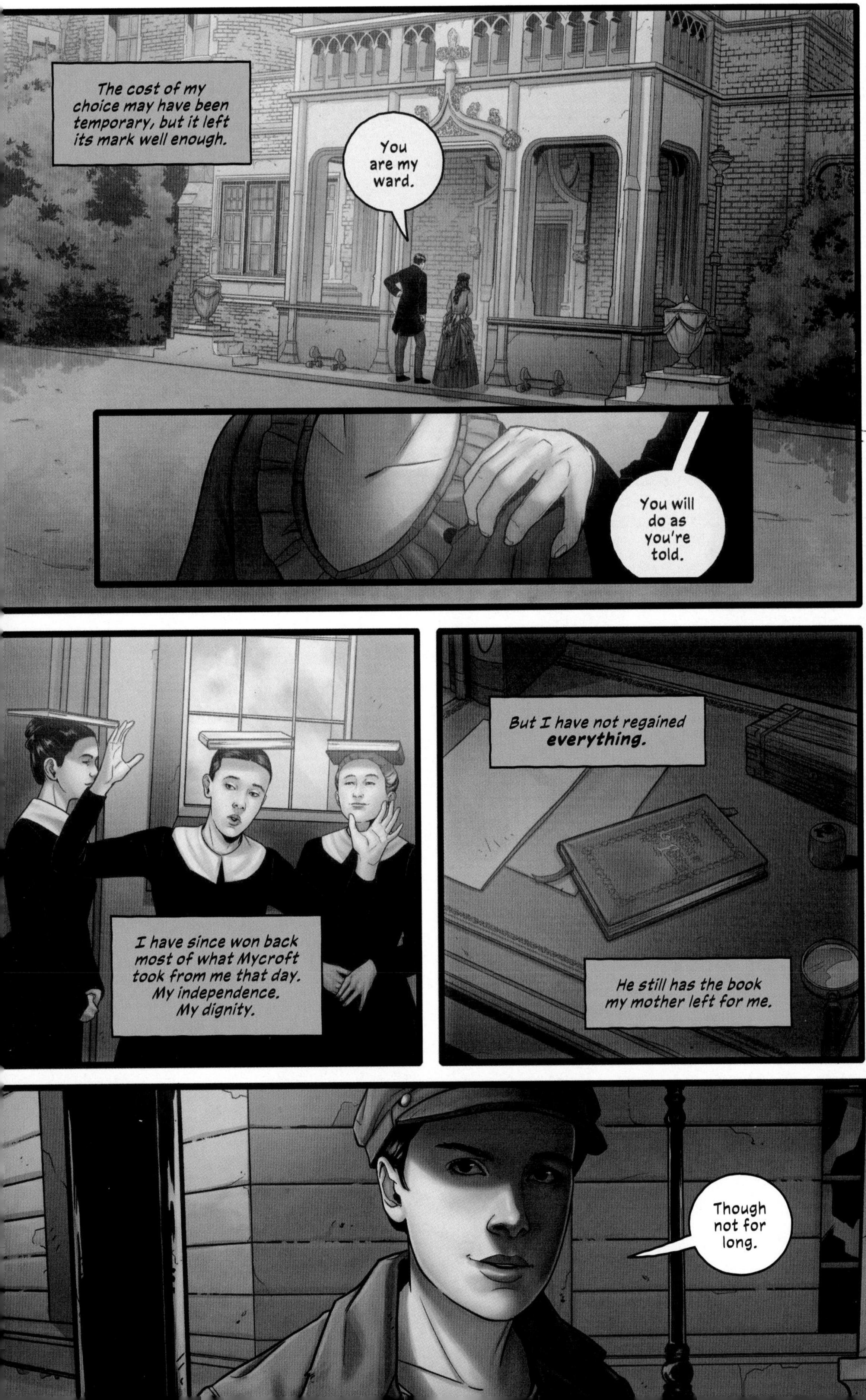
The cost of my choice may have been temporary, but it left its mark well enough.
You are my ward.
You will do as you're told.
I have since won back most of what Mycroft took from me that day. My independence. My dignity.
But I have not regained **everything.**
He still has the book my mother left for me.
Though not for long.

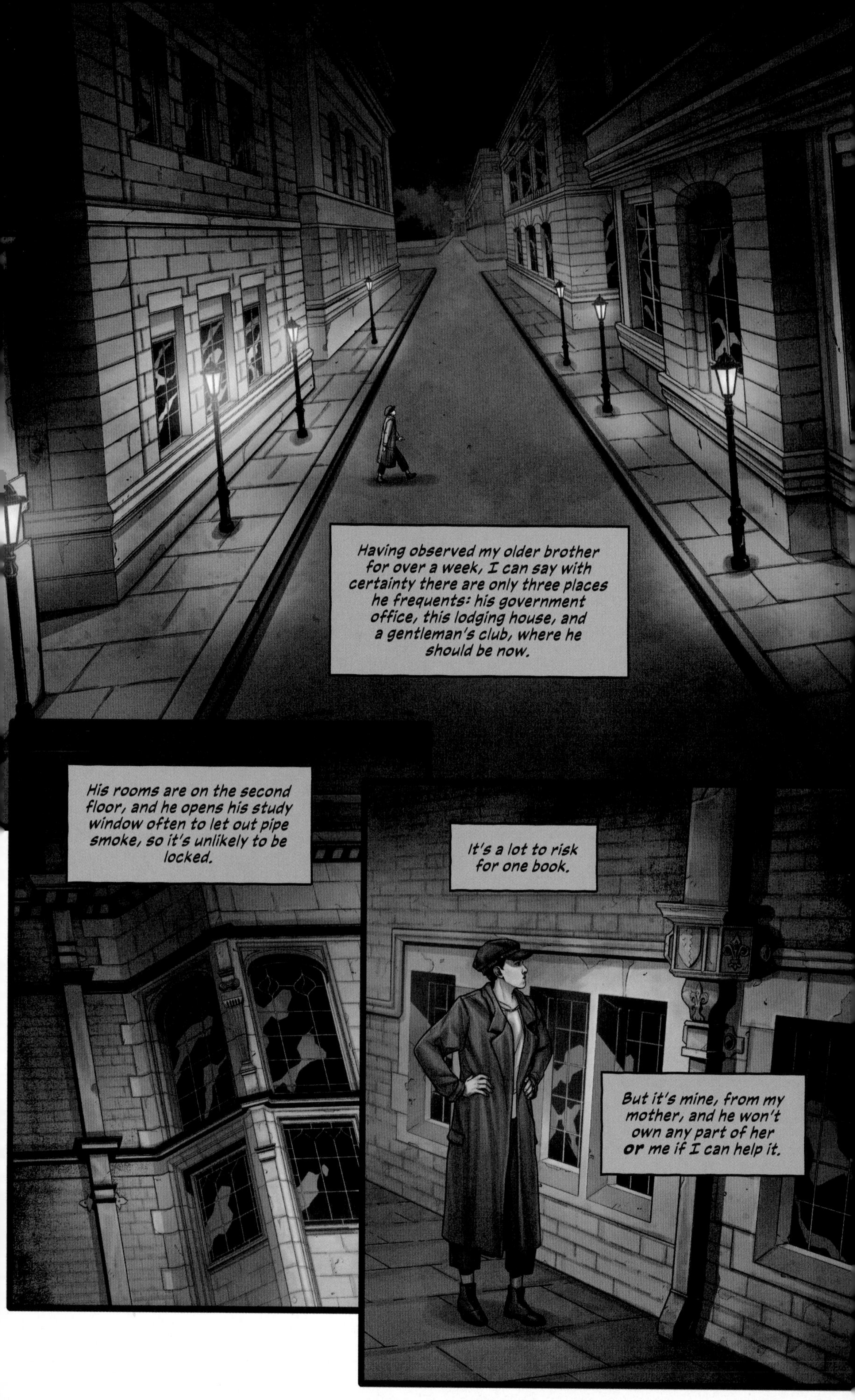
Having observed my older brother for over a week, I can say with certainty there are only three places he frequents: his government office, this lodging house, and a gentleman's club, where he should be now.
His rooms are on the second floor, and he opens his study window often to let out pipe smoke, so it's unlikely to be locked.
It's a lot to risk for one book.
But it's mine, from my mother, and he won't own any part of her **or** me if I can help it.

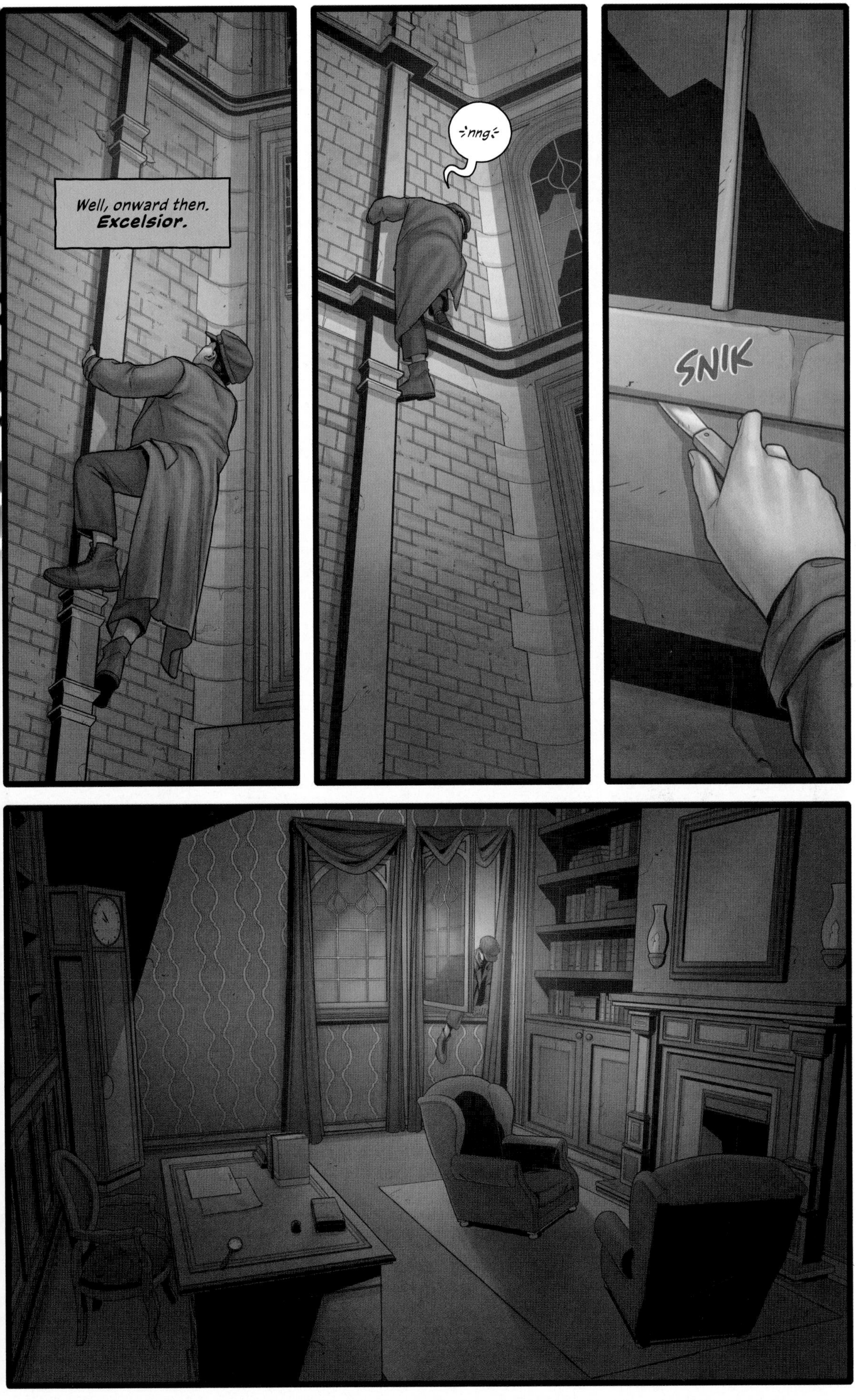
Well, onward then. **Excelsior.**
nng
SNIK

Where **is** the blasted thing?

If I were Sherlock, I'd be able to deduce where my book is simply by the way Mycroft keeps his study and what it reveals of his personality.

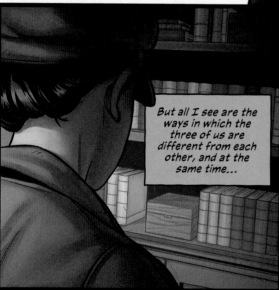

But all I see are the ways in which the three of us are different from each other, and at the same time...

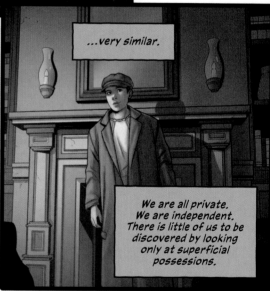

...very similar.

We are all private. We are independent. There is little of us to be discovered by looking only at superficial possessions.

THUMP THUMP THUMP

Oh, my stars and garters.

Martha, I am not to be disturbed. If anyone comes asking after me, send them away.

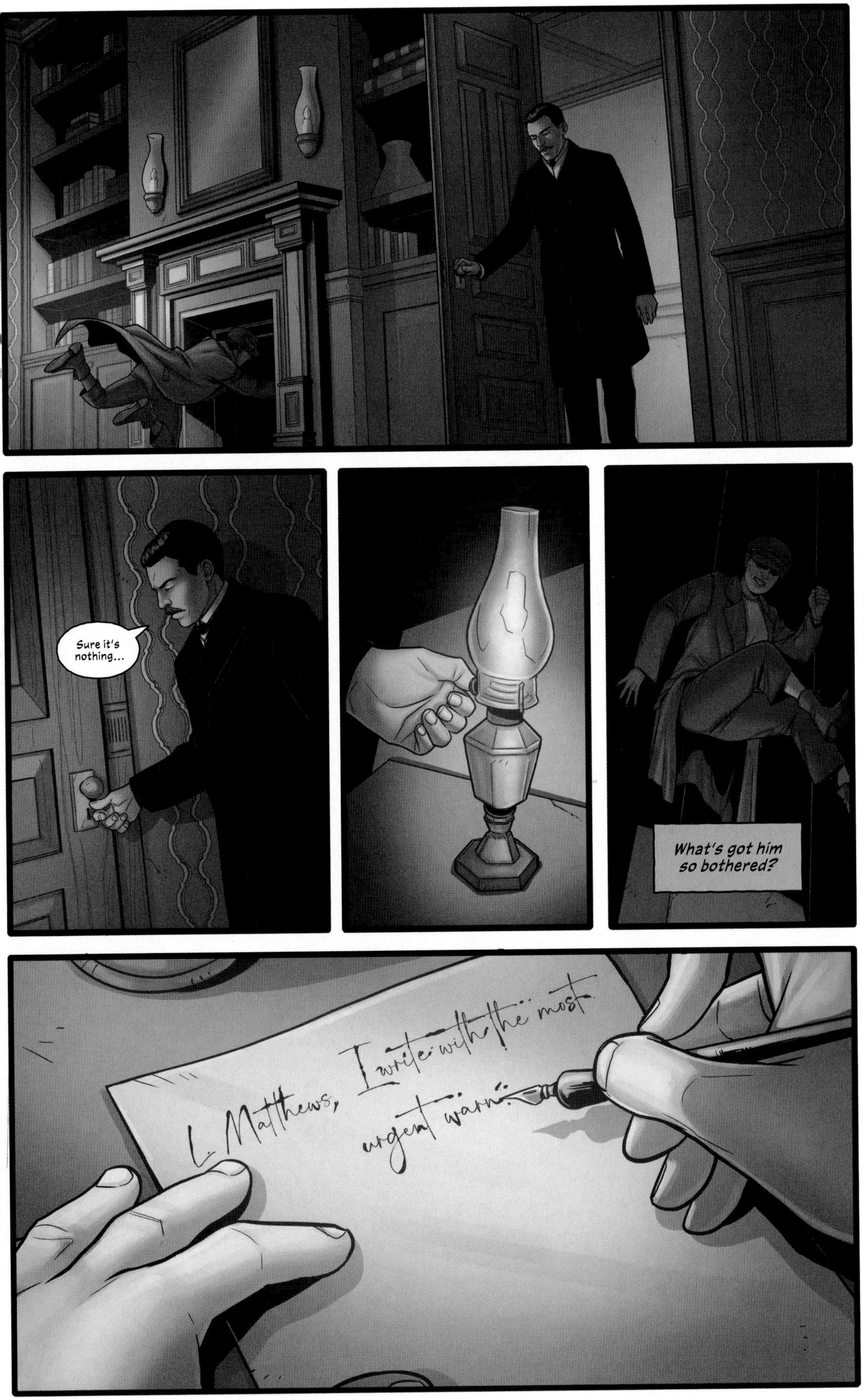
Sure it's nothing...
What's got him so bothered?
L. Matthews, I write with the most urgent warn

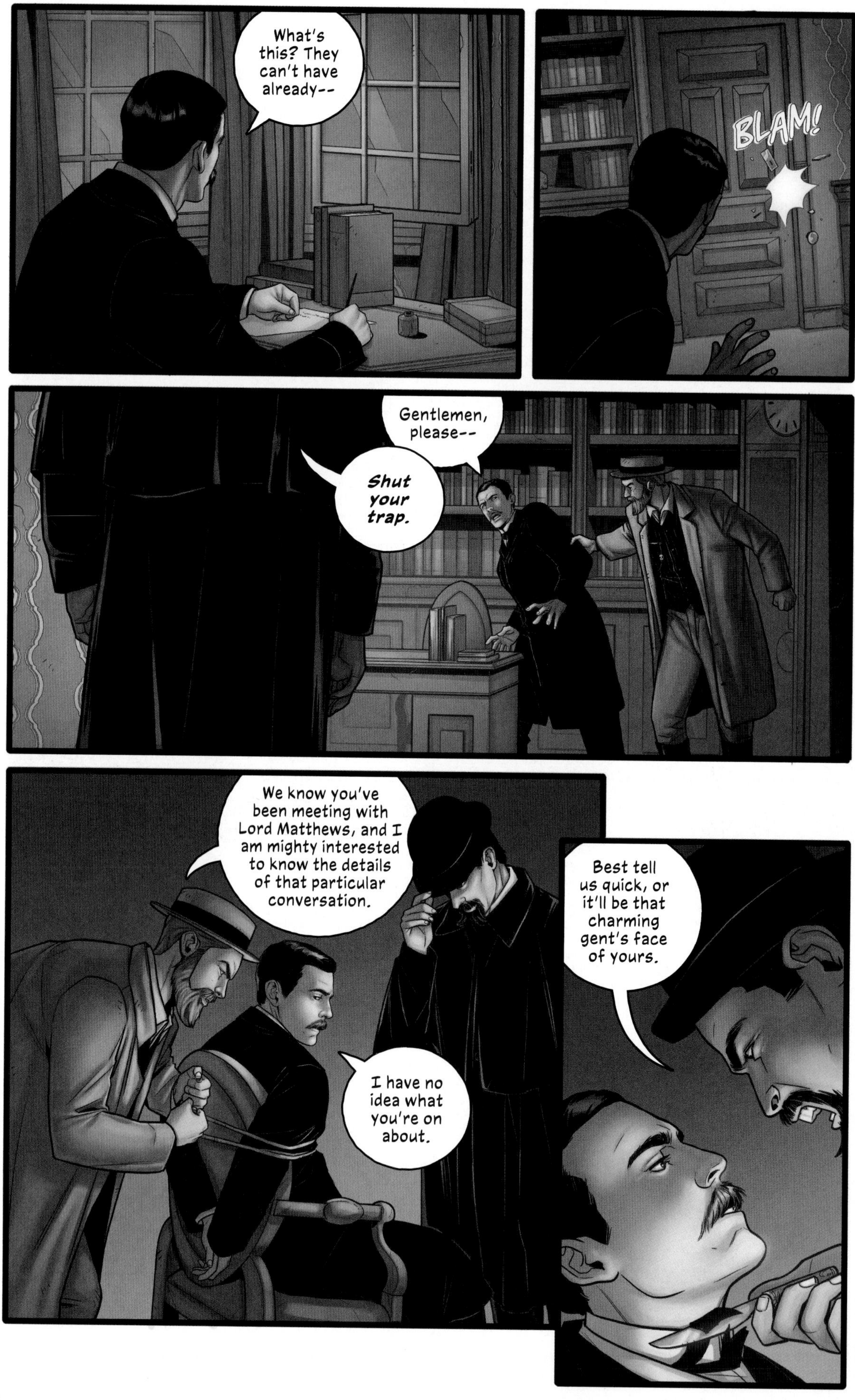
What's this? They can't have already--
BLAM!
Gentlemen, please--
Shut your trap.
We know you've been meeting with Lord Matthews, and I am mighty interested to know the details of that particular conversation.
I have no idea what you're on about.
Best tell us quick, or it'll be that charming gent's face of yours.

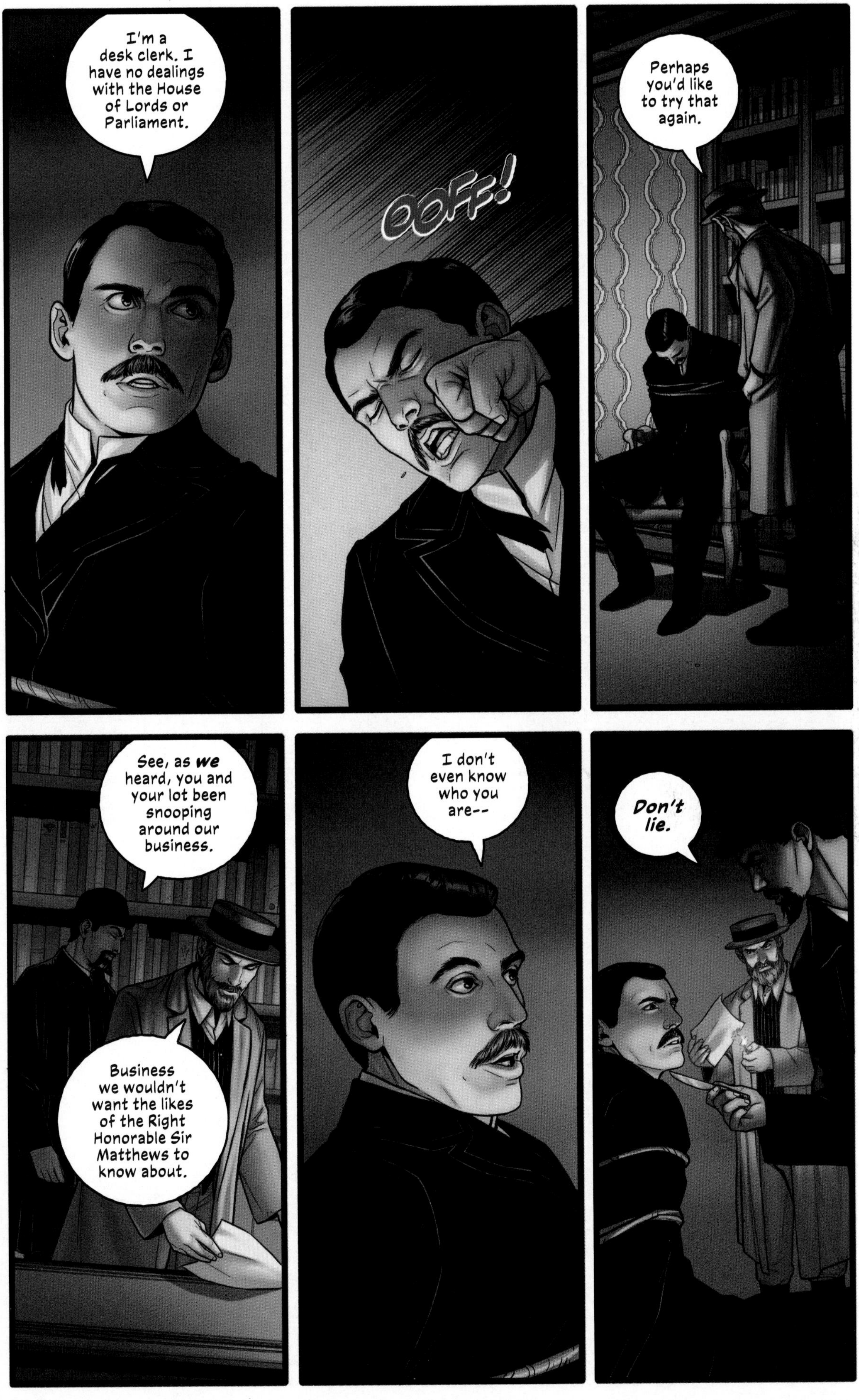
I'm a desk clerk. I have no dealings with the House of Lords or Parliament.
OOFF!
Perhaps you'd like to try that again.
See, as *we* heard, you and your lot been snooping around our business.
Business we wouldn't want the likes of the Right Honorable Sir Matthews to know about.
I don't even know who you are--
Don't lie.

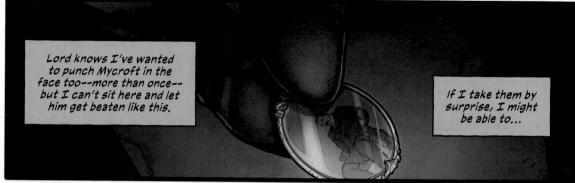

Lord knows I've wanted to punch Mycroft in the face too--more than once--but I can't sit here and let him get beaten like this.

If I take them by surprise, I might be able to...

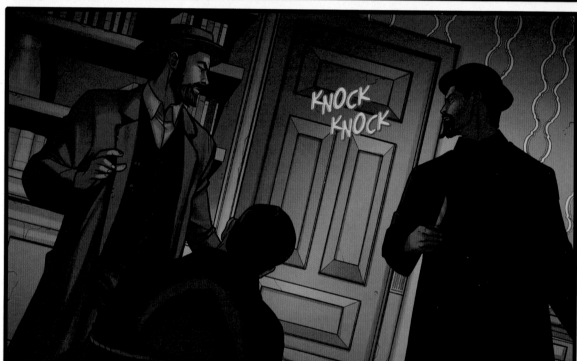

KNOCK KNOCK

Mr. Holmes, I'm quite alarmed by such uproar.

Whatever is going on? Shall I call Scotland Yard?

No, Martha, everything is fine. Please return to your rooms.

But I heard a gunshot!

Martha, as I've told you before, my business is my business.

Return to your rooms and do not disturb me again.

Alarmed, was she? We'll show her *Alarm.*

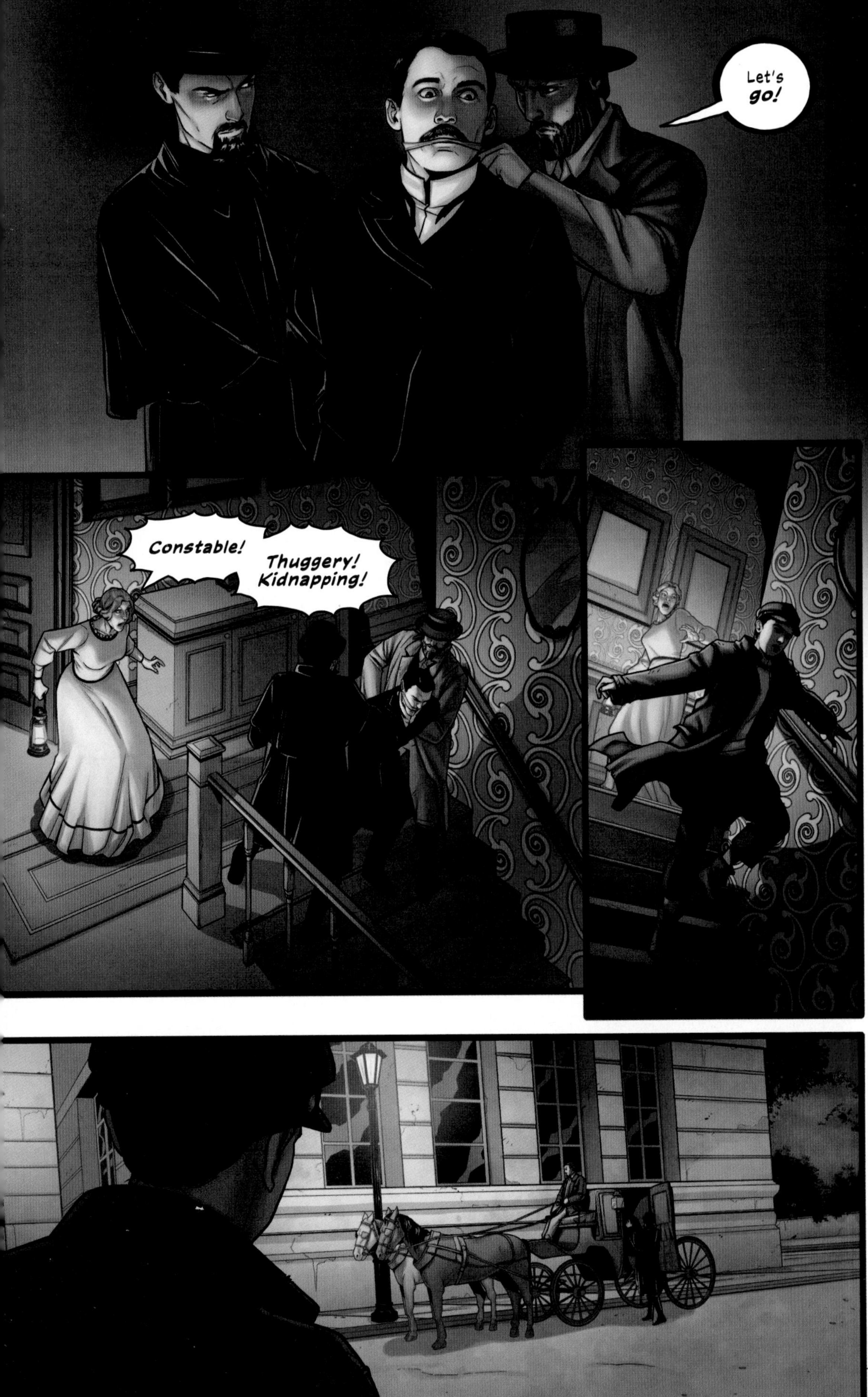
Let's go!
Constable!
Thuggery! Kidnapping!

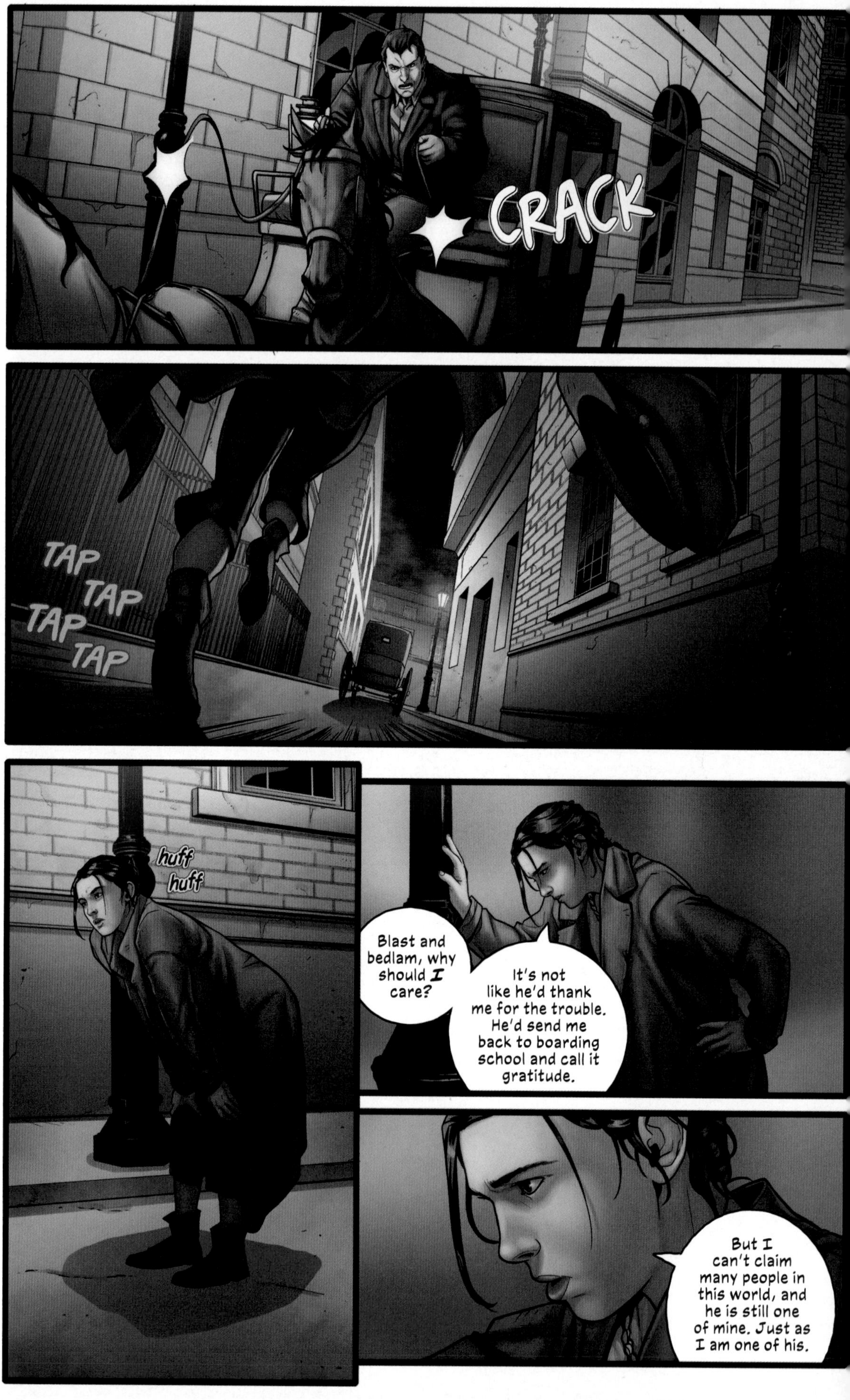
CRACK
TAP TAP TAP TAP
huff huff
Blast and bedlam, why should *I* care?
It's not like he'd thank me for the trouble. He'd send me back to boarding school and call it gratitude.
But I can't claim many people in this world, and he is still one of mine. Just as I am one of his.

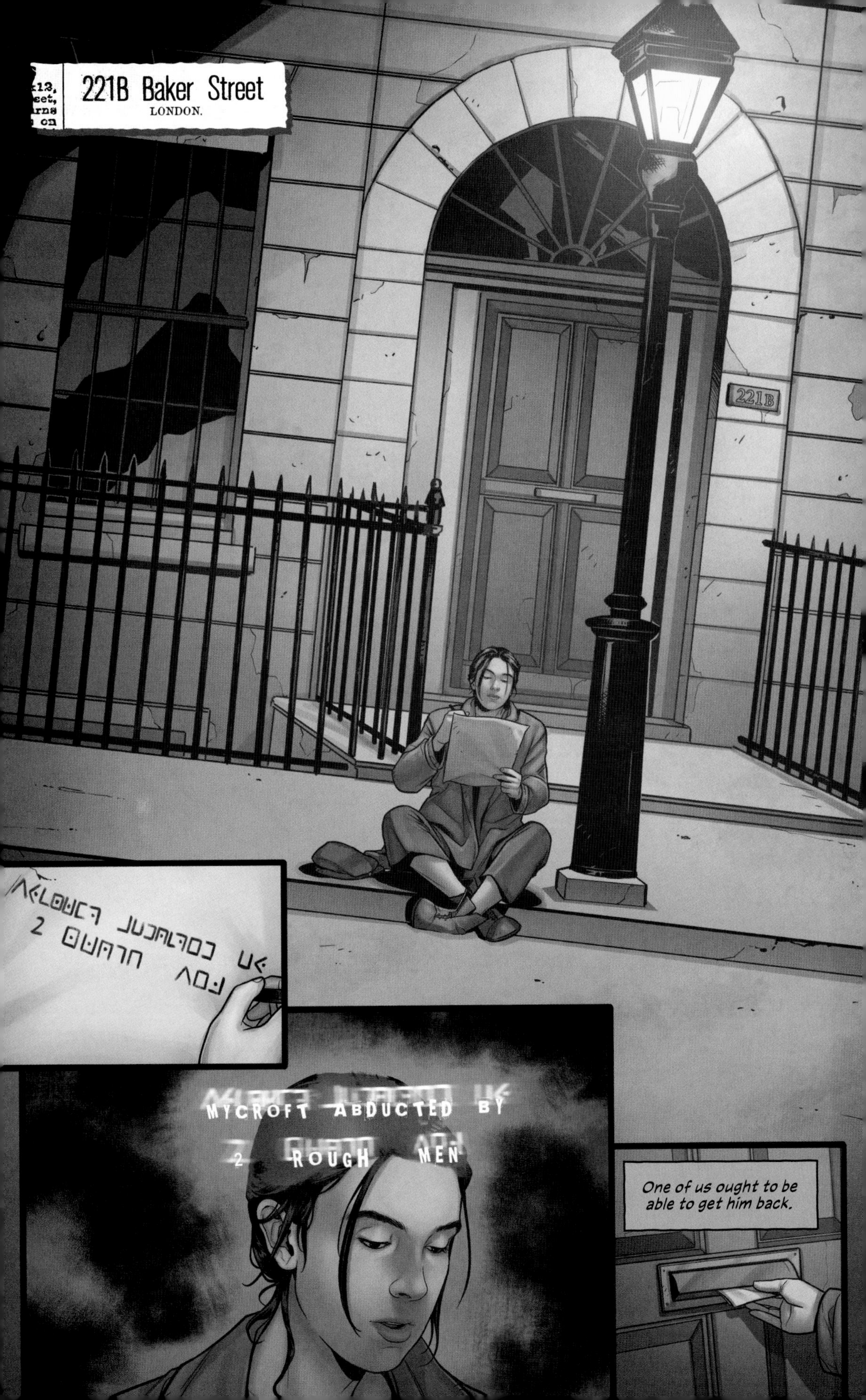
221B Baker Street
LONDON.
221B
MYCROFT ABDUCTED BY
2 ROUGH MEN
One of us ought to be able to get him back.

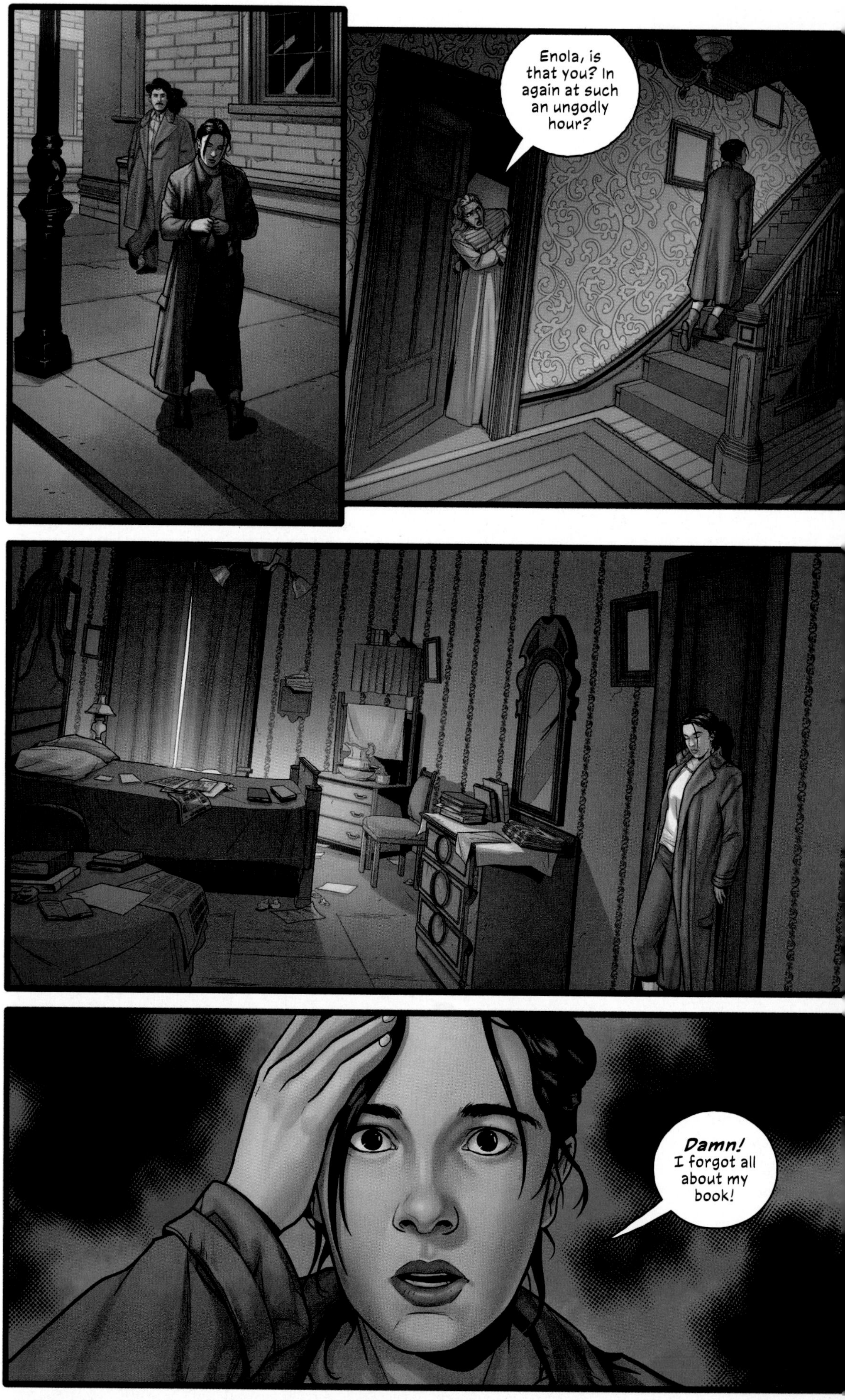
Enola, is that you? In again at such an ungodly hour?
Damn! I forgot all about my book!

[Chapter Two]

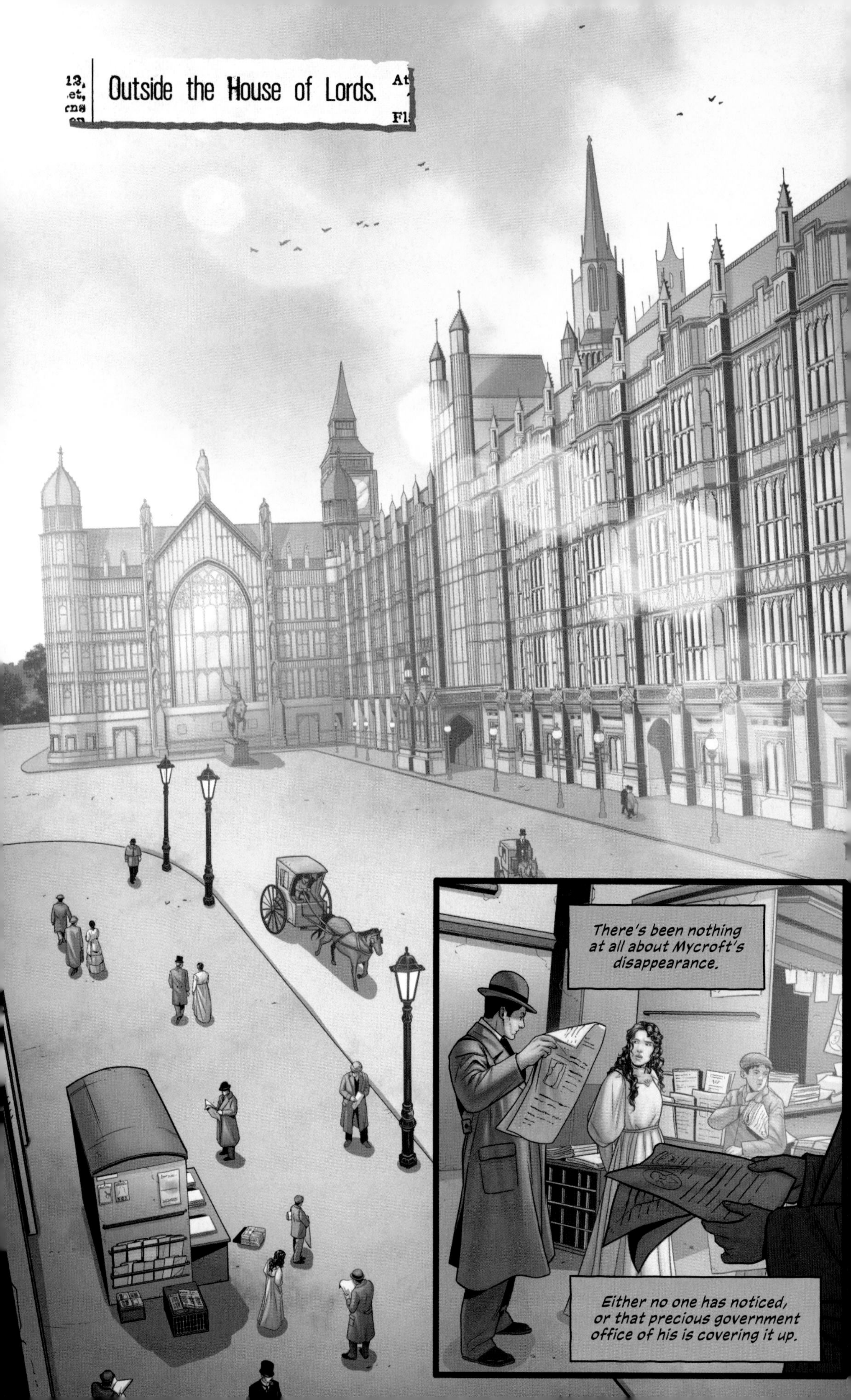
Outside the House of Lords.
There's been nothing at all about Mycroft's disappearance.
Either no one has noticed, or that precious government office of his is covering it up.

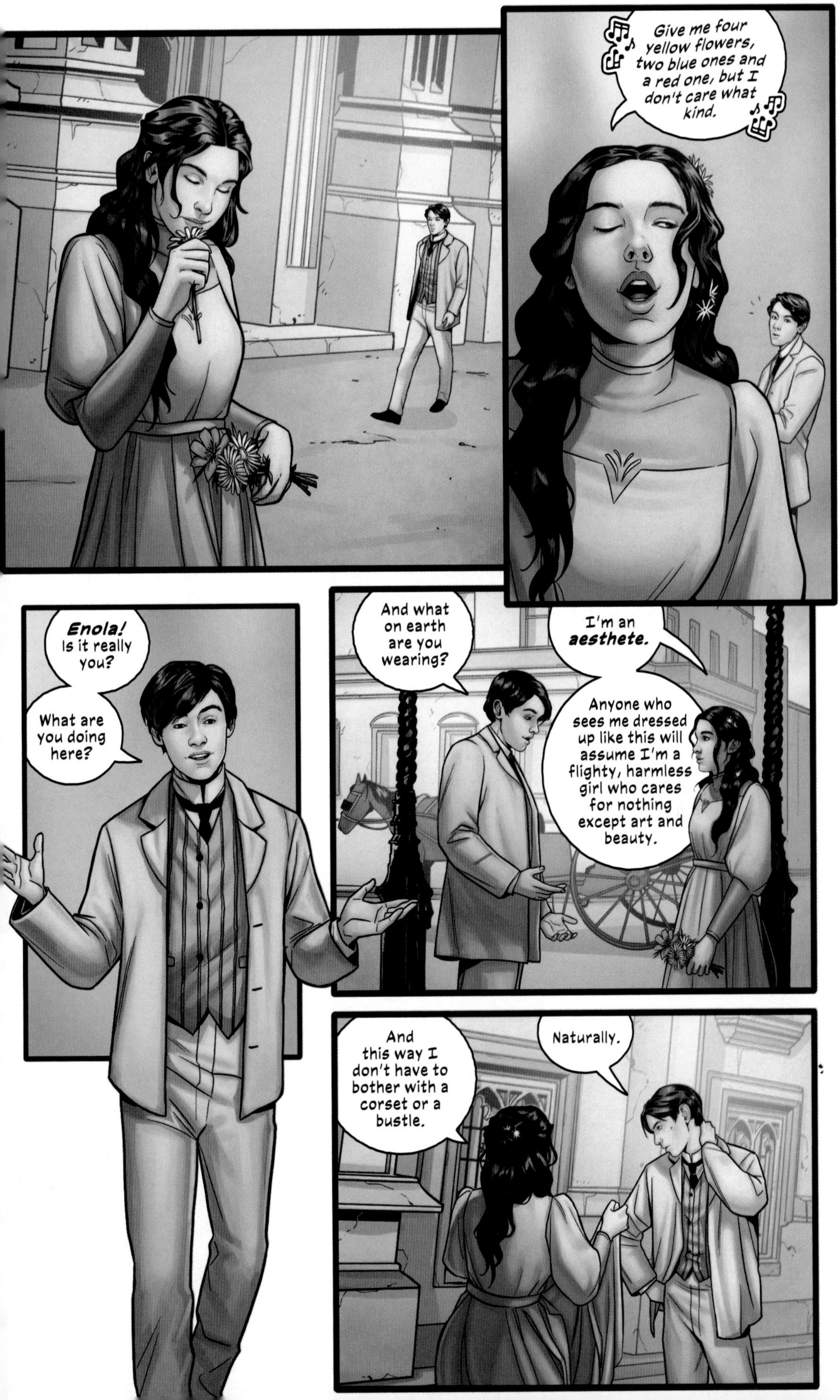
Give me four yellow flowers, two blue ones and a red one, but I don't care what kind.
Enola! Is it really you?
What are you doing here?
And what on earth are you wearing?
I'm an aesthete.
Anyone who sees me dressed up like this will assume I'm a flighty, harmless girl who cares for nothing except art and beauty.
And this way I don't have to bother with a corset or a bustle.
Naturally.

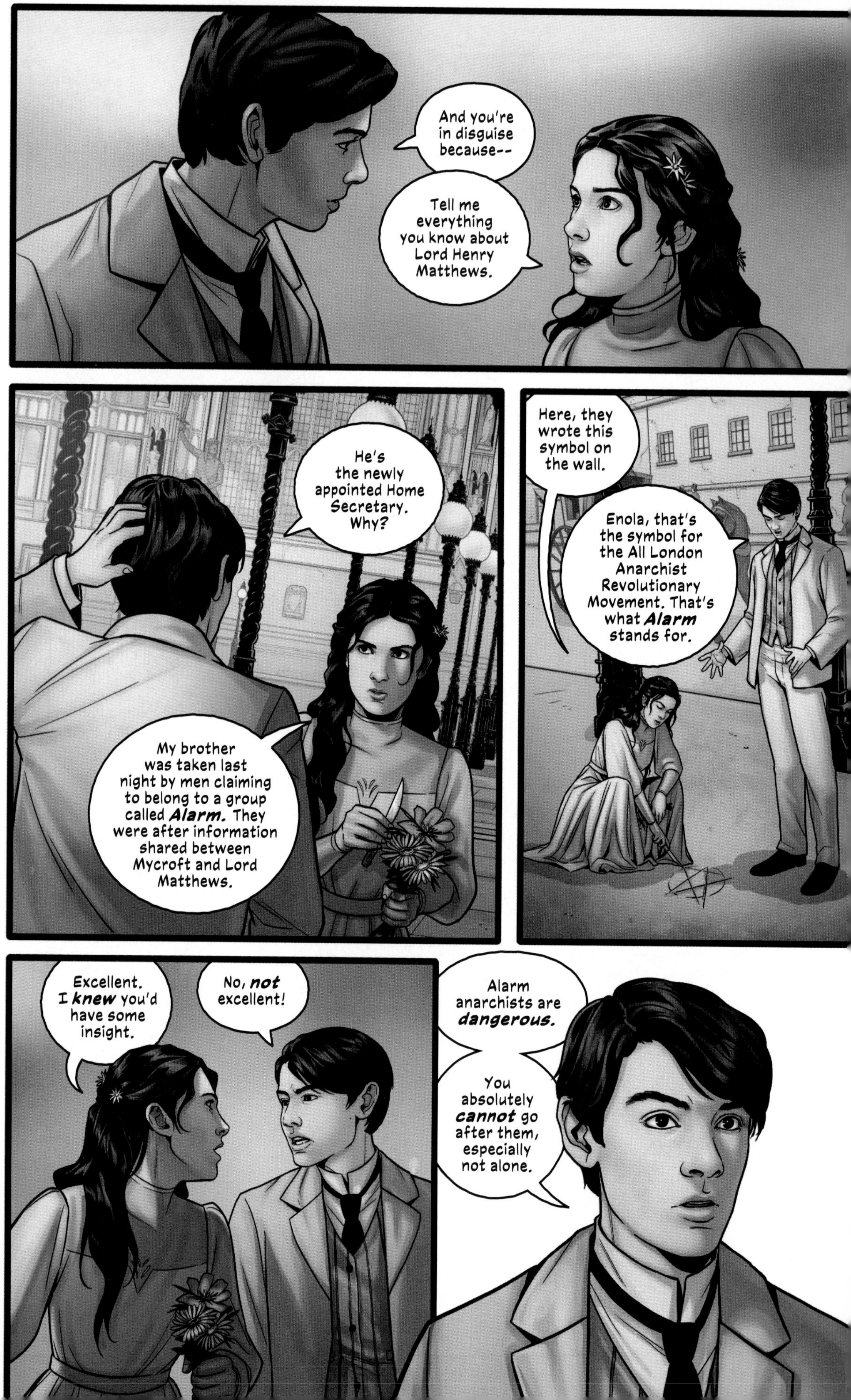
And you're in disguise because--
Tell me everything you know about Lord Henry Matthews.
He's the newly appointed Home Secretary. Why?
My brother was taken last night by men claiming to belong to a group called *Alarm.* They were after information shared between Mycroft and Lord Matthews.
Here, they wrote this symbol on the wall.
Enola, that's the symbol for the All London Anarchist Revolutionary Movement. That's what *Alarm* stands for.
Excellent. I *knew* you'd have some insight.
No, *not* excellent!
Alarm anarchists are *dangerous.*
You absolutely *cannot* go after them, especially not alone.

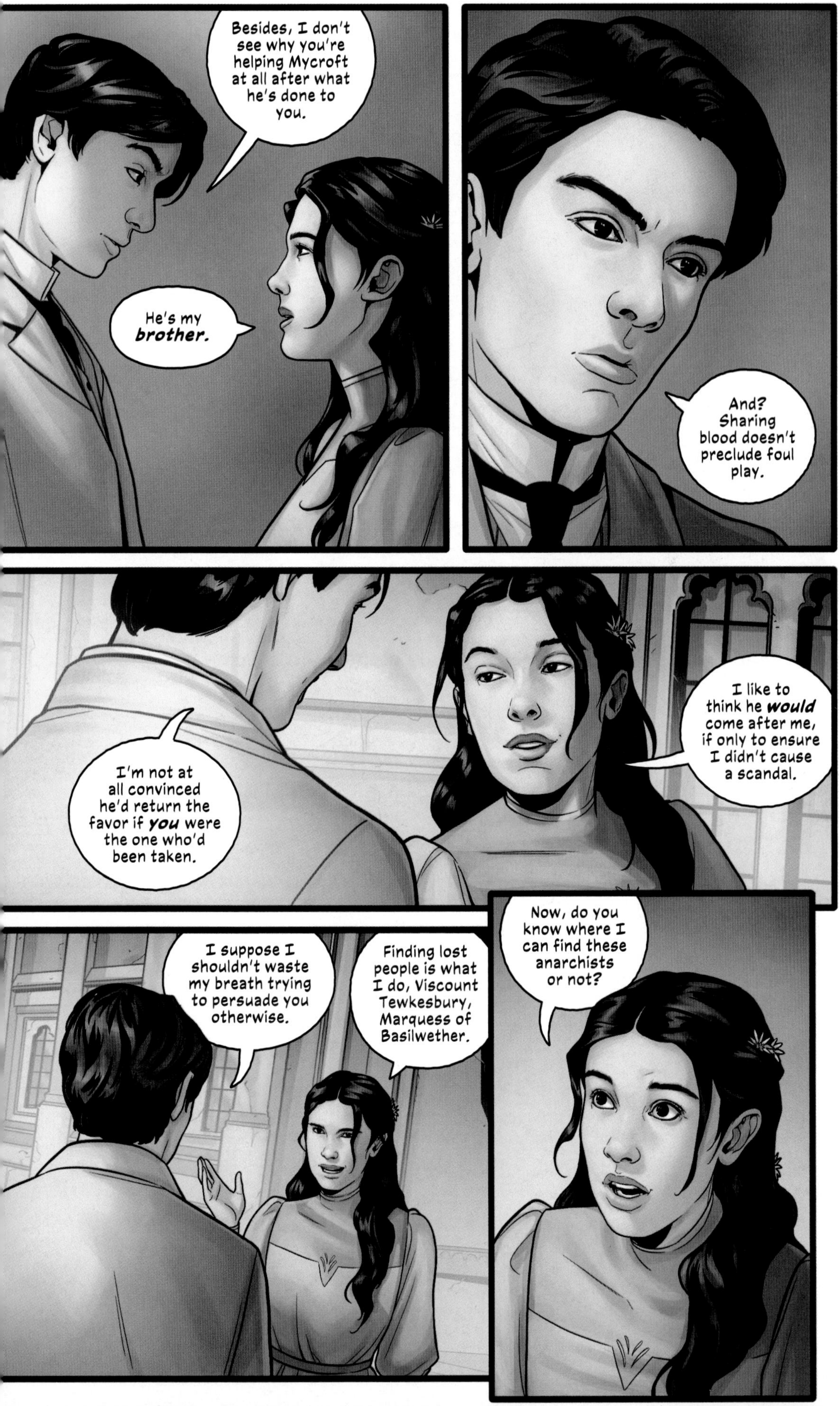

Besides, I don't see why you're helping Mycroft at all after what he's done to you.
He's my **brother.**
And? Sharing blood doesn't preclude foul play.
I like to think he ***would*** come after me, if only to ensure I didn't cause a scandal.
I'm not at all convinced he'd return the favor if ***you*** were the one who'd been taken.
I suppose I shouldn't waste my breath trying to persuade you otherwise.
Finding lost people is what I do, Viscount Tewkesbury, Marquess of Basilwether.
Now, do you know where I can find these anarchists or not?

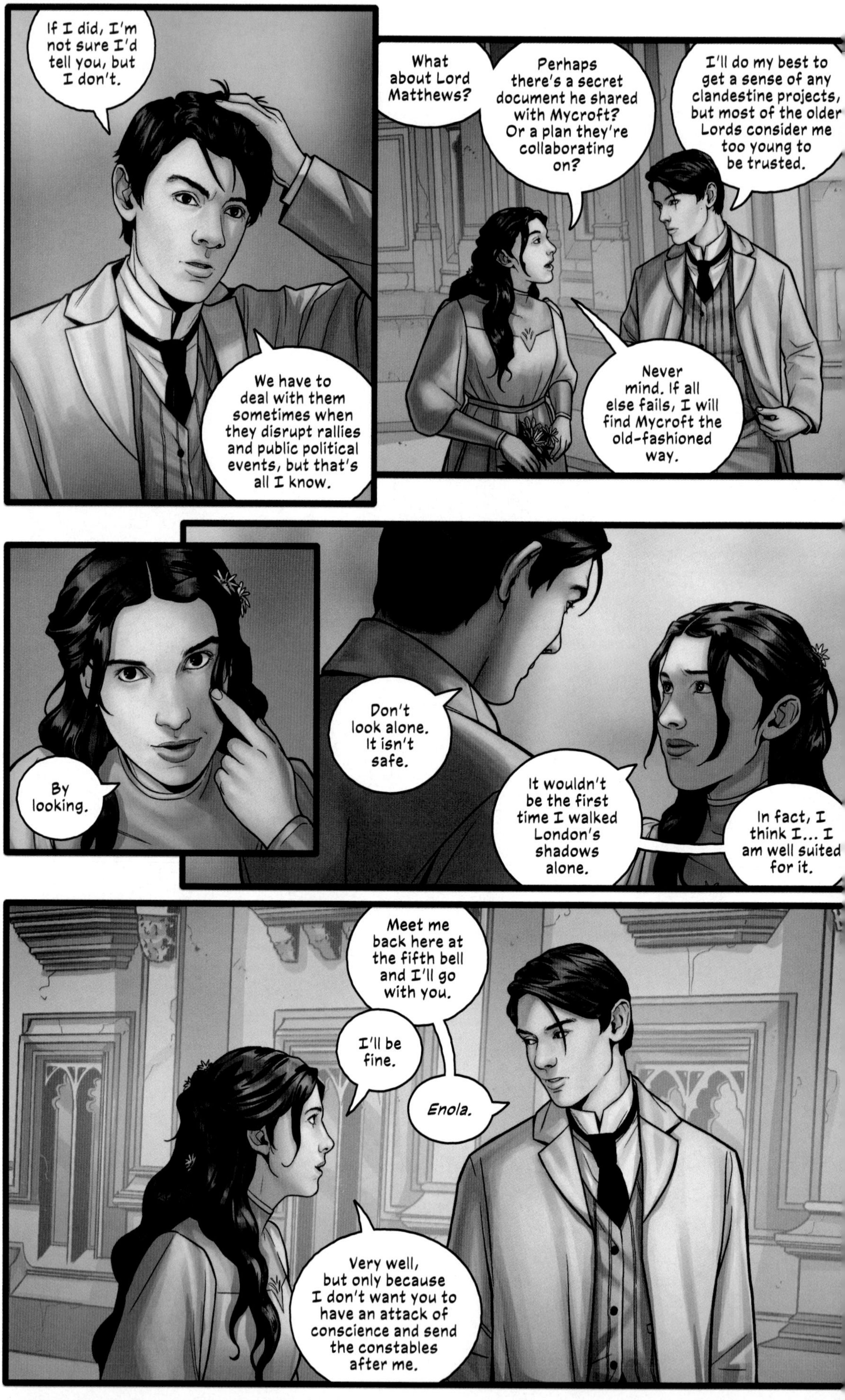
If I did, I'm not sure I'd tell you, but I don't.
We have to deal with them sometimes when they disrupt rallies and public political events, but that's all I know.
What about Lord Matthews?
Perhaps there's a secret document he shared with Mycroft? Or a plan they're collaborating on?
I'll do my best to get a sense of any clandestine projects, but most of the older Lords consider me too young to be trusted.
Never mind. If all else fails, I will find Mycroft the old-fashioned way.
By looking.
Don't look alone. It isn't safe.
It wouldn't be the first time I walked London's shadows alone.
In fact, I think I... I am well suited for it.
Meet me back here at the fifth bell and I'll go with you.
I'll be fine.
Enola.
Very well, but only because I don't want you to have an attack of conscience and send the constables after me.

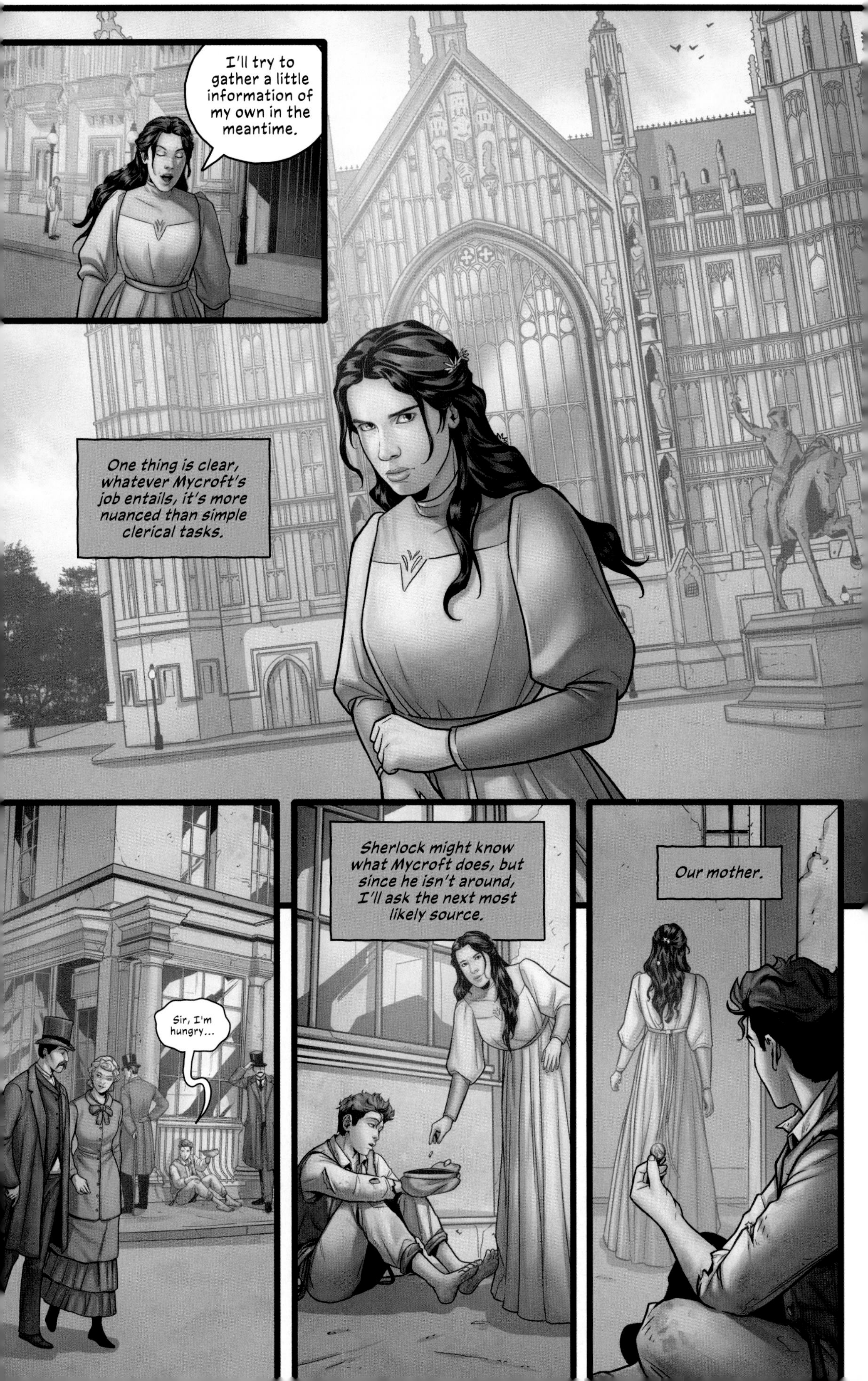
I'll try to gather a little information of my own in the meantime.
One thing is clear, whatever Mycroft's job entails, it's more nuanced than simple clerical tasks.
Sir, I'm hungry...
Sherlock might know what Mycroft does, but since he isn't around, I'll ask the next most likely source.
Our mother.

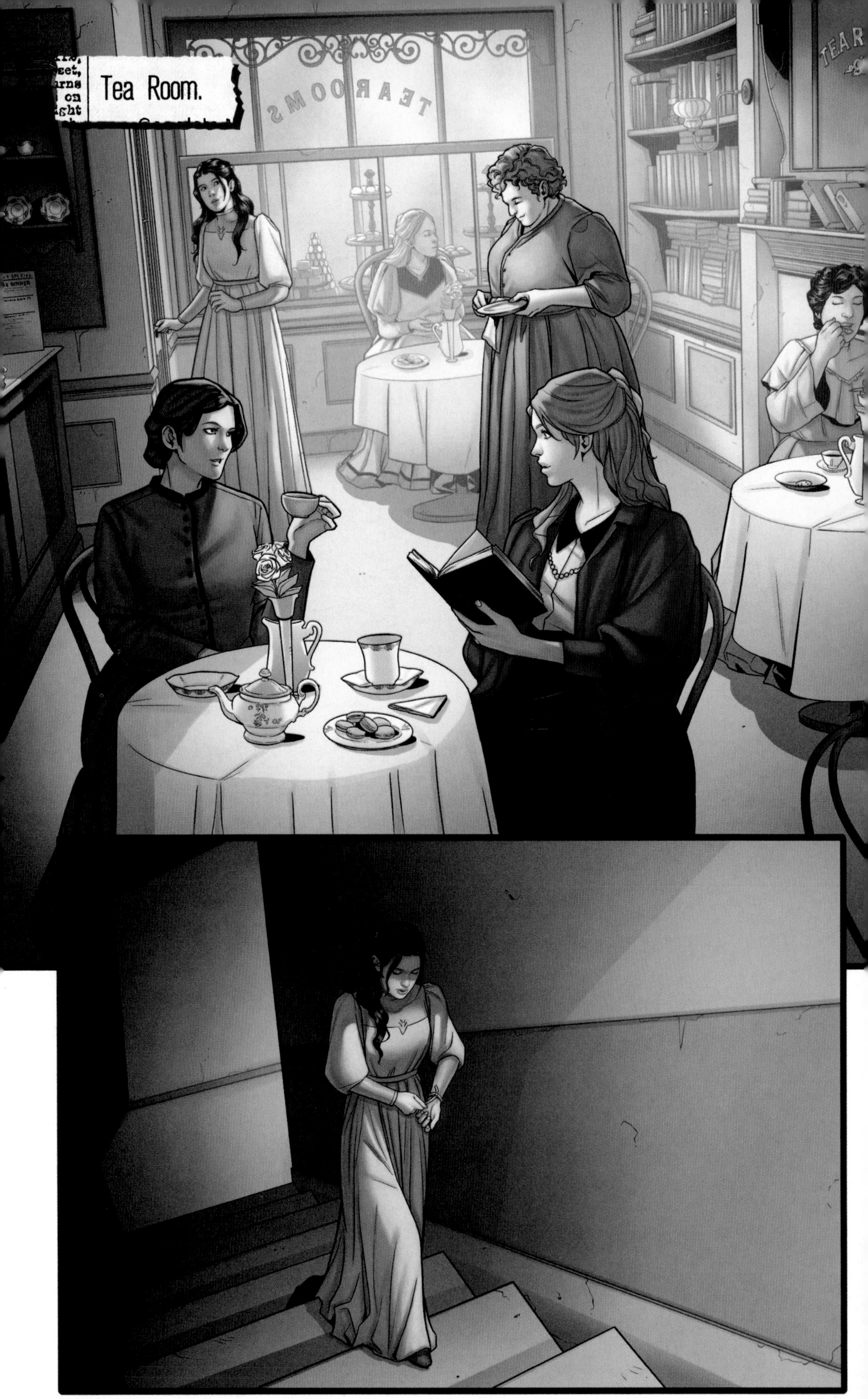
Tea Room.

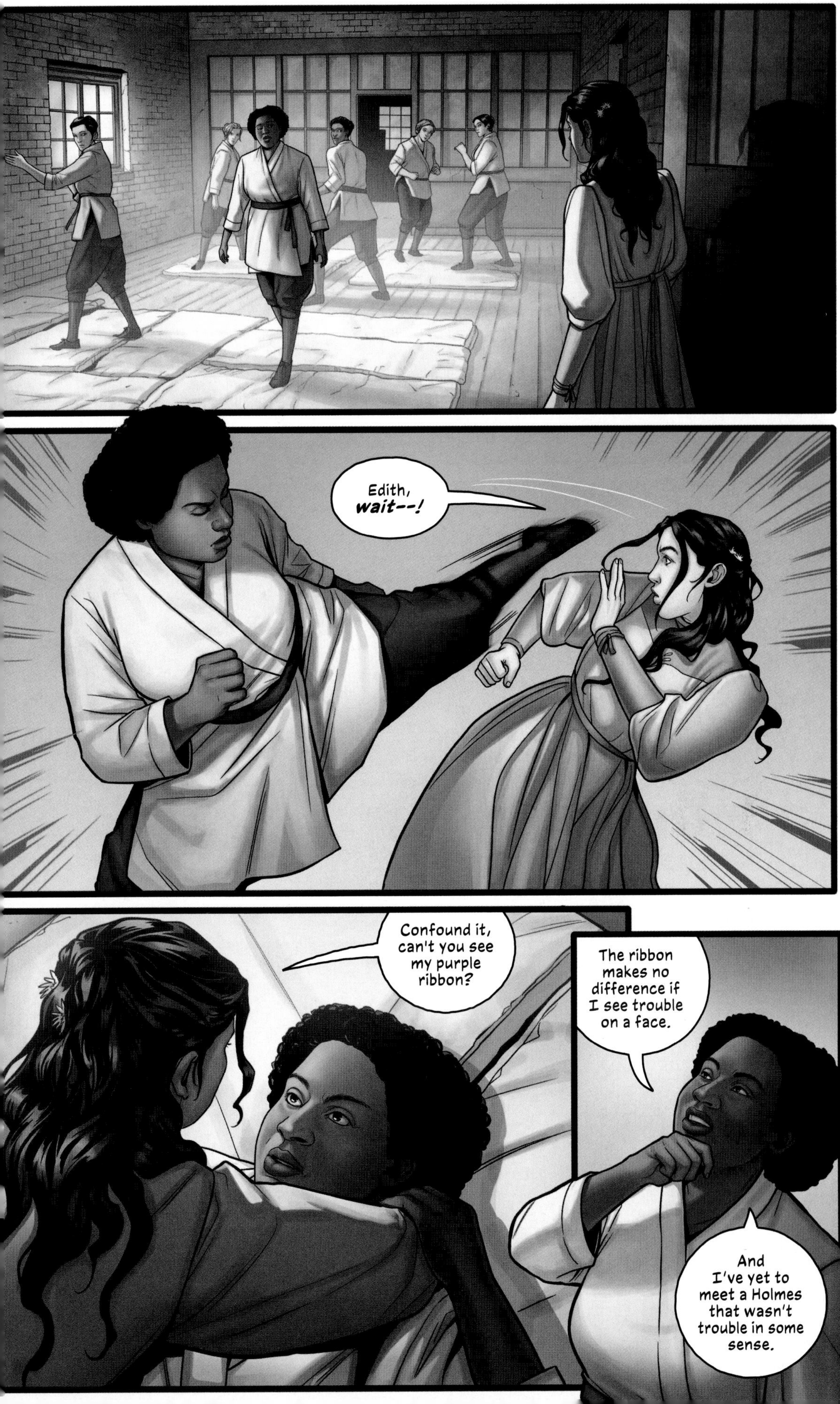
Edith, **wait--!**
Confound it, can't you see my purple ribbon?
The ribbon makes no difference if I see trouble on a face.
And I've yet to meet a Holmes that wasn't trouble in some sense.

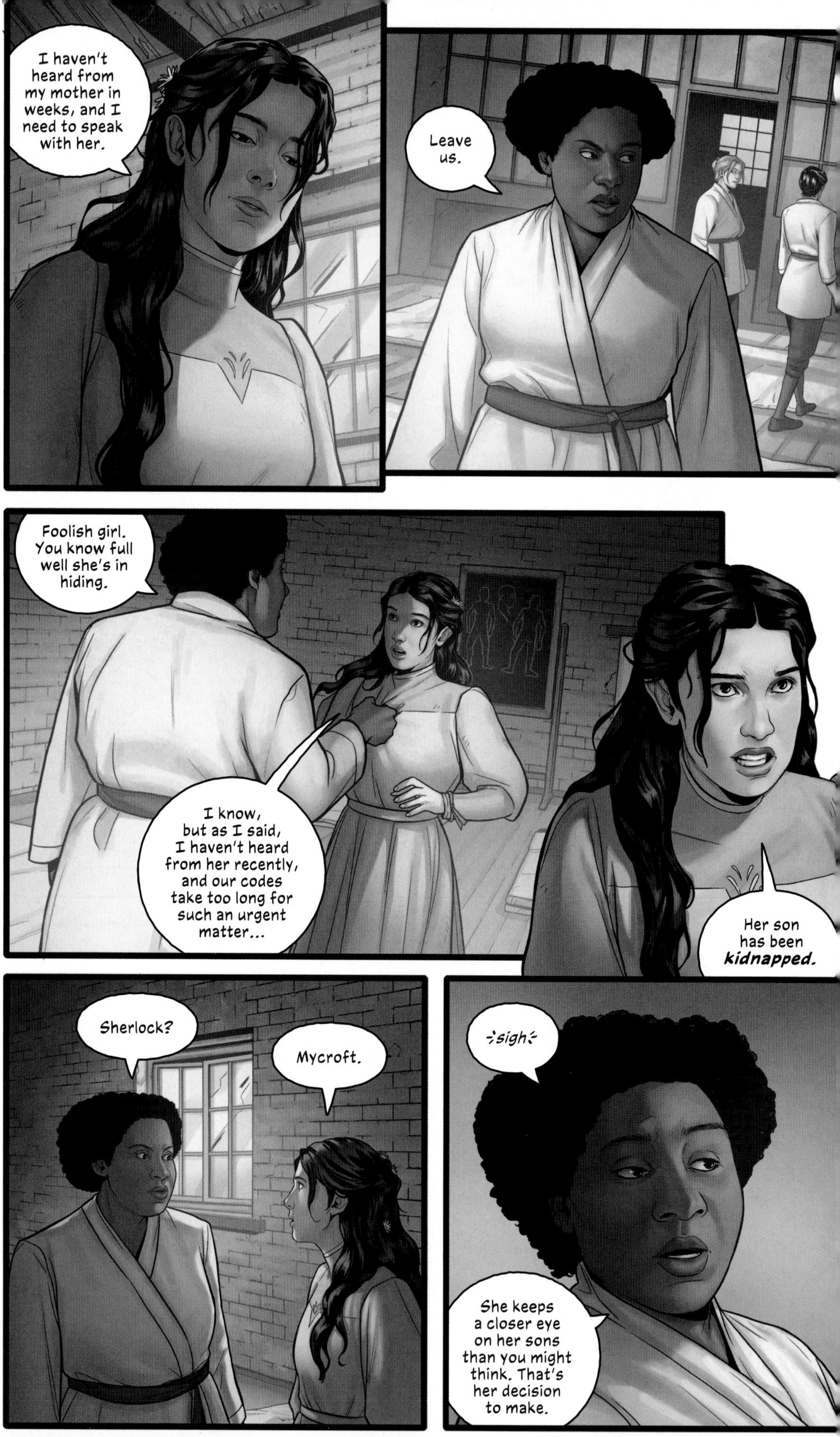
I haven't heard from my mother in weeks, and I need to speak with her.
Leave us.
Foolish girl. You know full well she's in hiding.
I know, but as I said, I haven't heard from her recently, and our codes take too long for such an urgent matter...
Her son has been ***kidnapped.***
Sherlock?
Mycroft.
sigh
She keeps a closer eye on her sons than you might think. That's her decision to make.

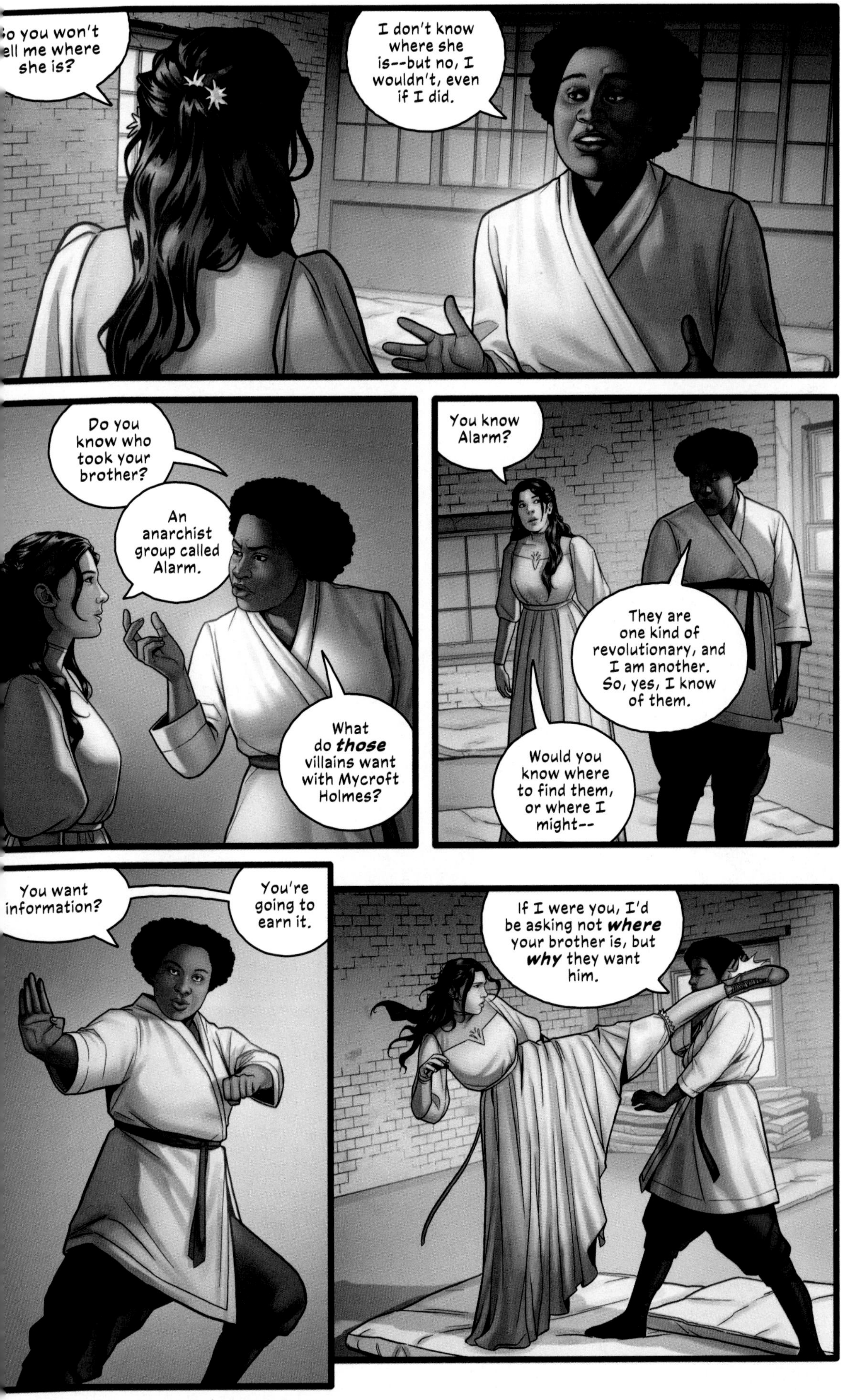

o you won't ell me where she is?
I don't know where she is--but no, I wouldn't, even if I did.
Do you know who took your brother?
An anarchist group called Alarm.
What do *those* villains want with Mycroft Holmes?
You know Alarm?
They are one kind of revolutionary, and I am another. So, yes, I know of them.
Would you know where to find them, or where I might--
You want information?
You're going to earn it.
If I were you, I'd be asking not *where* your brother is, but *why* they want him.

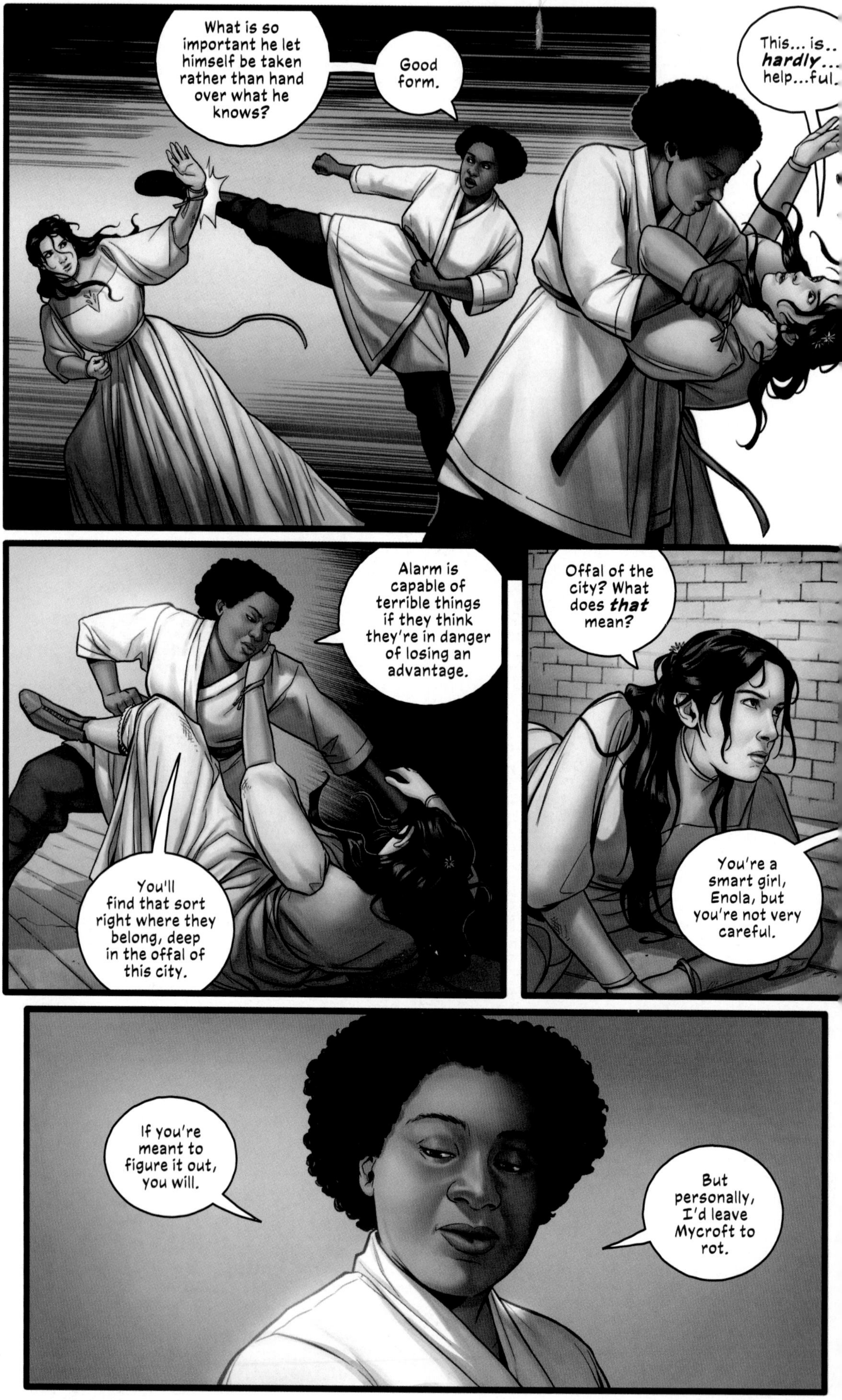
What is so important he let himself be taken rather than hand over what he knows?
Good form.
This... is.. hardly... help...ful.
Alarm is capable of terrible things if they think they're in danger of losing an advantage.
You'll find that sort right where they belong, deep in the offal of this city.
Offal of the city? What does that mean?
You're a smart girl, Enola, but you're not very careful.
If you're meant to figure it out, you will.
But personally, I'd leave Mycroft to rot.

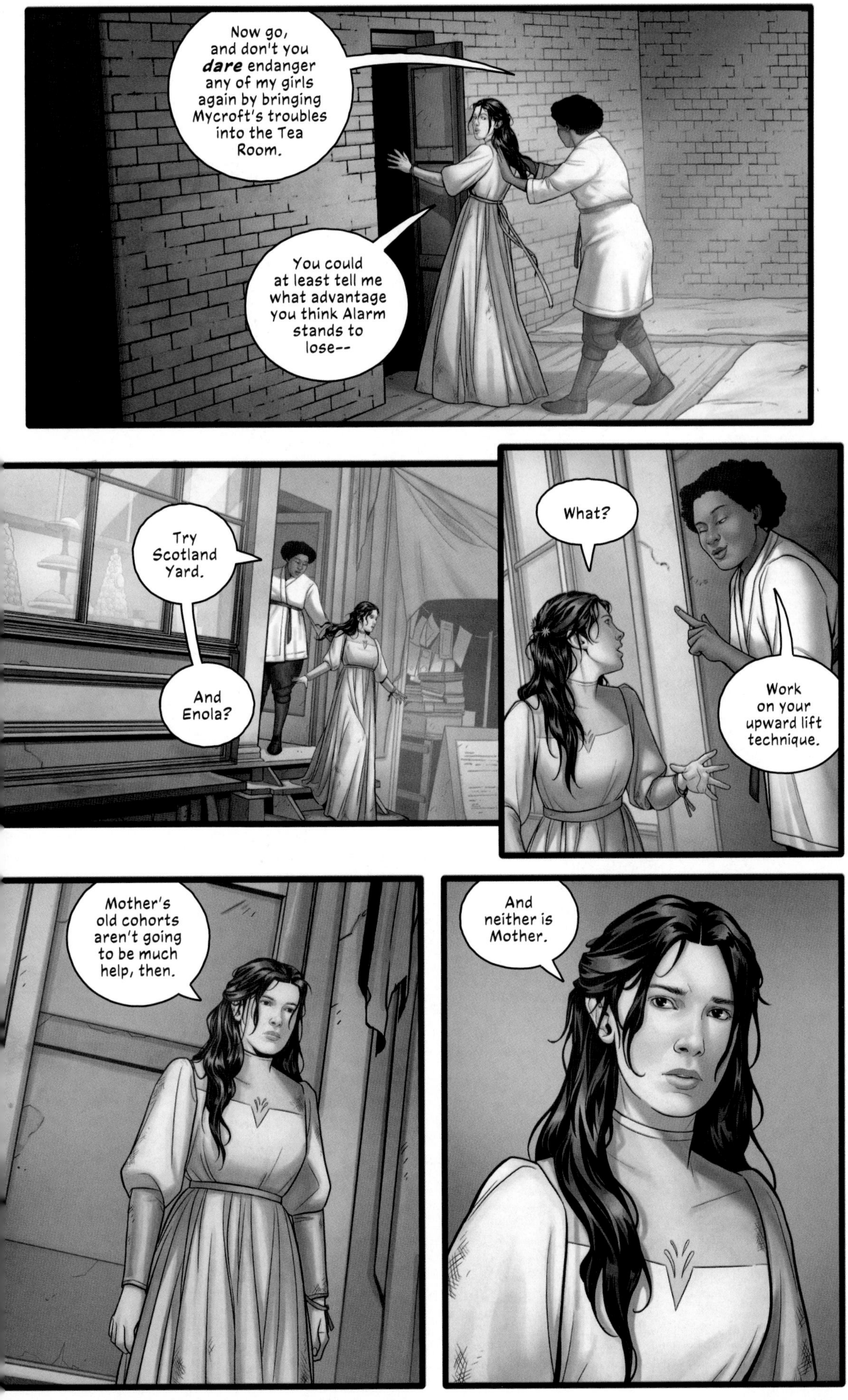
Now go, and don't you *dare* endanger any of my girls again by bringing Mycroft's troubles into the Tea Room.
You could at least tell me what advantage you think Alarm stands to lose--
Try Scotland Yard.
And Enola?
What?
Work on your upward lift technique.
Mother's old cohorts aren't going to be much help, then.
And neither is Mother.

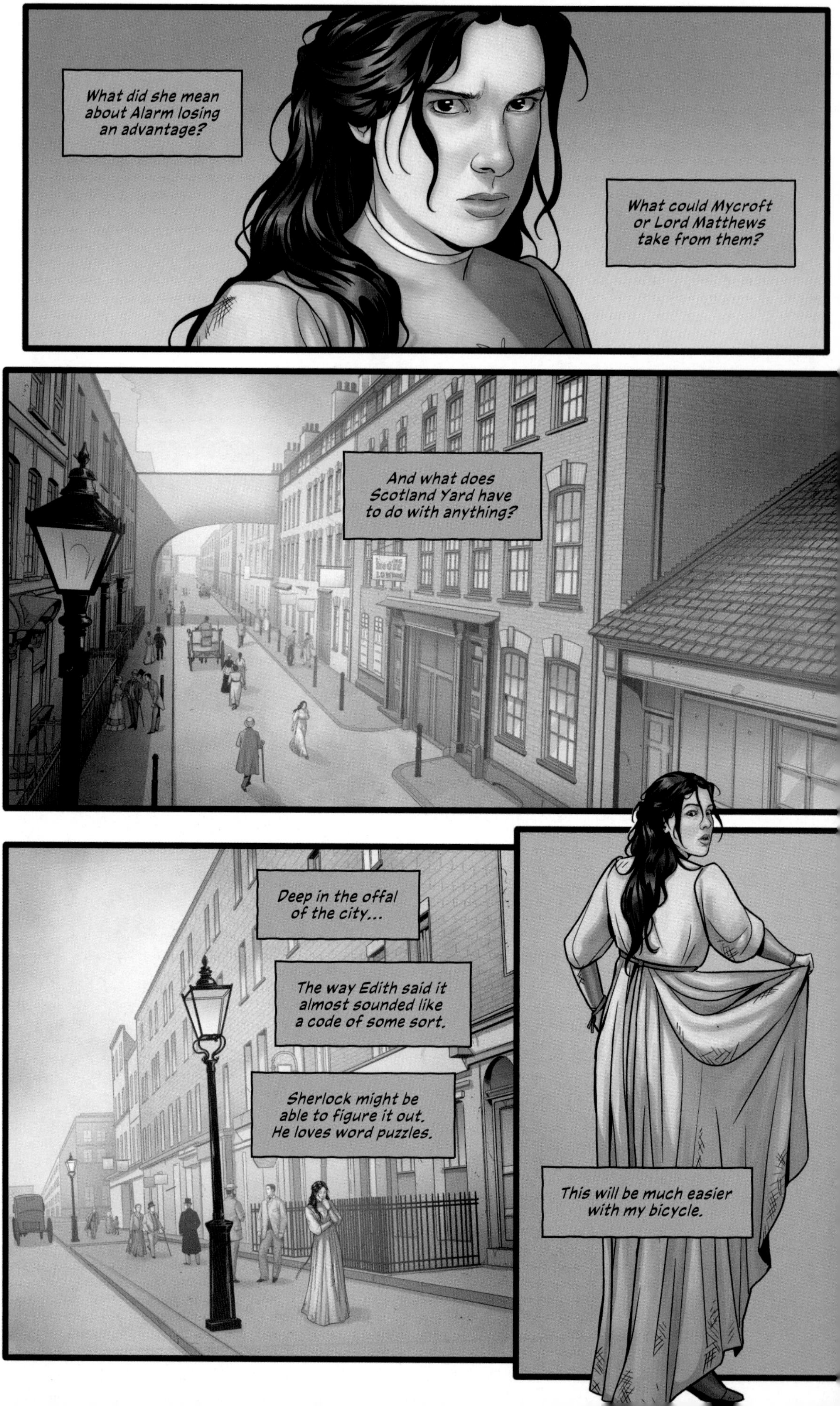
What did she mean about Alarm losing an advantage?
What could Mycroft or Lord Matthews take from them?
And what does Scotland Yard have to do with anything?
Deep in the offal of the city...
The way Edith said it almost sounded like a code of some sort.
Sherlock might be able to figure it out. He loves word puzzles.
This will be much easier with my bicycle.

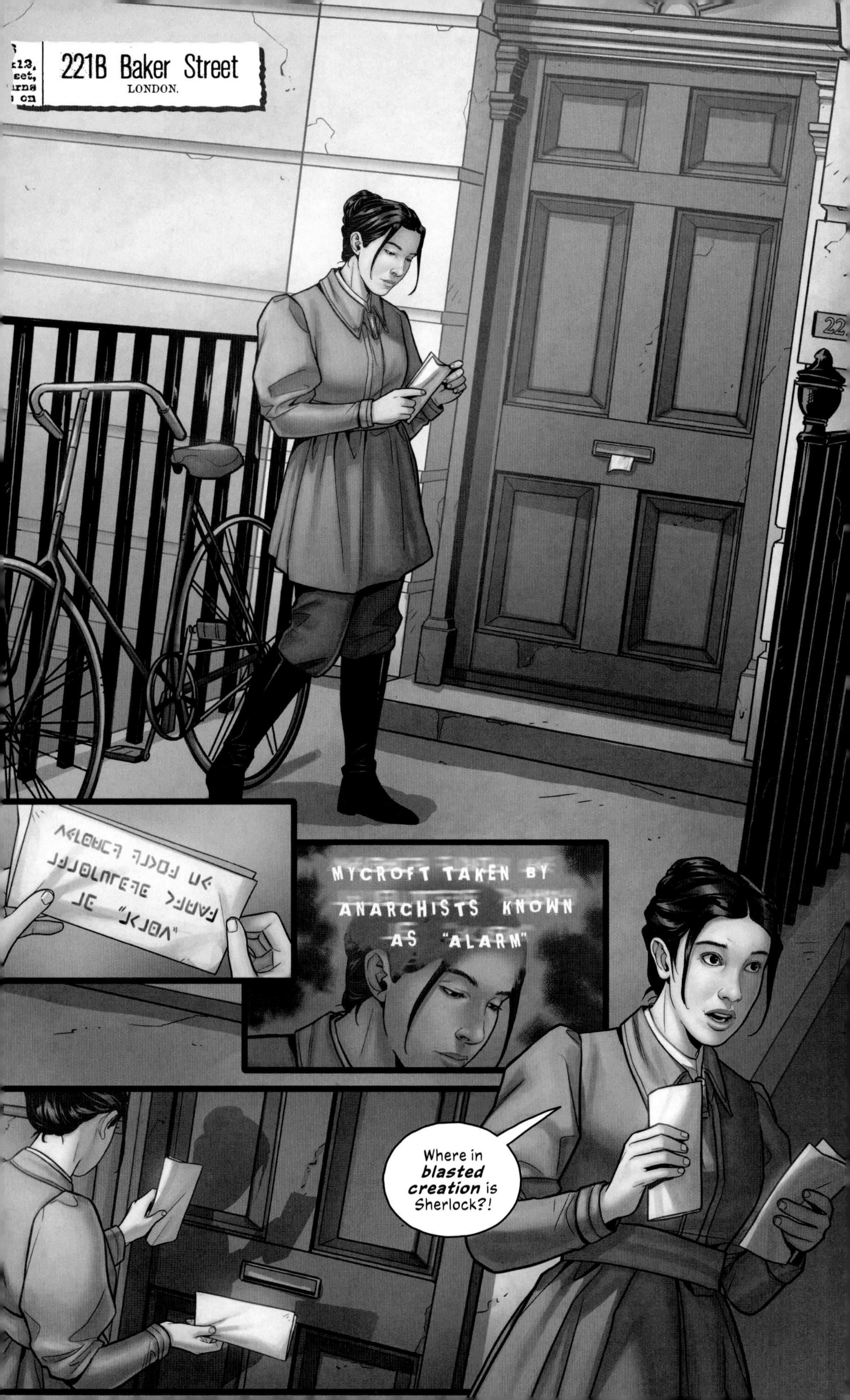
221B Baker Street
LONDON.
MYCROFT TAKEN BY ANARCHISTS KNOWN AS "ALARM"
Where in blasted creation is Sherlock?!

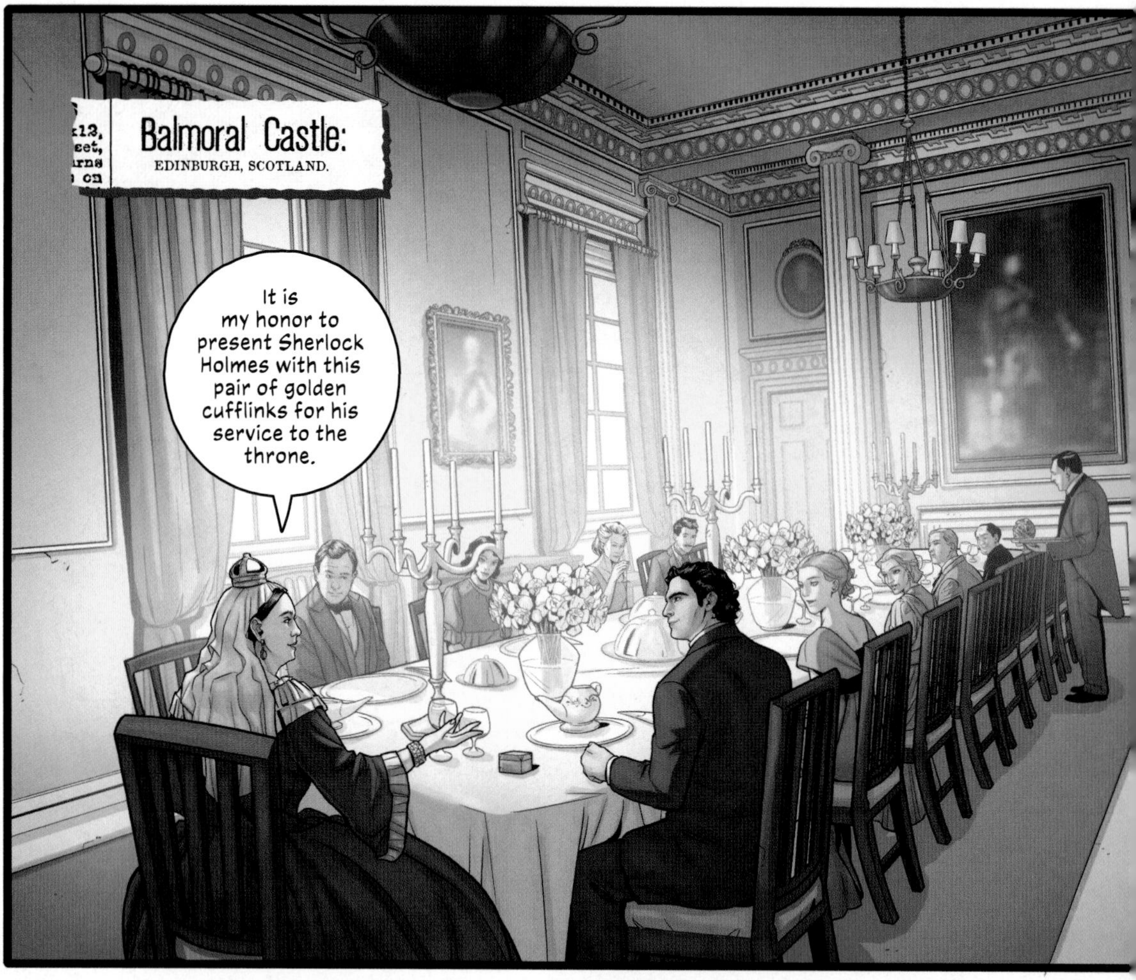
Balmoral Castle:
EDINBURGH, SCOTLAND.
It is my honor to present Sherlock Holmes with this pair of golden cufflinks for his service to the throne.

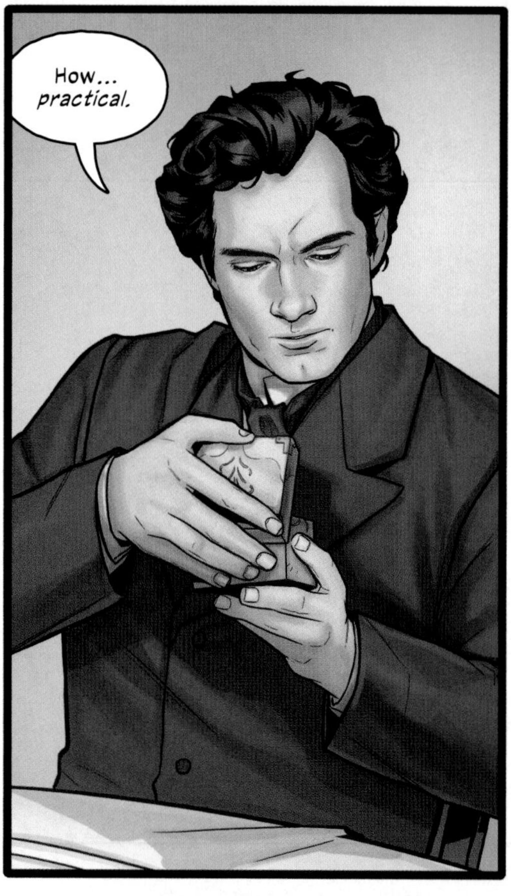
How... *practical.*

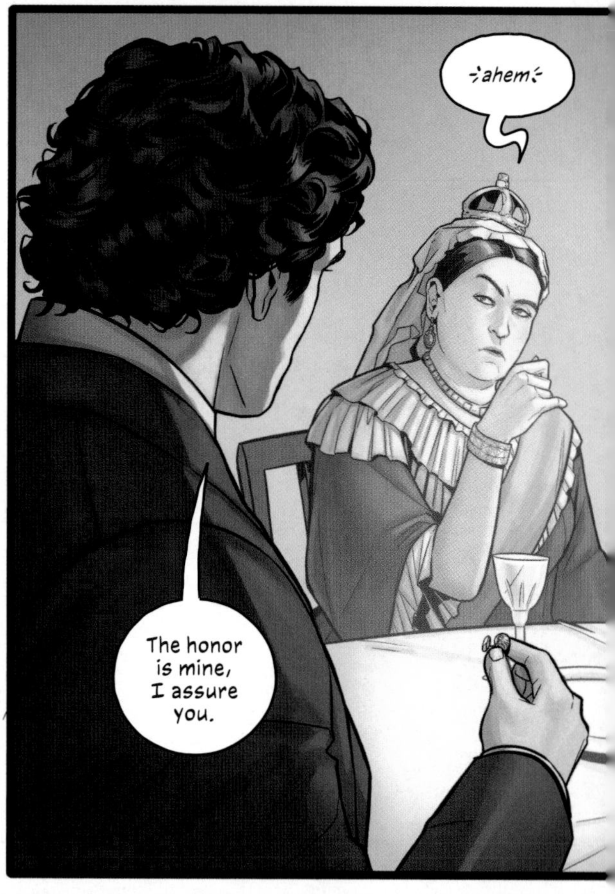
ahem
The honor is mine, I assure you.

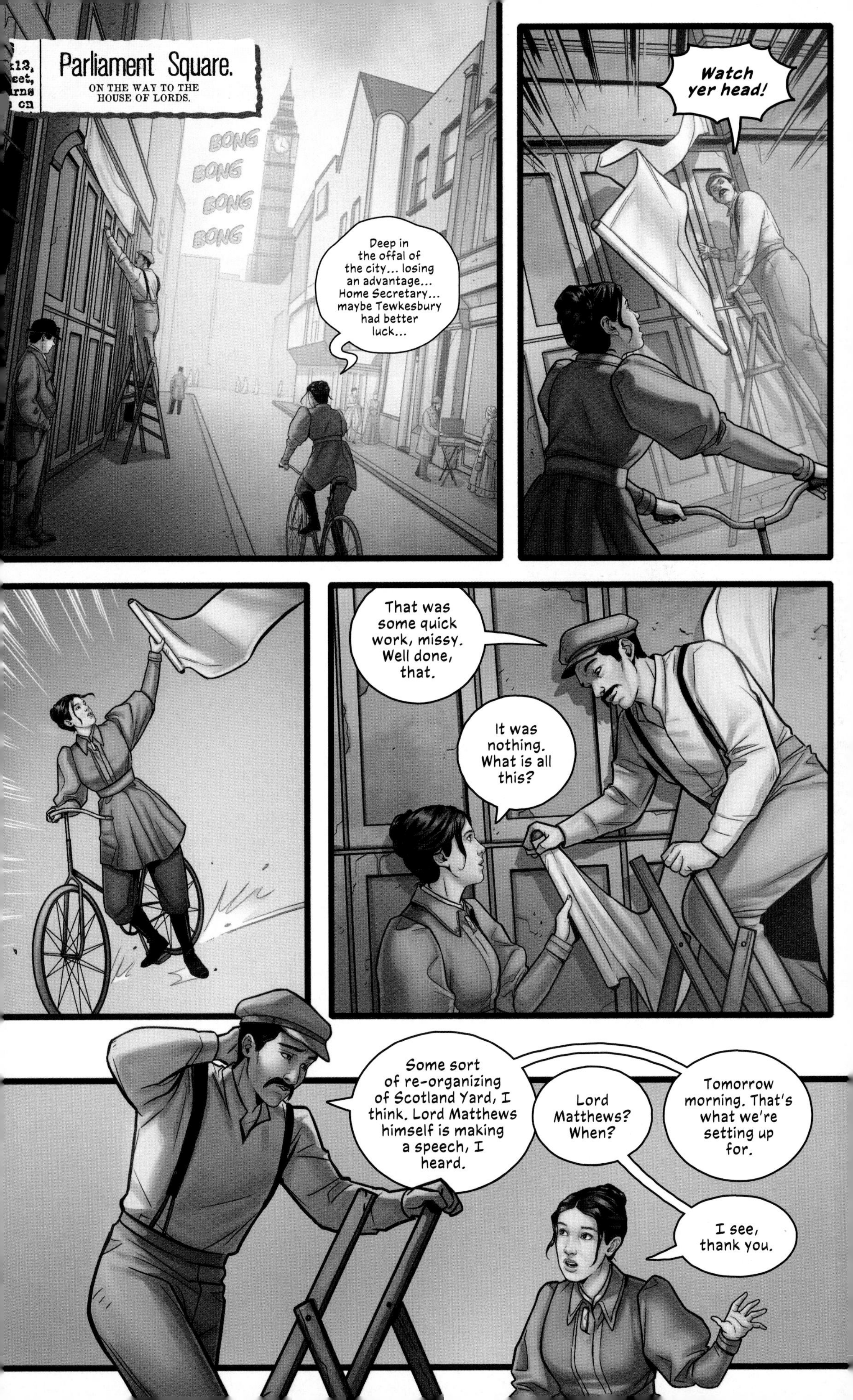
Parliament Square.
ON THE WAY TO THE HOUSE OF LORDS.
BONG BONG BONG BONG
Deep in the offal of the city... losing an advantage... Home Secretary... maybe Tewkesbury had better luck...
Watch yer head!
That was some quick work, missy. Well done, that.
It was nothing. What is all this?
Some sort of re-organizing of Scotland Yard, I think. Lord Matthews himself is making a speech, I heard.
Lord Matthews? When?
Tomorrow morning. That's what we're setting up for.
I see, thank you.

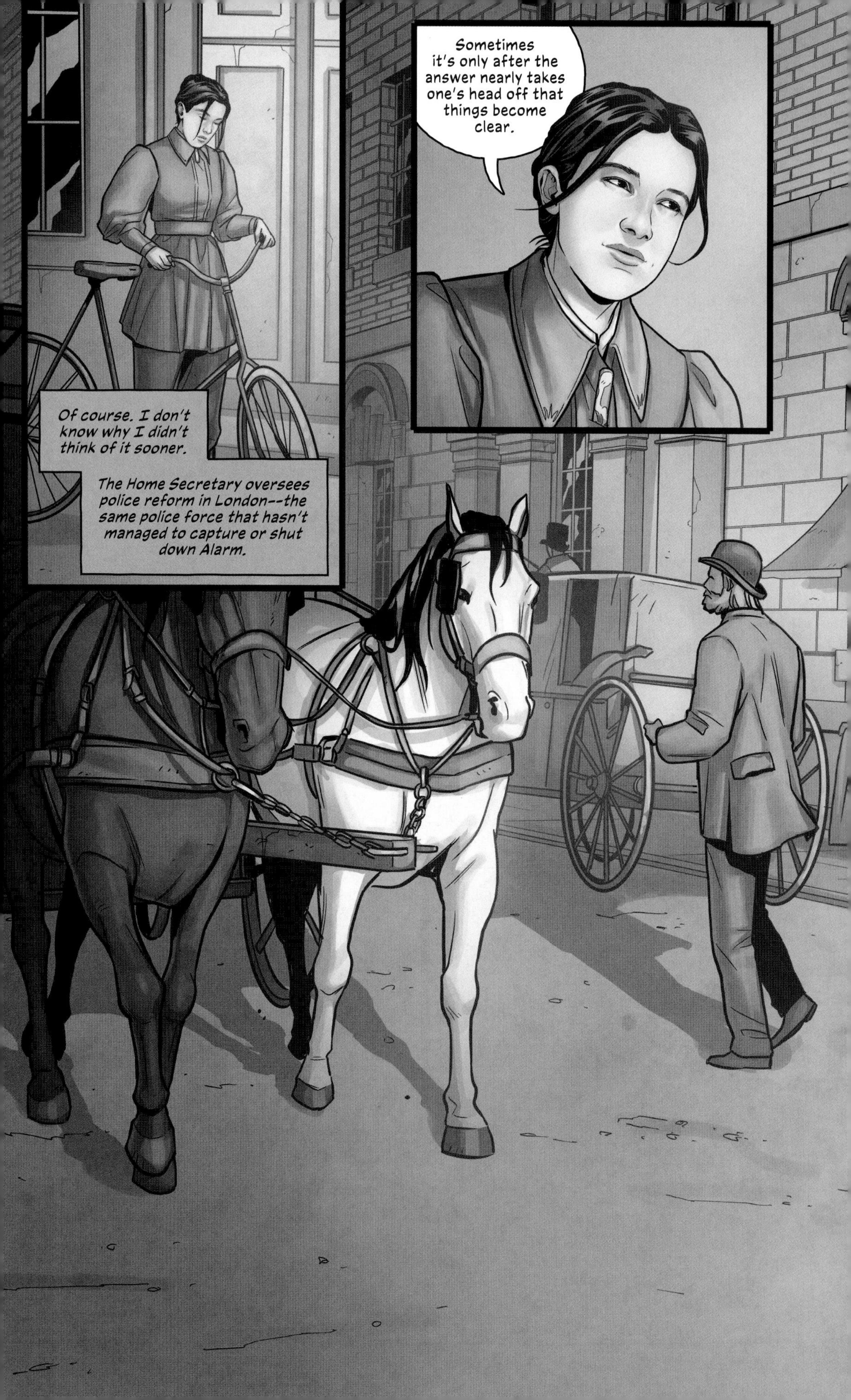
Of course. I don't know why I didn't think of it sooner.
The Home Secretary oversees police reform in London--the same police force that hasn't managed to capture or shut down Alarm.
Sometimes it's only after the answer nearly takes one's head off that things become clear.

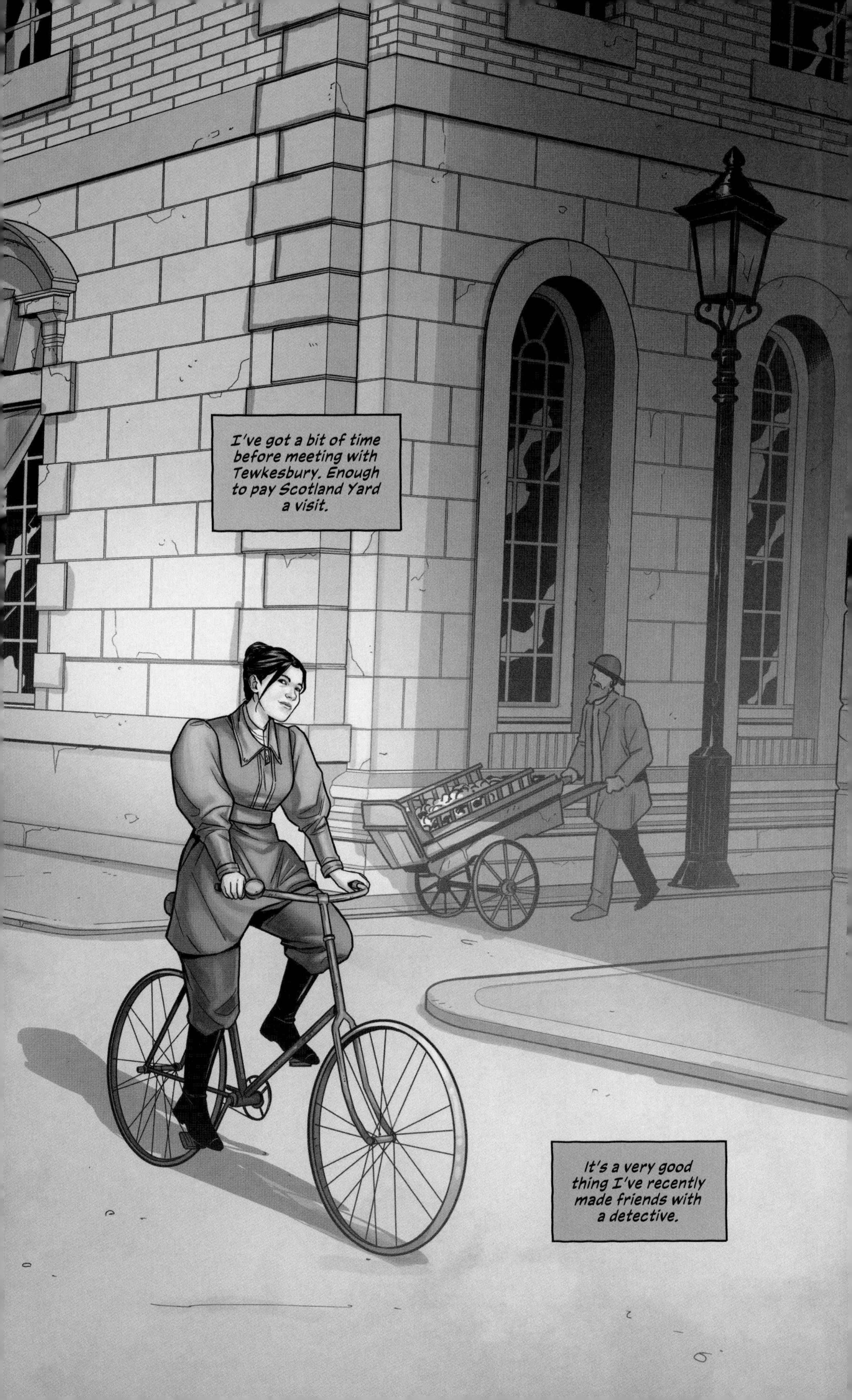
I've got a bit of time before meeting with Tewkesbury. Enough to pay Scotland Yard a visit.
It's a very good thing I've recently made friends with a detective.

[Chapter Three]

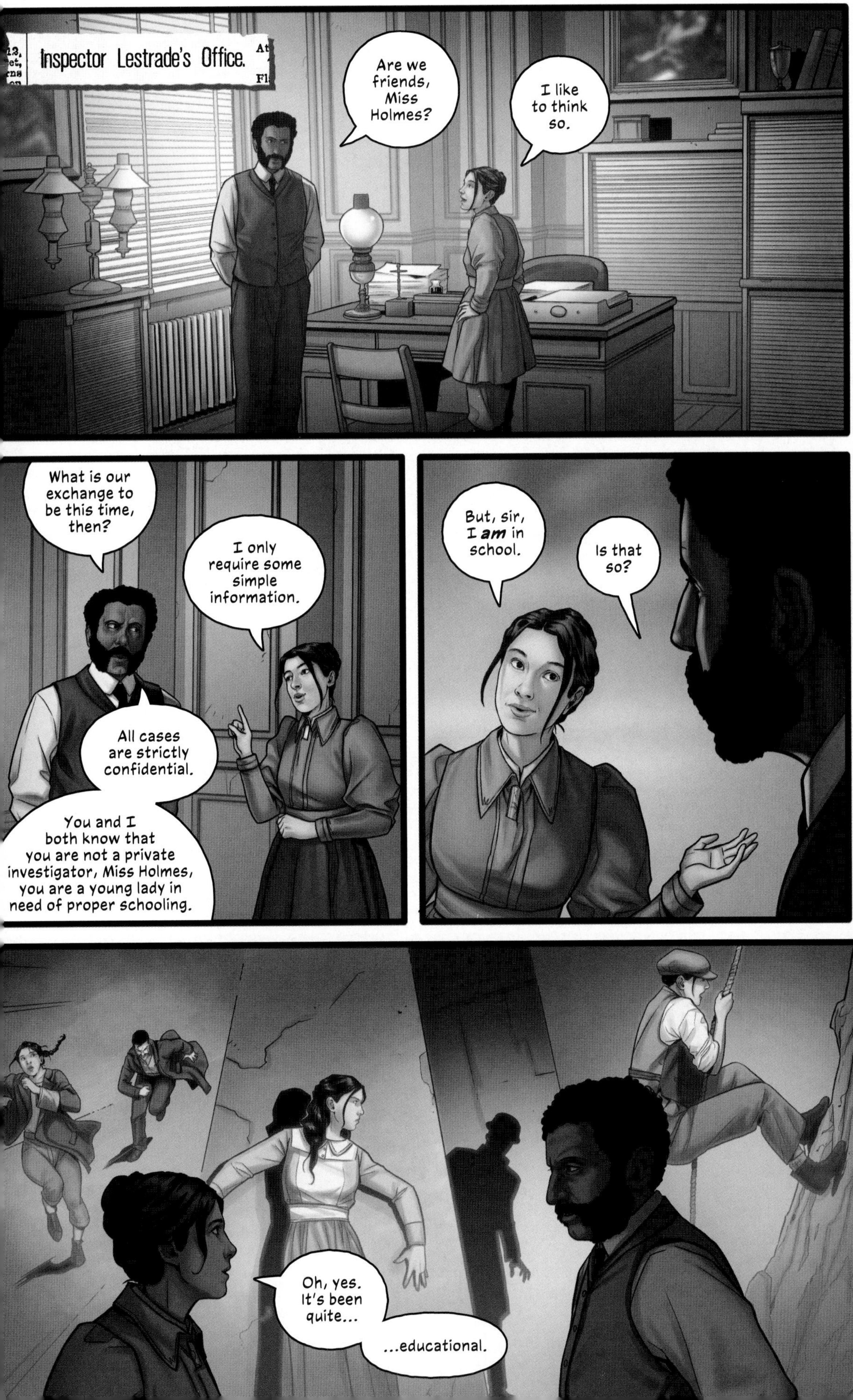
Inspector Lestrade's Office.
Are we friends, Miss Holmes?
I like to think so.
What is our exchange to be this time, then?
I only require some simple information.
All cases are strictly confidential.
You and I both know that you are not a private investigator, Miss Holmes, you are a young lady in need of proper schooling.
But, sir, I *am* in school.
Is that so?
Oh, yes. It's been quite...
...educational.

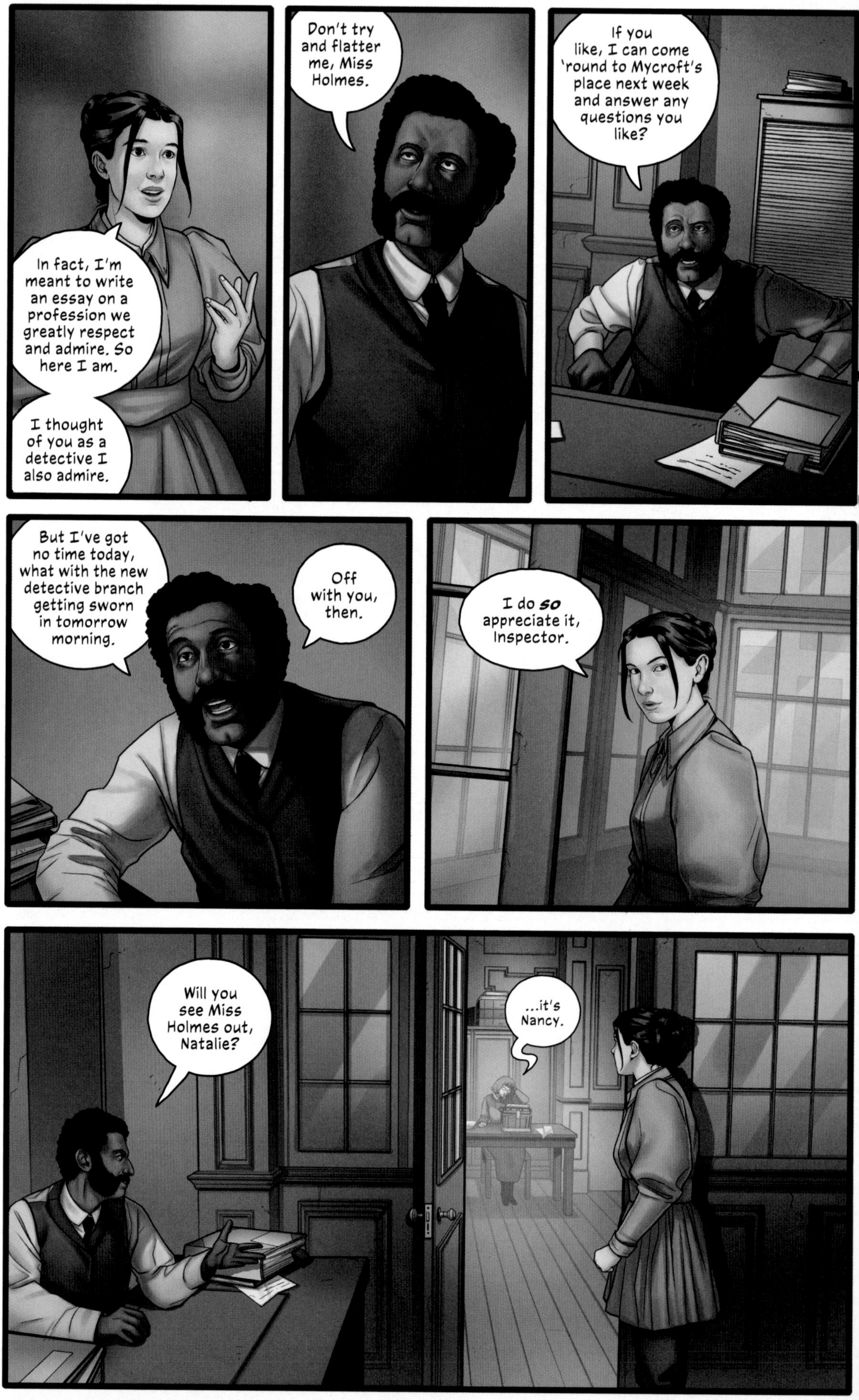
In fact, I'm meant to write an essay on a profession we greatly respect and admire. So here I am.
I thought of you as a detective I also admire.
Don't try and flatter me, Miss Holmes.
If you like, I can come 'round to Mycroft's place next week and answer any questions you like?
But I've got no time today, what with the new detective branch getting sworn in tomorrow morning.
Off with you, then.
I do *so* appreciate it, Inspector.
Will you see Miss Holmes out, Natalie?
...it's Nancy.

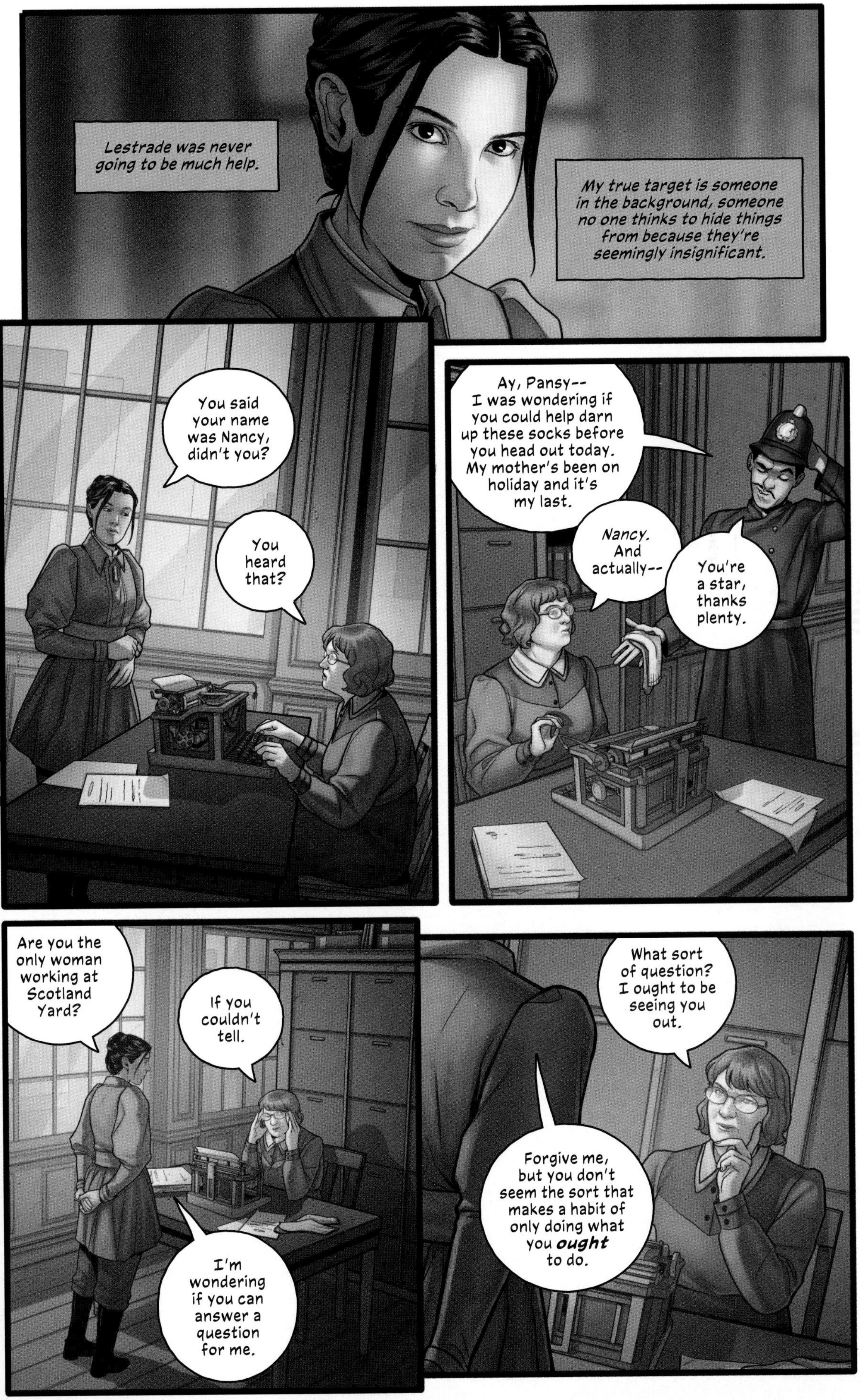
Lestrade was never going to be much help.
My true target is someone in the background, someone no one thinks to hide things from because they're seemingly insignificant.
You said your name was Nancy, didn't you?
You heard that?
Ay, Pansy-- I was wondering if you could help darn up these socks before you head out today. My mother's been on holiday and it's my last.
Nancy. And actually--
You're a star, thanks plenty.
Are you the only woman working at Scotland Yard?
If you couldn't tell.
I'm wondering if you can answer a question for me.
What sort of question? I ought to be seeing you out.
Forgive me, but you don't seem the sort that makes a habit of only doing what you ***ought*** to do.

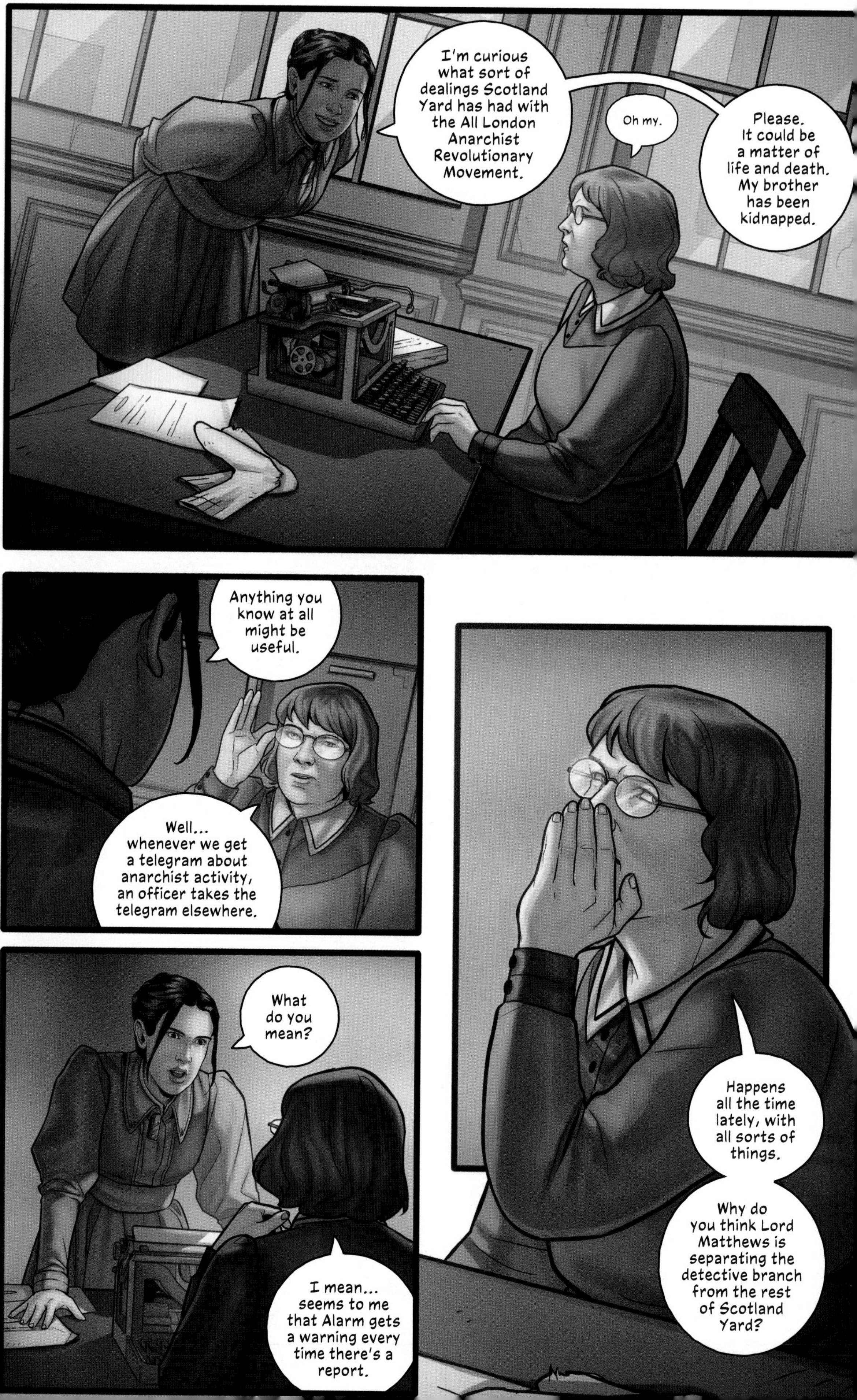
I'm curious what sort of dealings Scotland Yard has had with the All London Anarchist Revolutionary Movement.
Oh my.
Please. It could be a matter of life and death. My brother has been kidnapped.
Anything you know at all might be useful.
Well... whenever we get a telegram about anarchist activity, an officer takes the telegram elsewhere.
What do you mean?
I mean... seems to me that Alarm gets a warning every time there's a report.
Happens all the time lately, with all sorts of things.
Why do you think Lord Matthews is separating the detective branch from the rest of Scotland Yard?

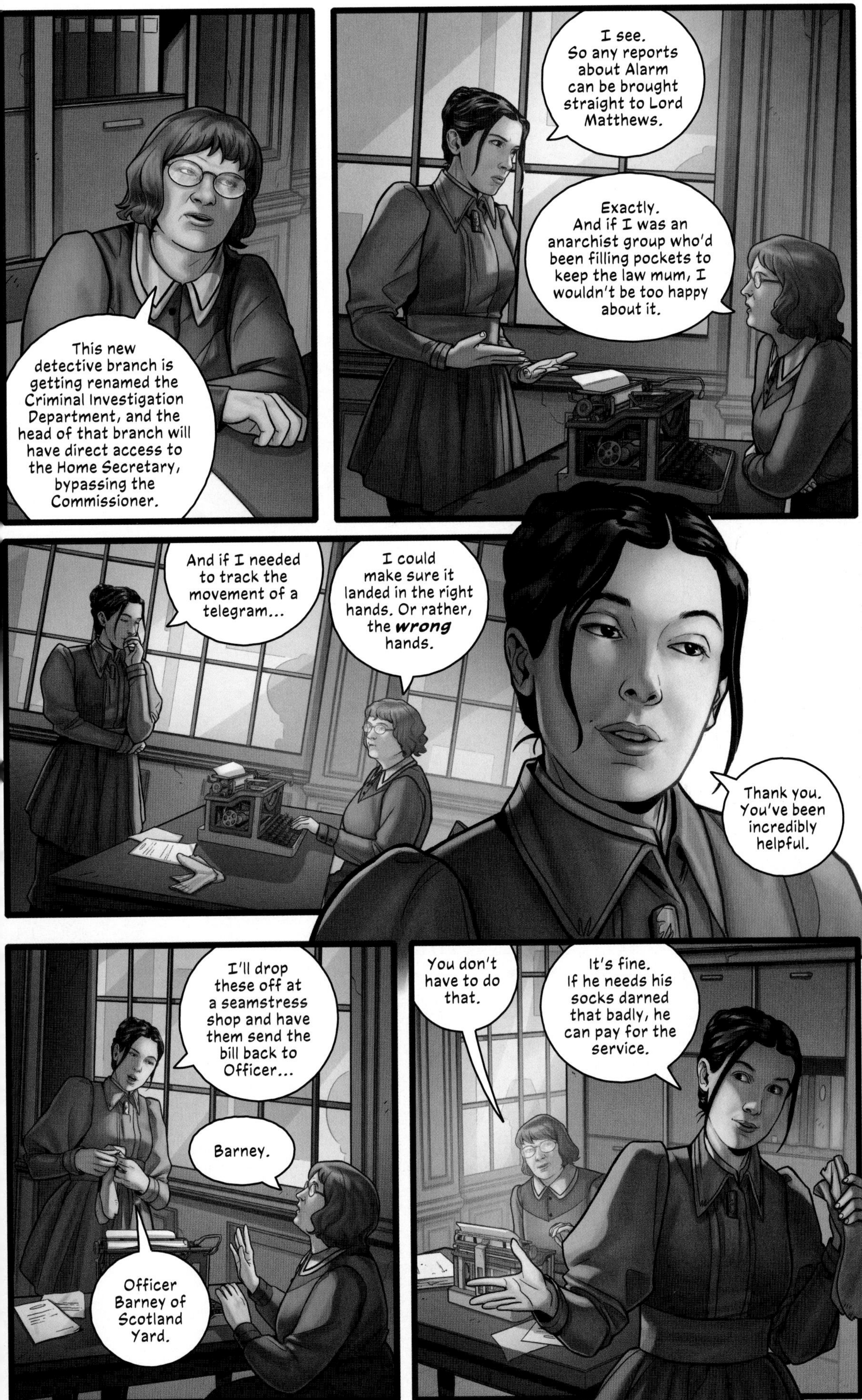
This new detective branch is getting renamed the Criminal Investigation Department, and the head of that branch will have direct access to the Home Secretary, bypassing the Commissioner.
I see. So any reports about Alarm can be brought straight to Lord Matthews.
Exactly. And if I was an anarchist group who'd been filling pockets to keep the law mum, I wouldn't be too happy about it.
And if I needed to track the movement of a telegram...
I could make sure it landed in the right hands. Or rather, the *wrong* hands.
Thank you. You've been incredibly helpful.
I'll drop these off at a seamstress shop and have them send the bill back to Officer...
Barney.
Officer Barney of Scotland Yard.
You don't have to do that.
It's fine. If he needs his socks darned that badly, he can pay for the service.

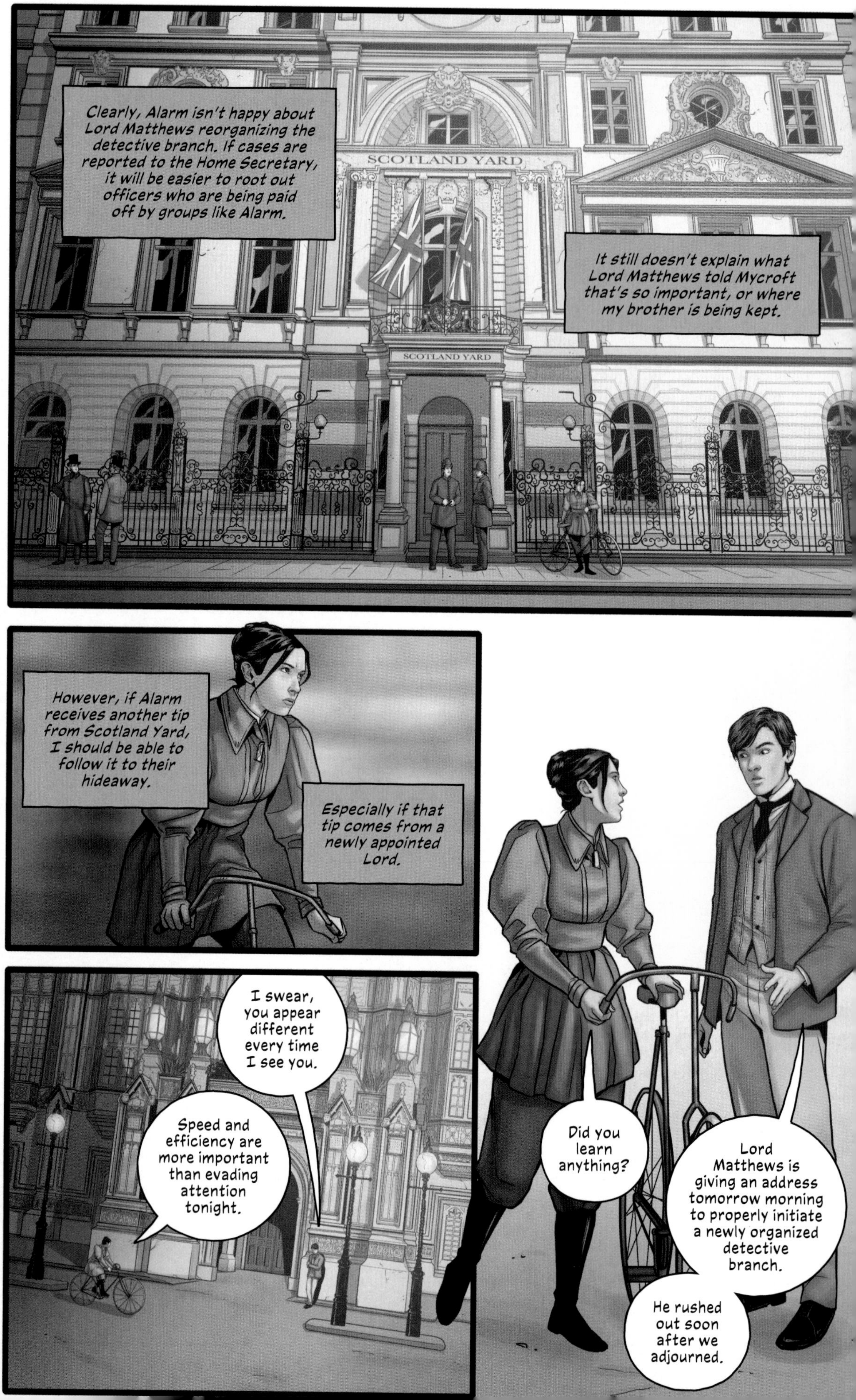
SCOTLAND YARD
Clearly, Alarm isn't happy about Lord Matthews reorganizing the detective branch. If cases are reported to the Home Secretary, it will be easier to root out officers who are being paid off by groups like Alarm.
It still doesn't explain what Lord Matthews told Mycroft that's so important, or where my brother is being kept.
SCOTLAND YARD
However, if Alarm receives another tip from Scotland Yard, I should be able to follow it to their hideaway.
Especially if that tip comes from a newly appointed Lord.
I swear, you appear different every time I see you.
Speed and efficiency are more important than evading attention tonight.
Did you learn anything?
Lord Matthews is giving an address tomorrow morning to properly initiate a newly organized detective branch.
He rushed out soon after we adjourned.

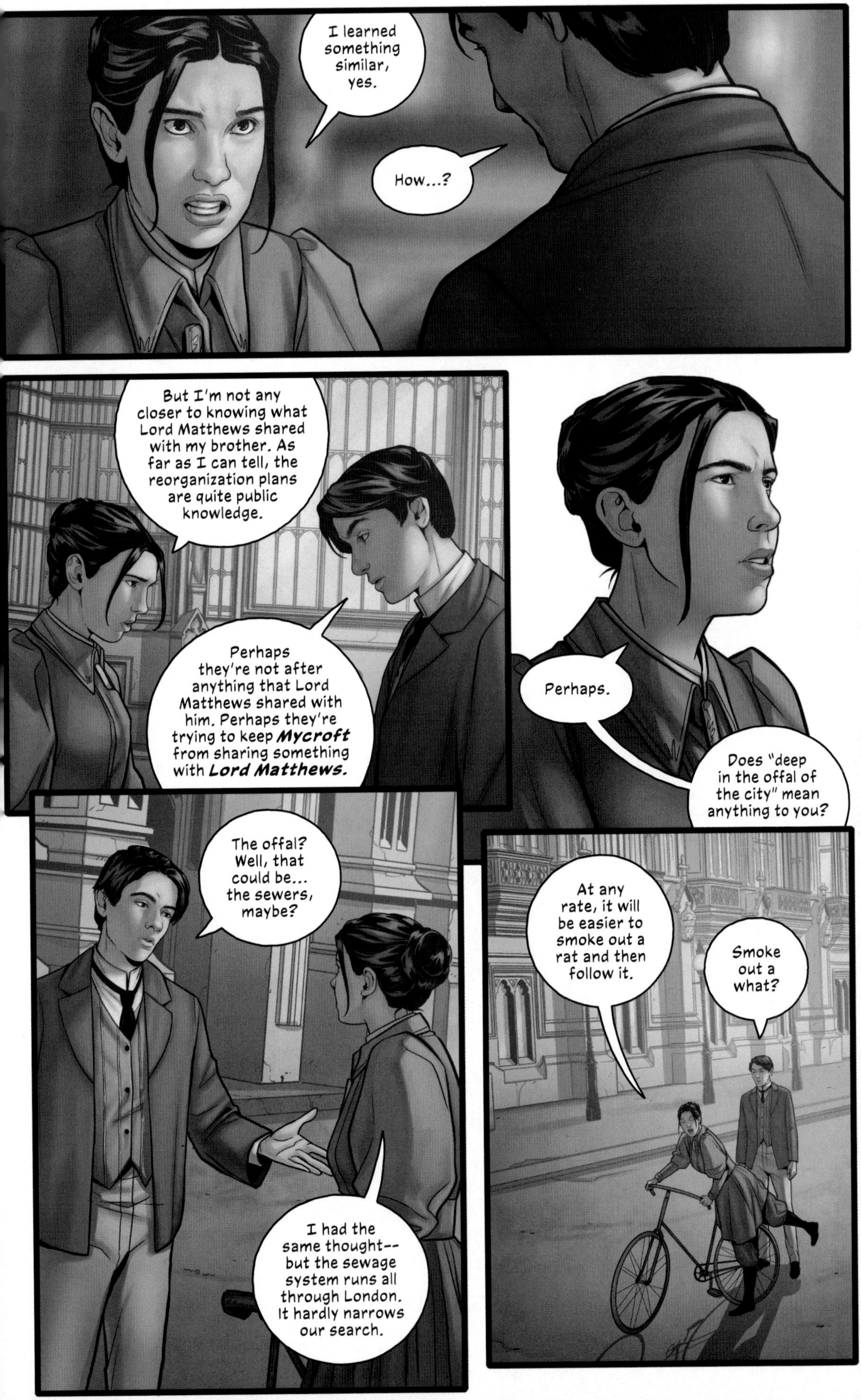
I learned something similar, yes.
How...?
But I'm not any closer to knowing what Lord Matthews shared with my brother. As far as I can tell, the reorganization plans are quite public knowledge.
Perhaps they're not after anything that Lord Matthews shared with him. Perhaps they're trying to keep **Mycroft** from sharing something with **Lord Matthews.**
Perhaps.
Does "deep in the offal of the city" mean anything to you?
The offal? Well, that could be... the sewers, maybe?
I had the same thought--but the sewage system runs all through London. It hardly narrows our search.
At any rate, it will be easier to smoke out a rat and then follow it.
Smoke out a what?

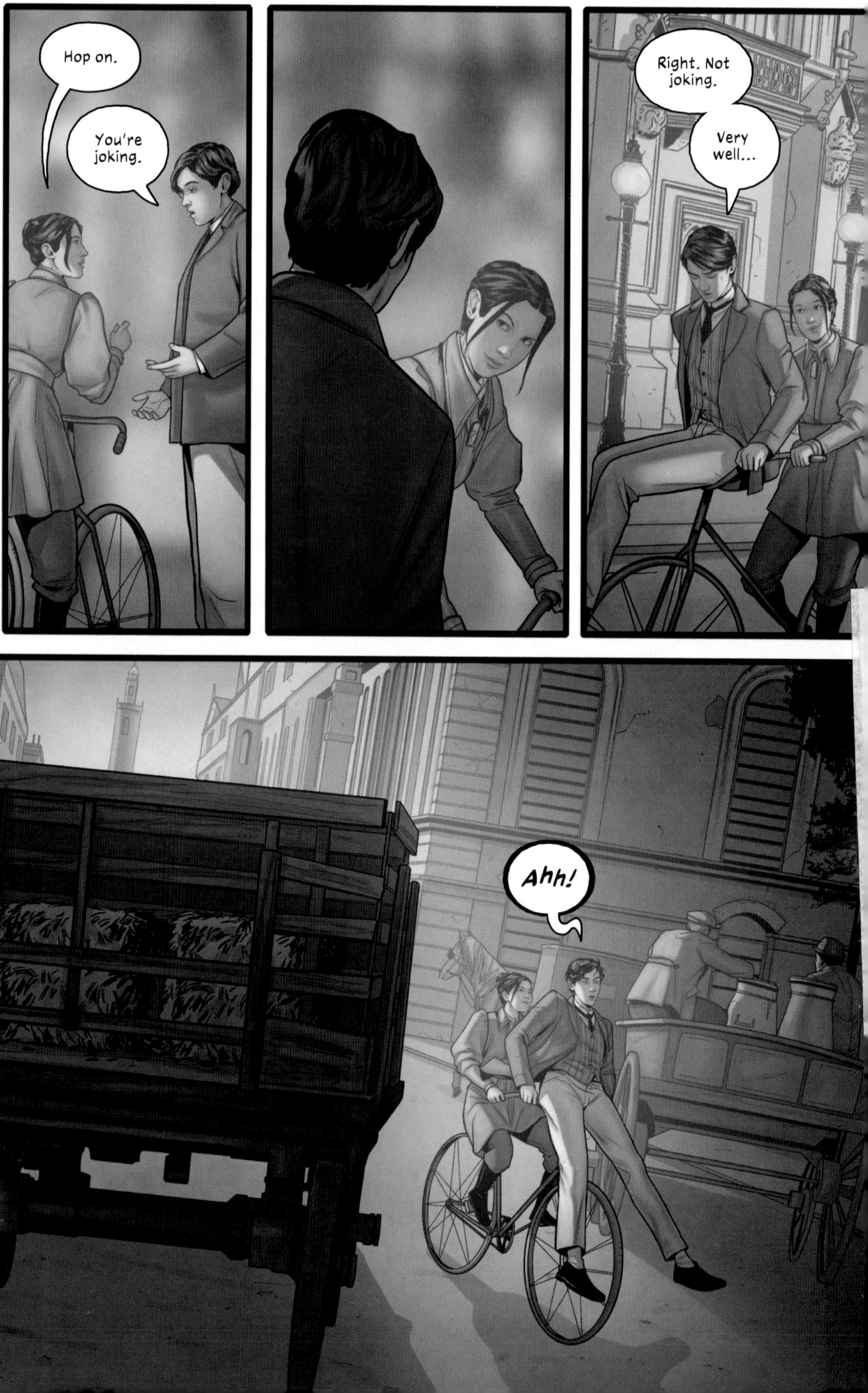
Hop on.
You're joking.
Right. Not joking.
Very well...
Ahh!

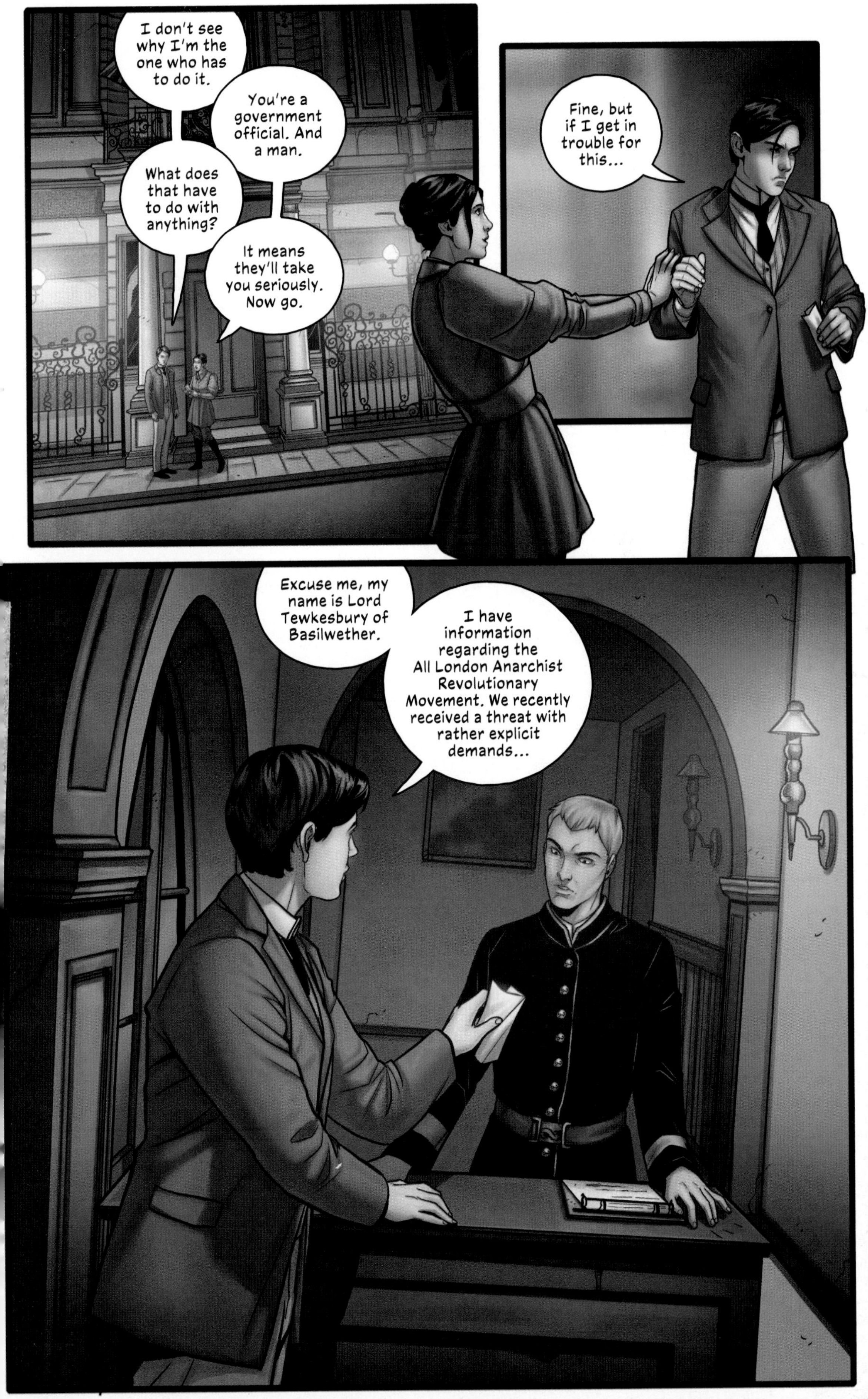
I don't see why I'm the one who has to do it.
You're a government official. And a man.
What does that have to do with anything?
It means they'll take you seriously. Now go.
Fine, but if I get in trouble for this...
Excuse me, my name is Lord Tewkesbury of Basilwether.
I have information regarding the All London Anarchist Revolutionary Movement. We recently received a threat with rather explicit demands...

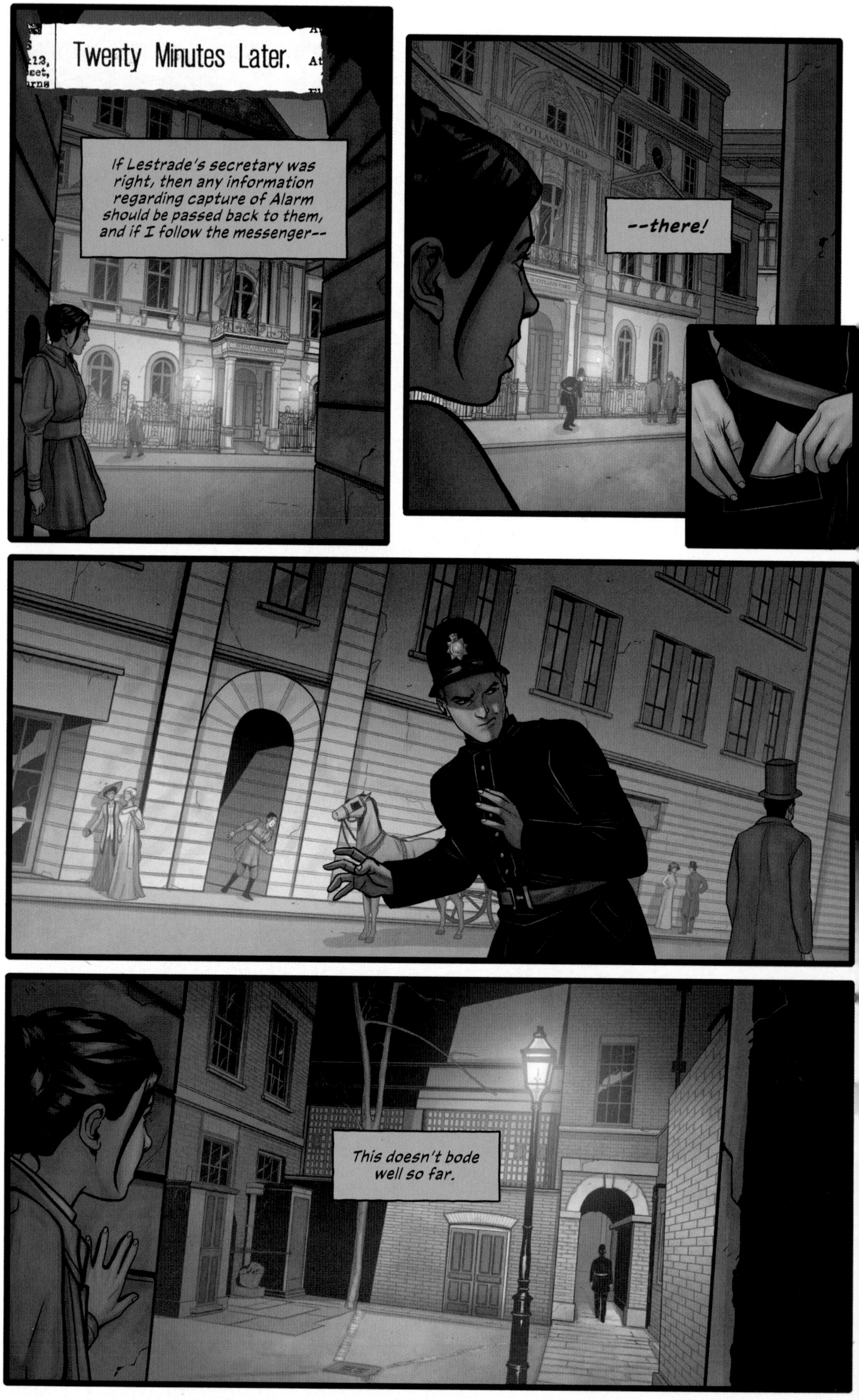
Twenty Minutes Later.
If Lestrade's secretary was right, then any information regarding capture of Alarm should be passed back to them, and if I follow the messenger--
SCOTLAND YARD
--there!
This doesn't bode well so far.

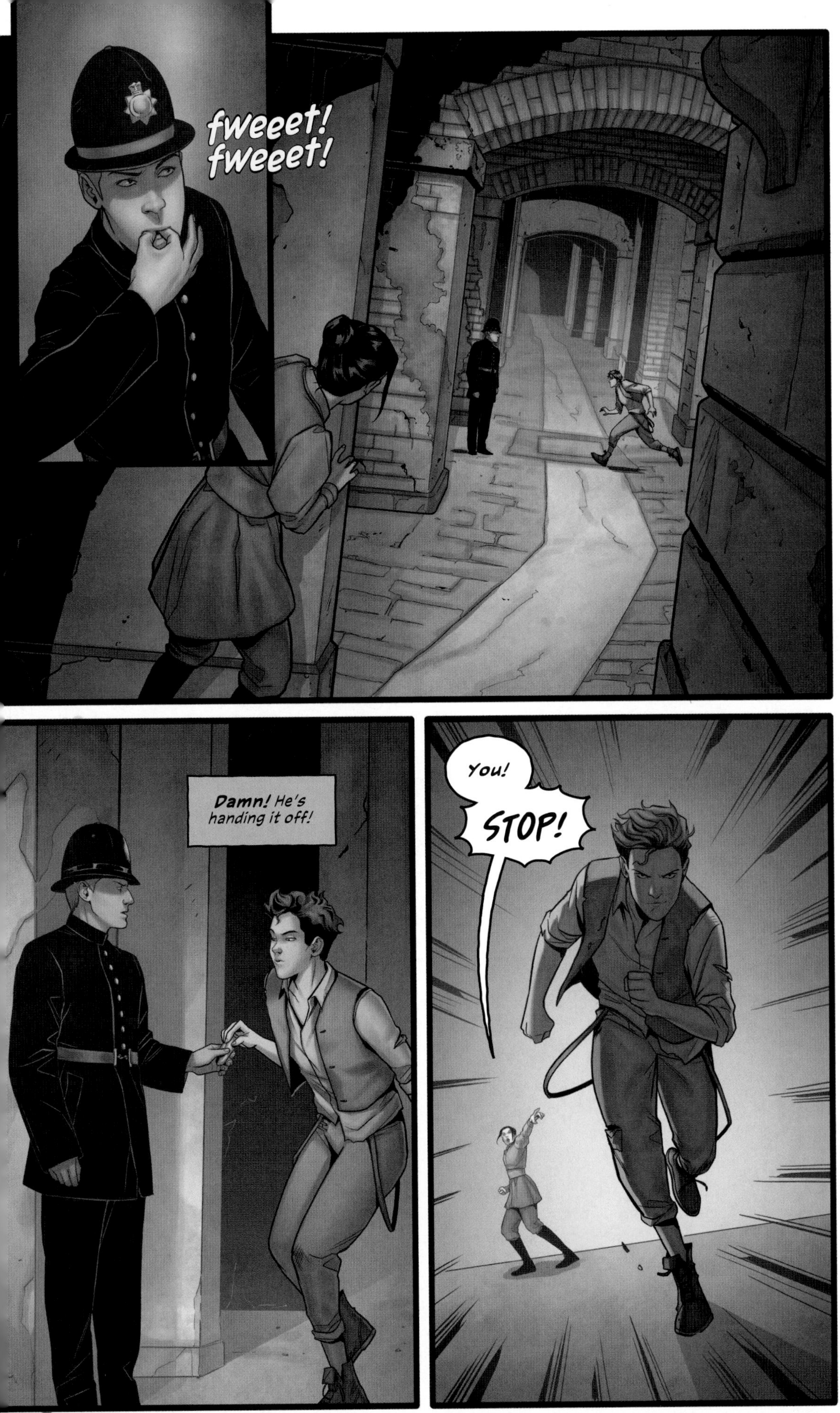
fweeet!
fweeet!
Damn! He's handing it off!
You!
STOP!

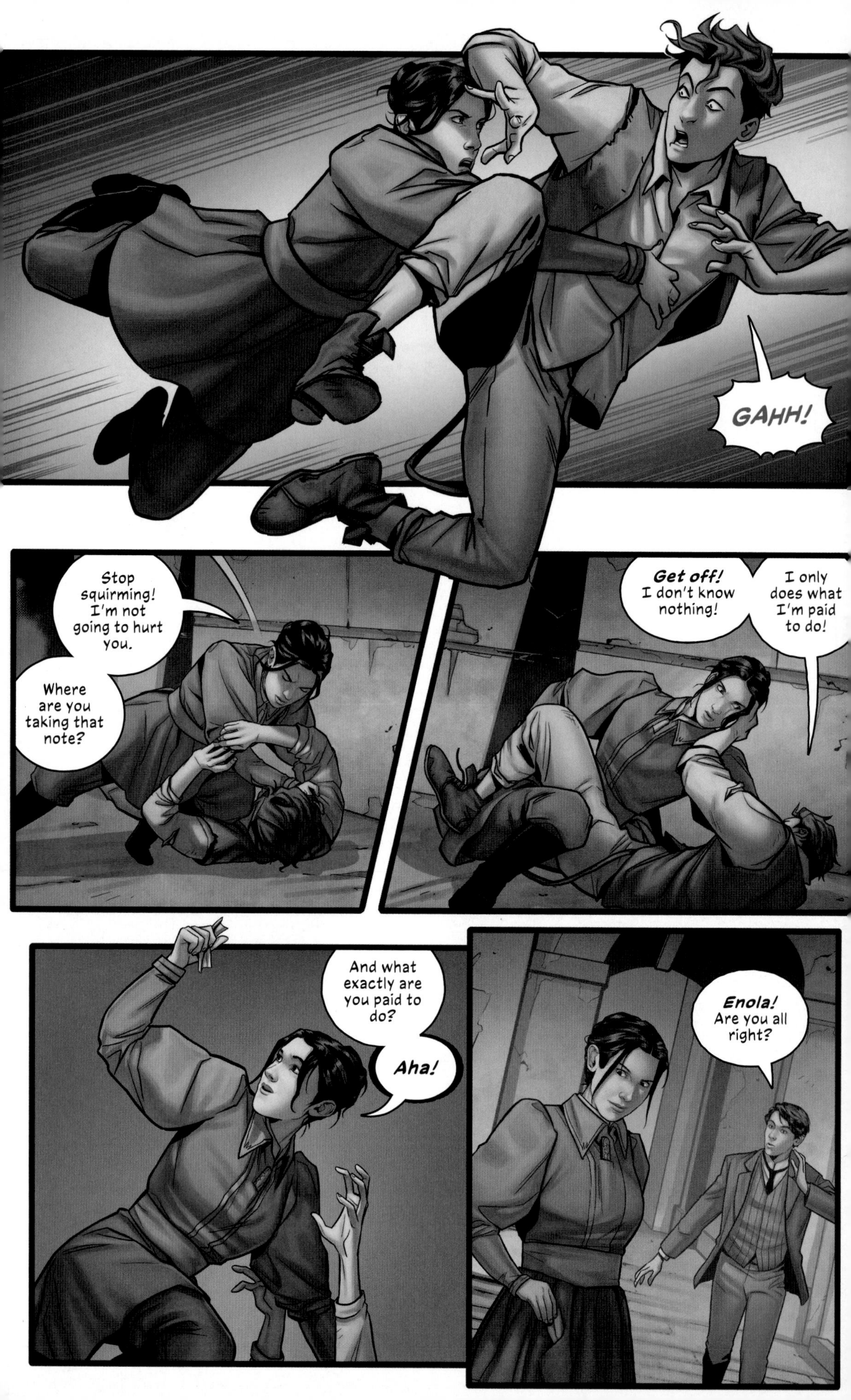
GAHH!
Stop squirming! I'm not going to hurt you.
Where are you taking that note?
Get off! I don't know nothing!
I only does what I'm paid to do!
And what exactly are you paid to do?
Aha!
Enola! Are you all right?

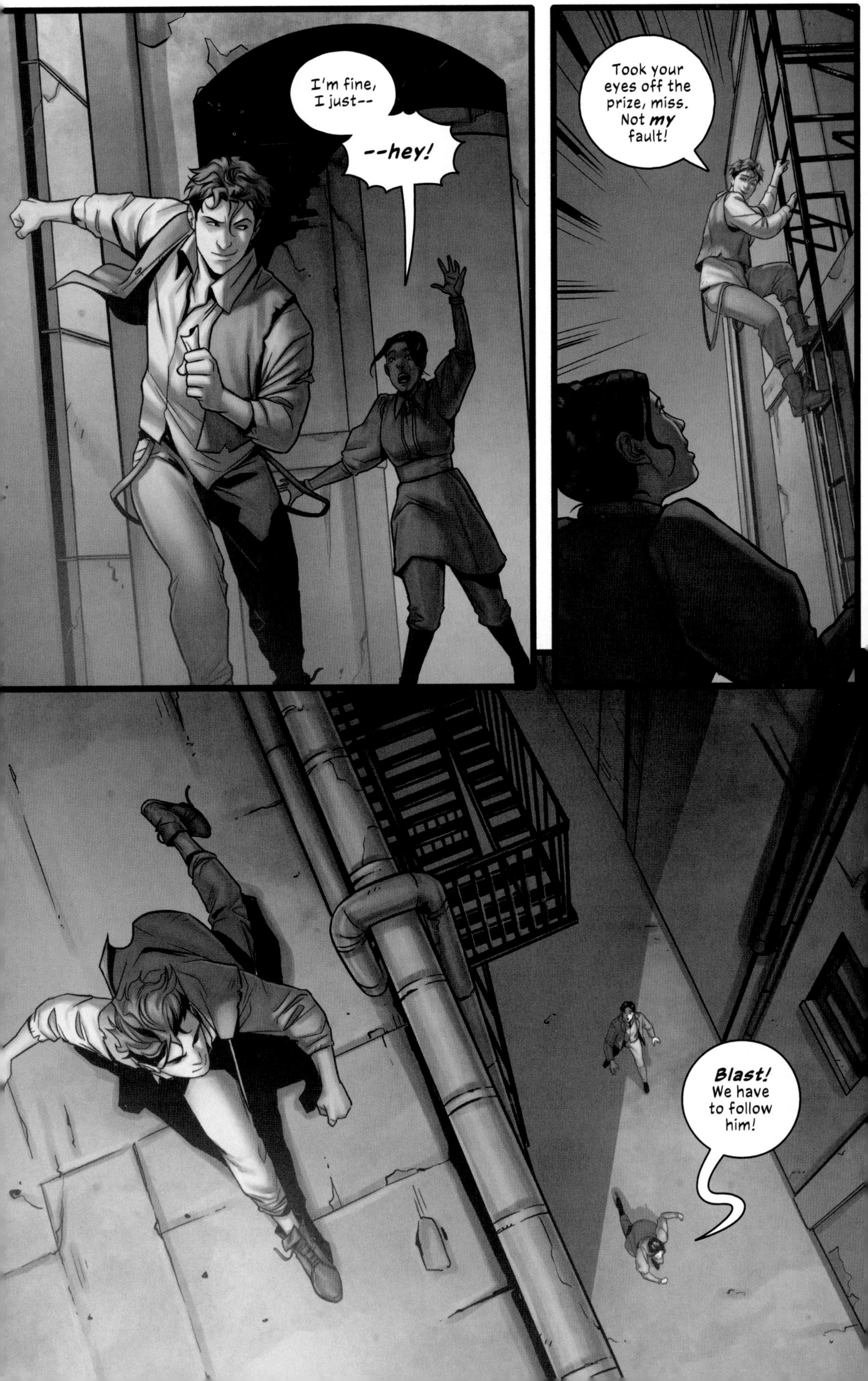
I'm fine, I just--
--hey!
Took your eyes off the prize, miss. Not my fault!
Blast! We have to follow him!

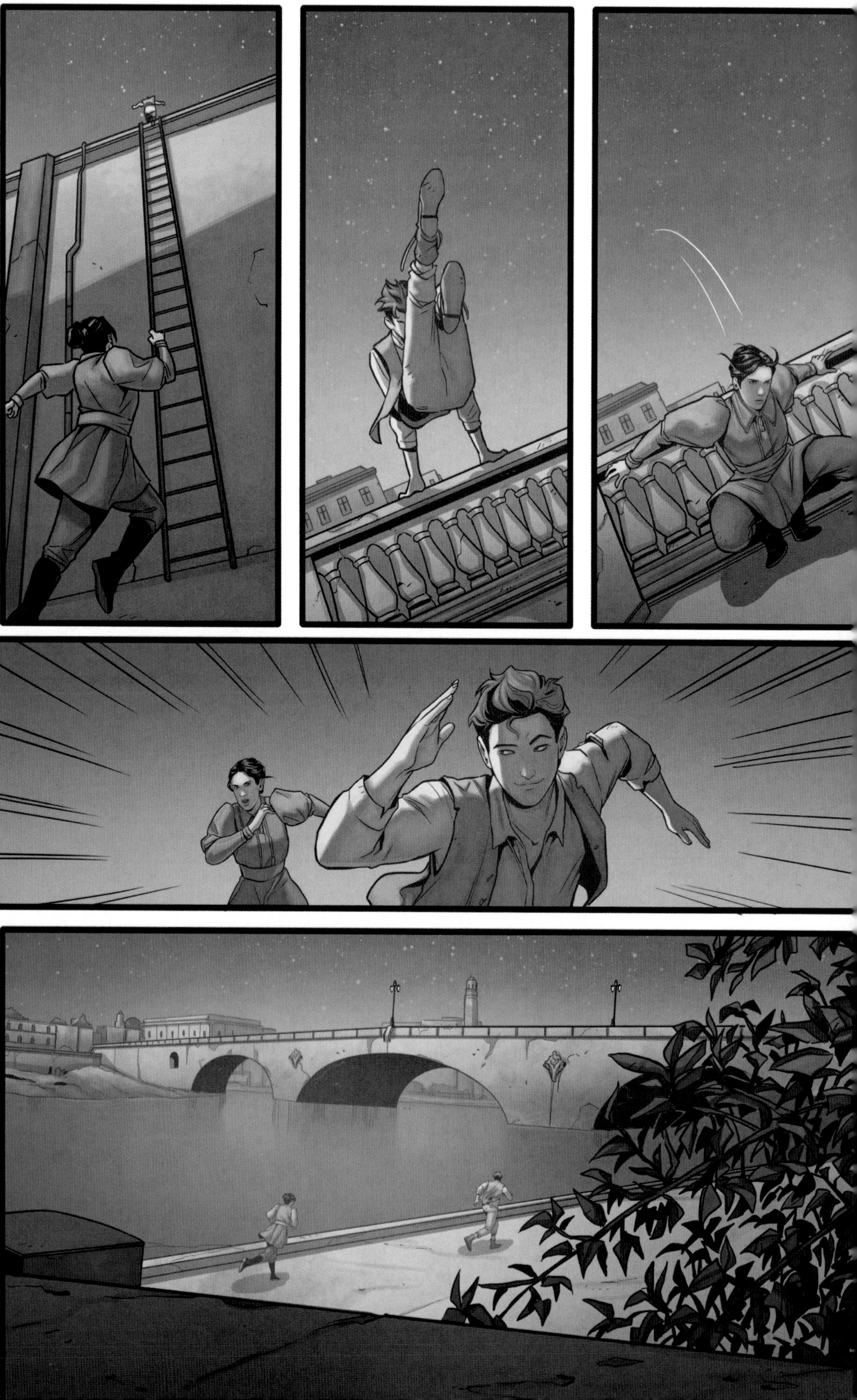

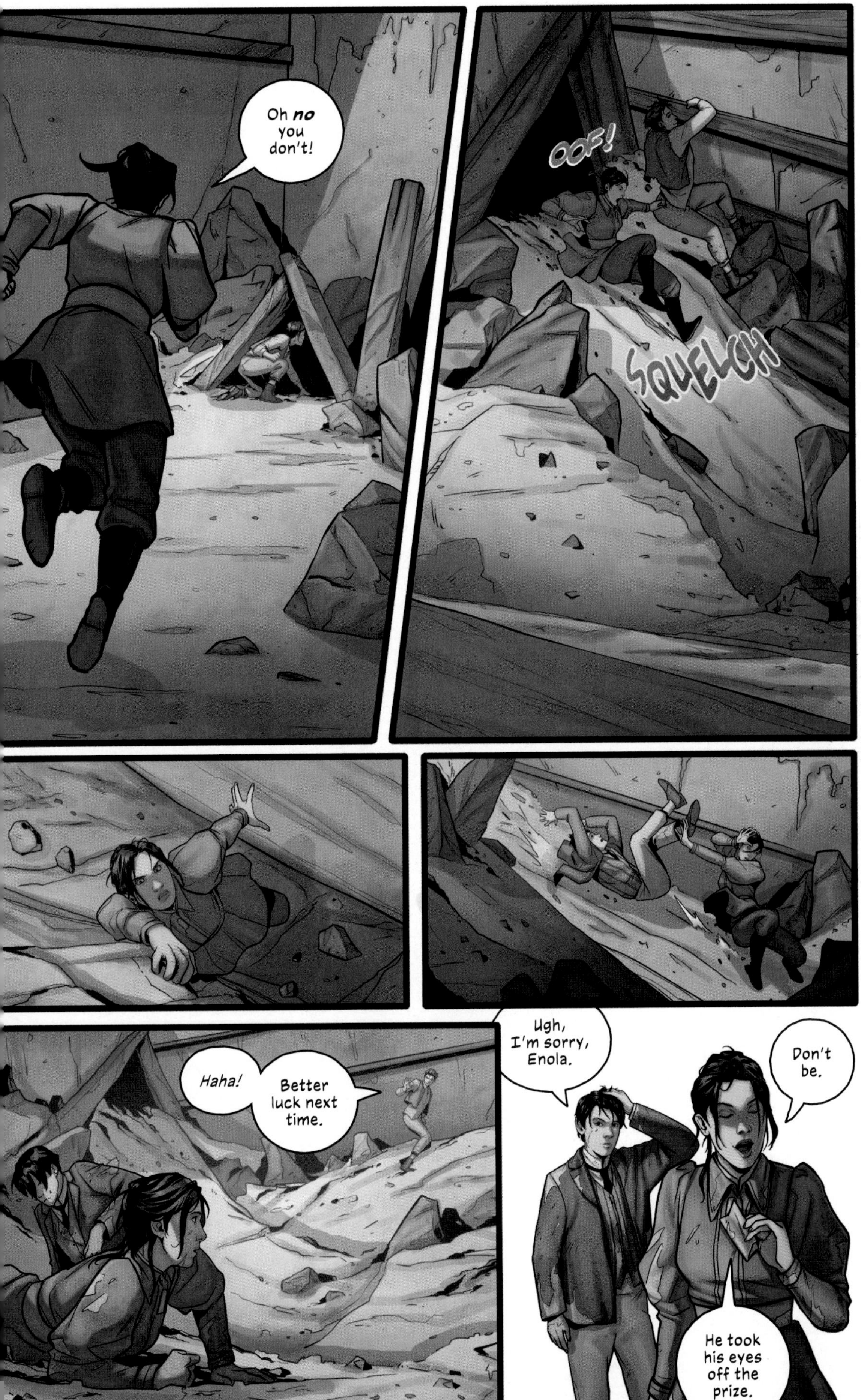
Oh no you don't!
OOF!
SQUELCH
Haha!
Better luck next time.
Ugh, I'm sorry, Enola.
Don't be.
He took his eyes off the prize.

[Chapter Four]

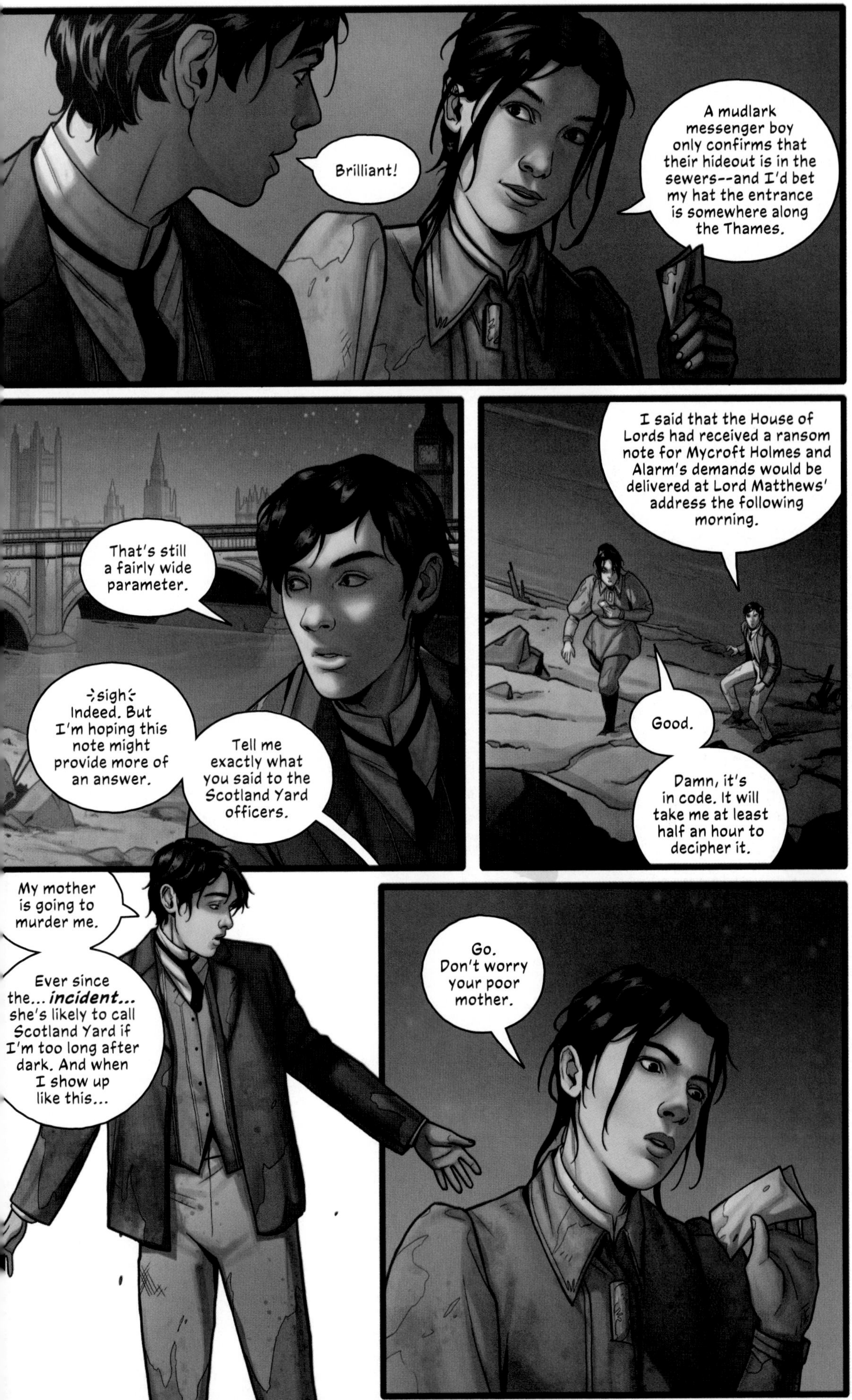
Brilliant!
A mudlark messenger boy only confirms that their hideout is in the sewers--and I'd bet my hat the entrance is somewhere along the Thames.
That's still a fairly wide parameter.
-sigh- Indeed. But I'm hoping this note might provide more of an answer.
Tell me exactly what you said to the Scotland Yard officers.
I said that the House of Lords had received a ransom note for Mycroft Holmes and Alarm's demands would be delivered at Lord Matthews' address the following morning.
Good.
Damn, it's in code. It will take me at least half an hour to decipher it.
My mother is going to murder me.
Ever since the... *incident*... she's likely to call Scotland Yard if I'm too long after dark. And when I show up like this...
Go. Don't worry your poor mother.

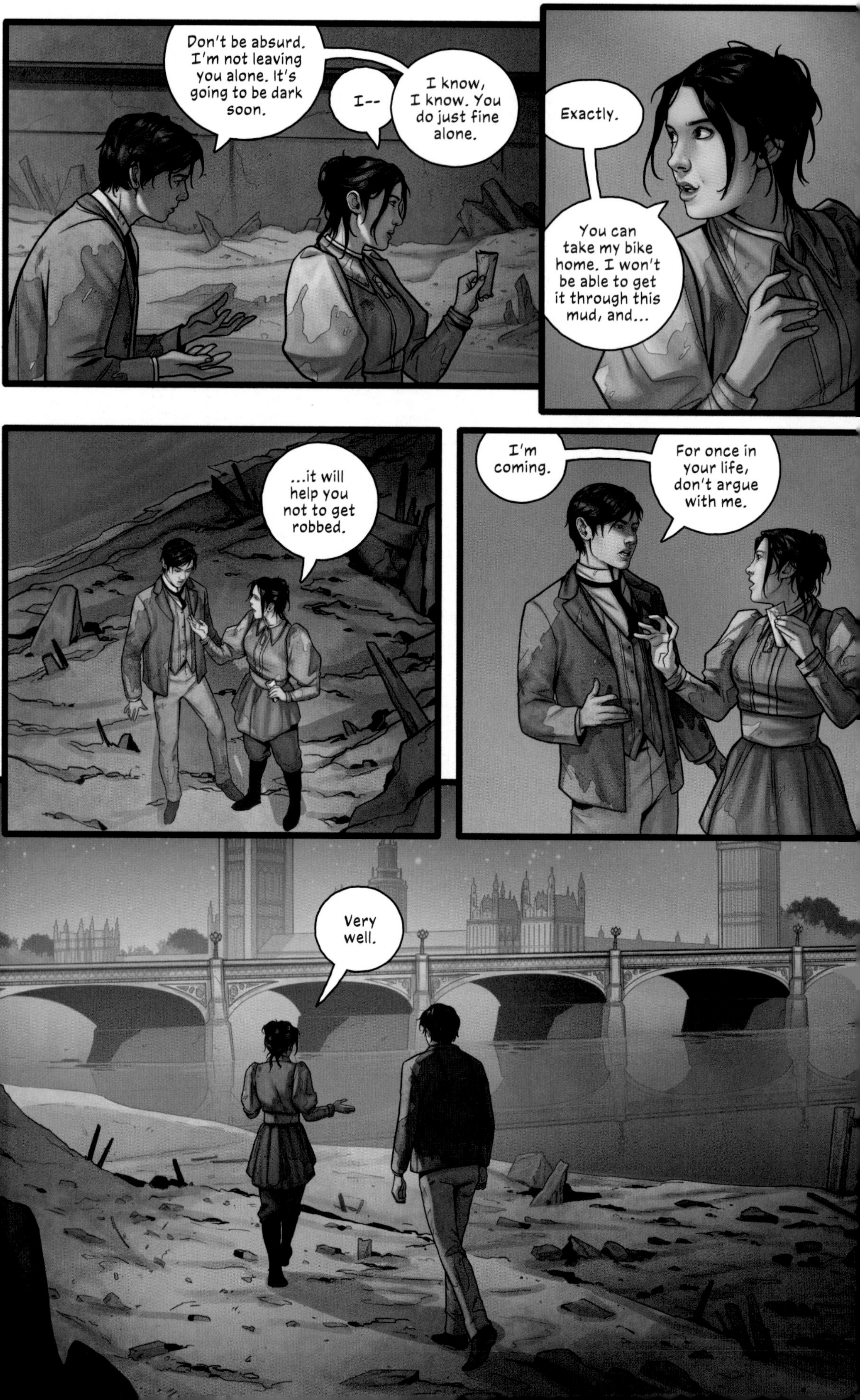
Don't be absurd. I'm not leaving you alone. It's going to be dark soon.
I--
I know, I know. You do just fine alone.
Exactly.
You can take my bike home. I won't be able to get it through this mud, and...
...it will help you not to get robbed.
I'm coming.
For once in your life, don't argue with me.
Very well.

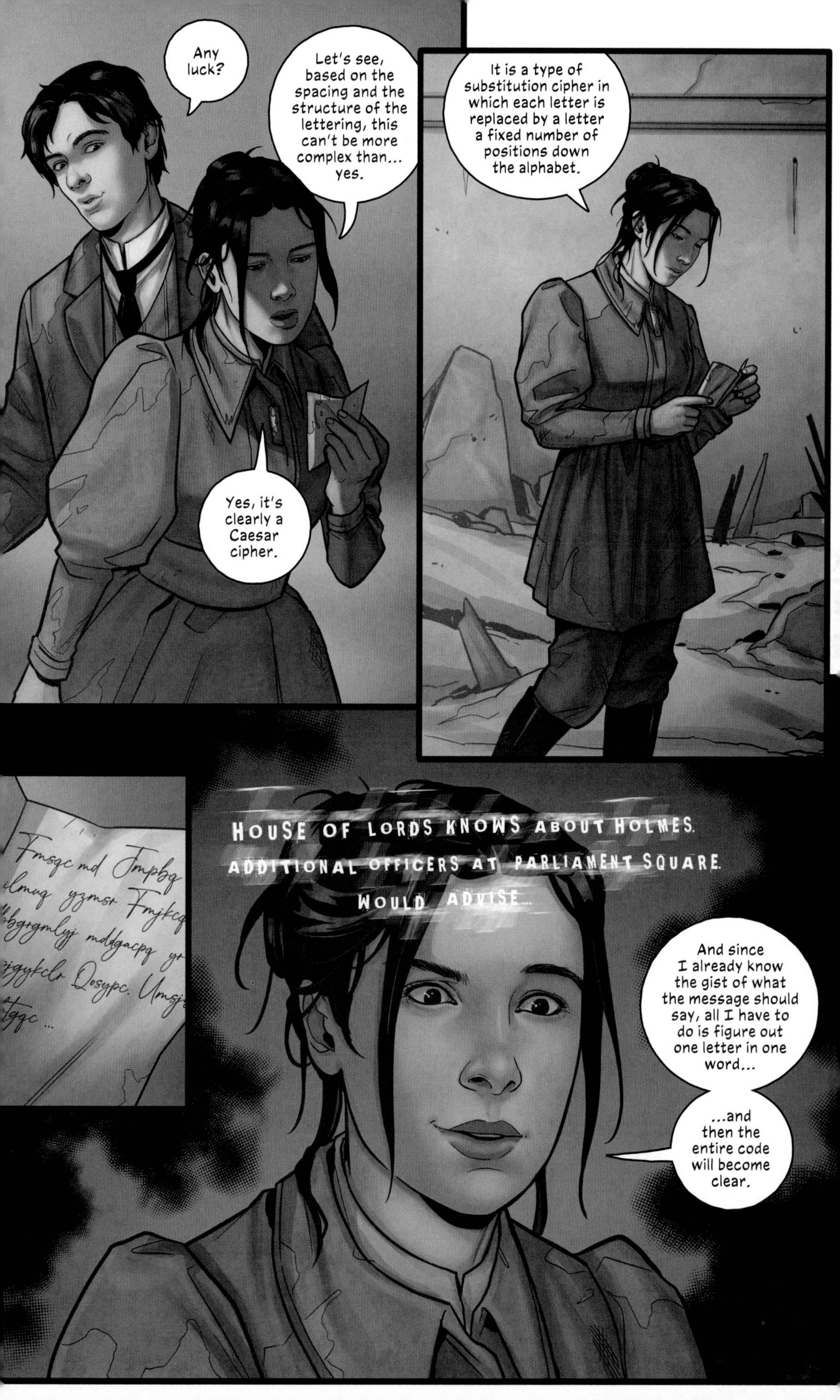

Any luck?
Let's see, based on the spacing and the structure of the lettering, this can't be more complex than... yes.
Yes, it's clearly a Caesar cipher.
It is a type of substitution cipher in which each letter is replaced by a letter a fixed number of positions down the alphabet.
Fmsqc md Jmpbq
ilmuq yzmsr Fmjkcq
bbgrgmlyj mddgacpq yr
jgykclr Qosypc. Umsj
tgqc ...
HOUSE OF LORDS KNOWS ABOUT HOLMES.
ADDITIONAL OFFICERS AT PARLIAMENT SQUARE.
WOULD ADVISE...
And since I already know the gist of what the message should say, all I have to do is figure out one letter in one word...
...and then the entire code will become clear.

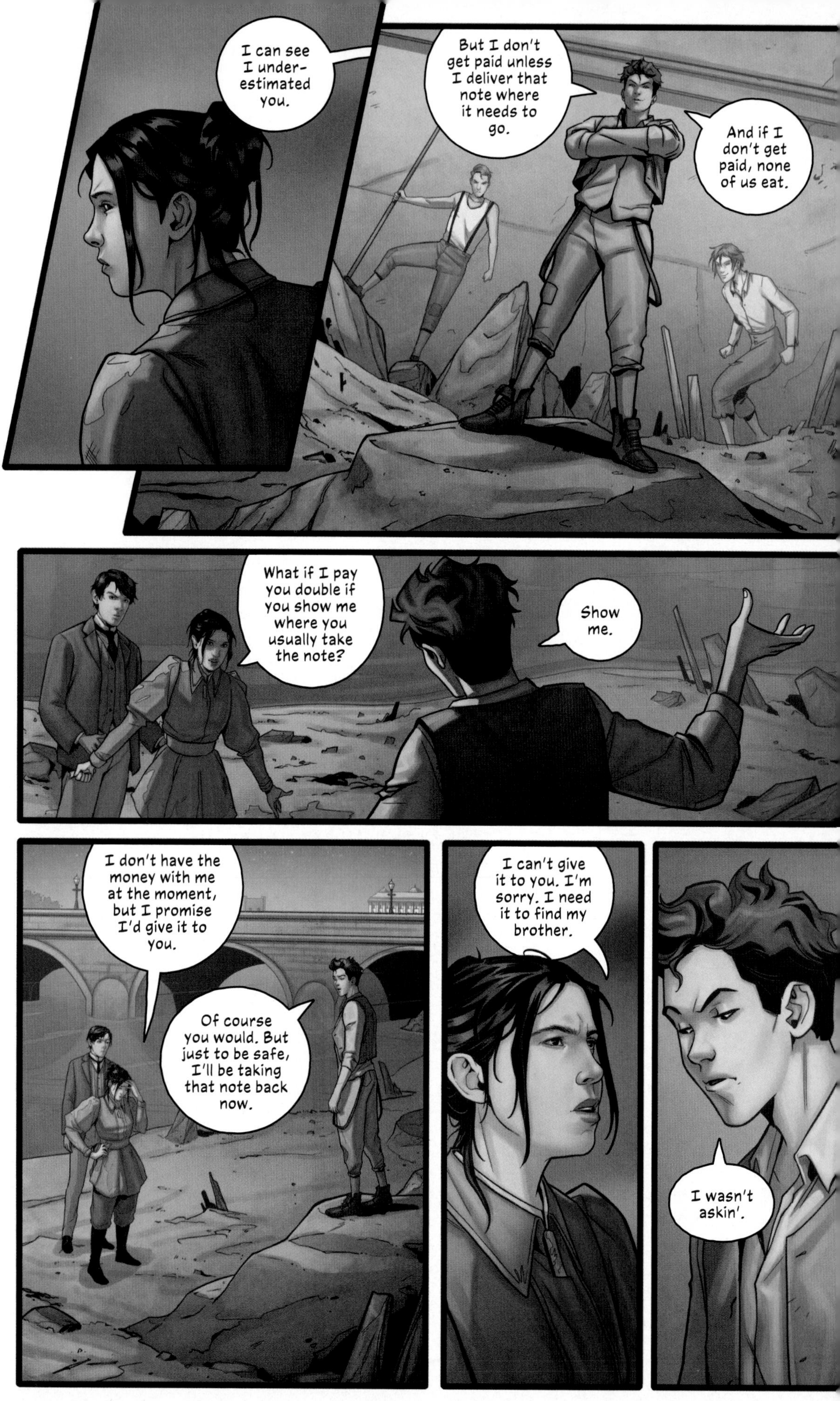
I can see I under-estimated you.
But I don't get paid unless I deliver that note where it needs to go.
And if I don't get paid, none of us eat.
What if I pay you double if you show me where you usually take the note?
Show me.
I don't have the money with me at the moment, but I promise I'd give it to you.
Of course you would. But just to be safe, I'll be taking that note back now.
I can't give it to you. I'm sorry. I need it to find my brother.
I wasn't askin'.

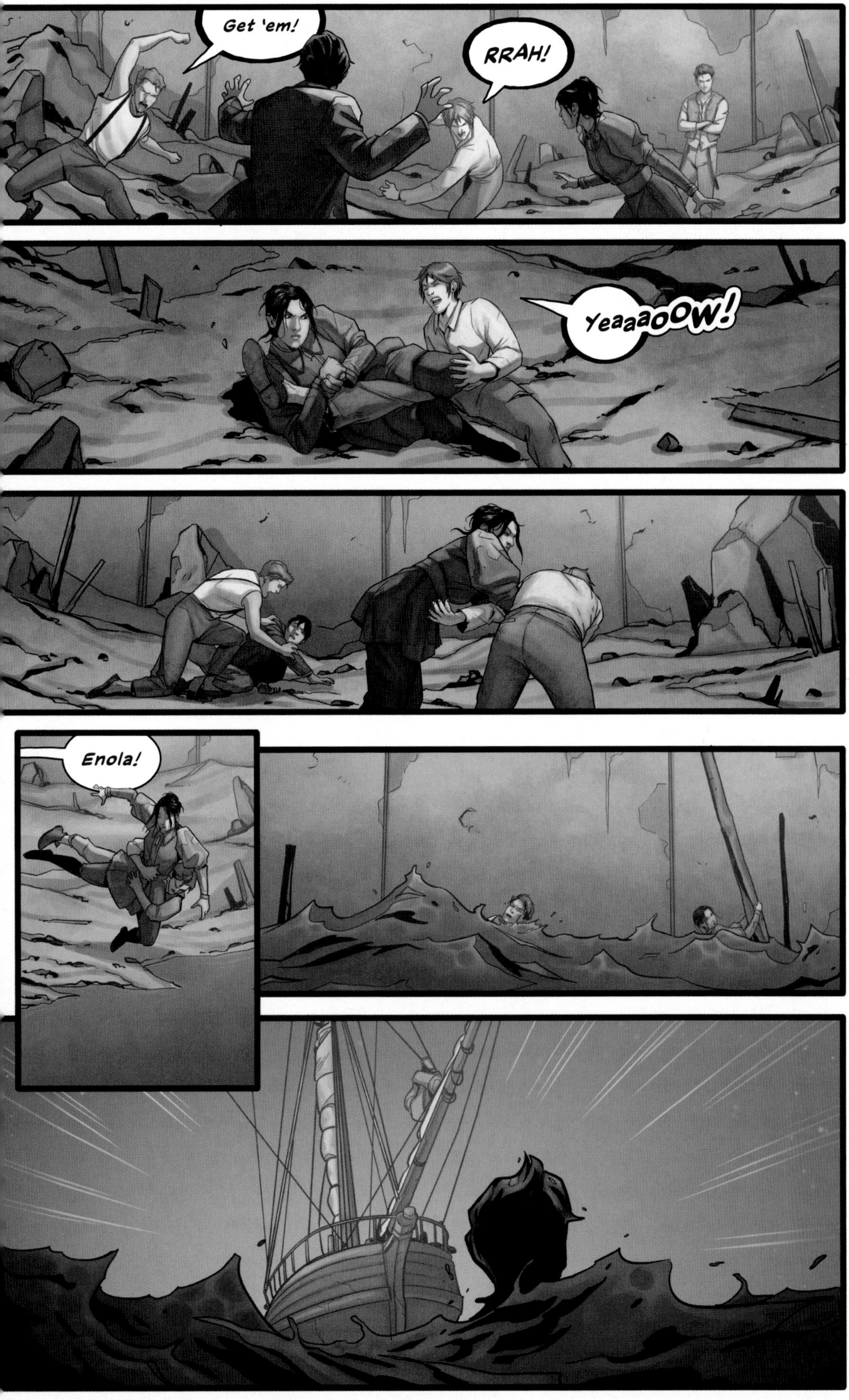
Get 'em!
RRAH!
YeaaaoOW!
Enola!

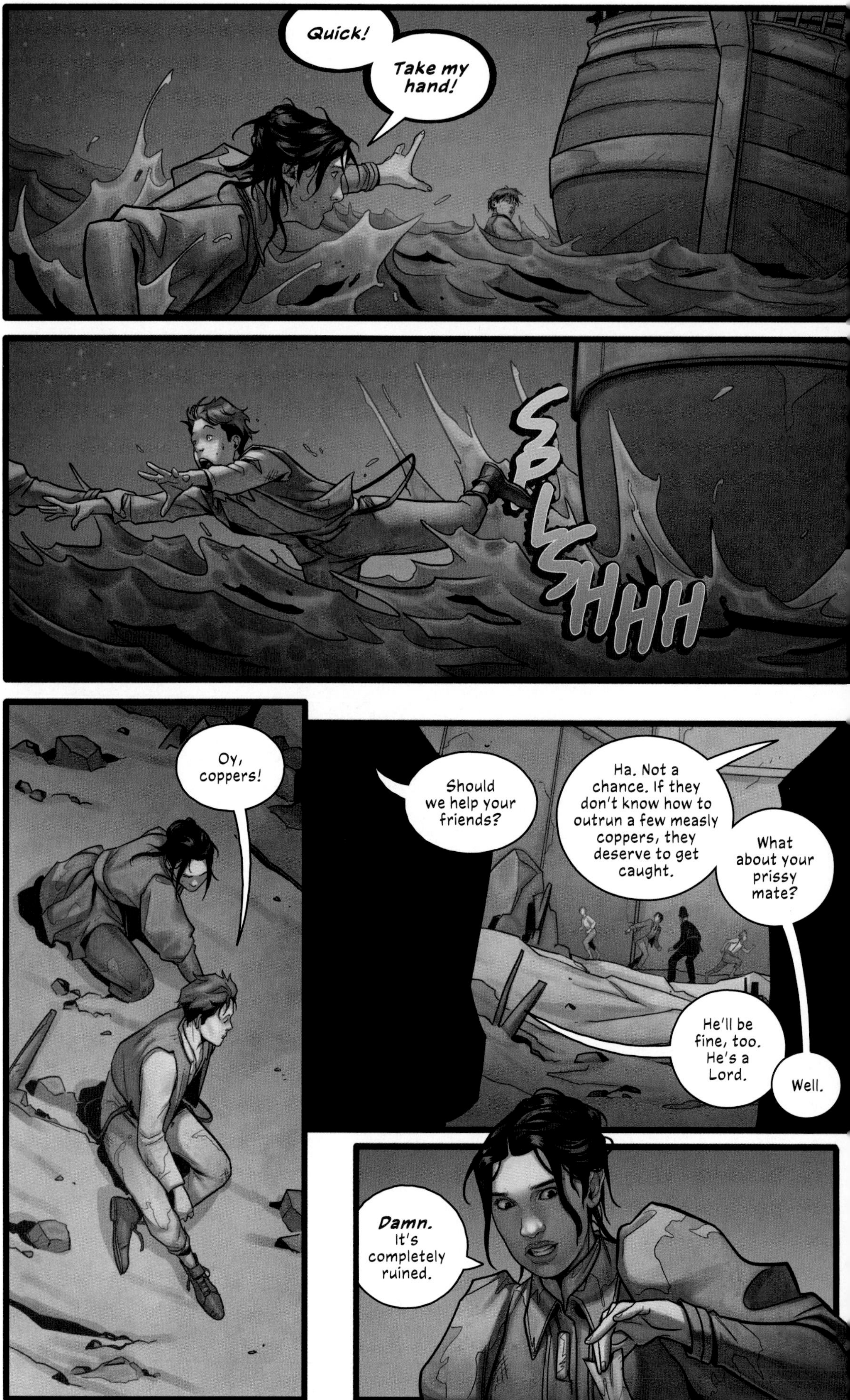
Quick!
Take my hand!
SBLSHHH
Oy, coppers!
Should we help your friends?
Ha. Not a chance. If they don't know how to outrun a few measly coppers, they deserve to get caught.
What about your prissy mate?
He'll be fine, too. He's a Lord.
Well.
Damn. It's completely ruined.

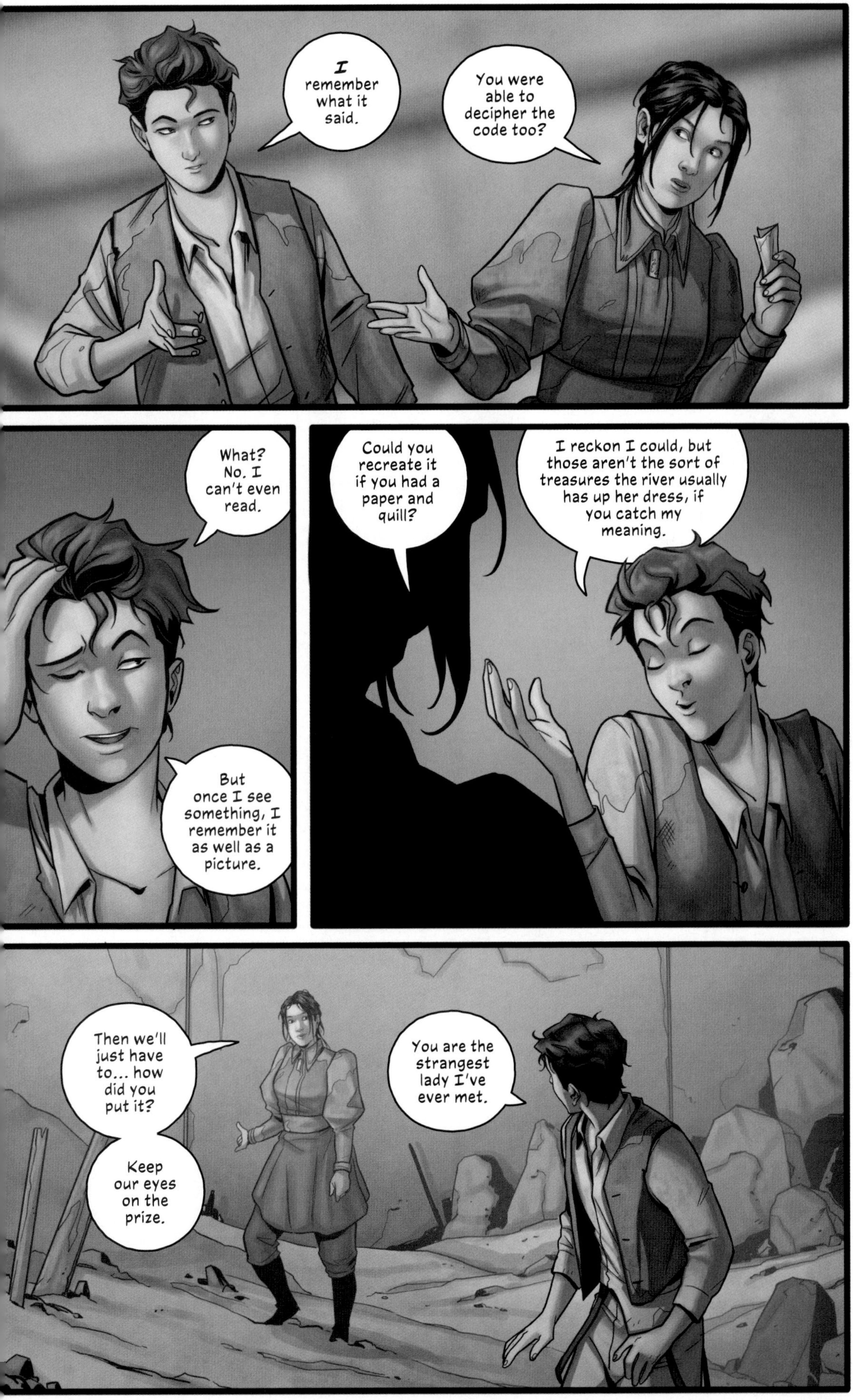
I remember what it said.
You were able to decipher the code too?
What? No. I can't even read.
But once I see something, I remember it as well as a picture.
Could you recreate it if you had a paper and quill?
I reckon I could, but those aren't the sort of treasures the river usually has up her dress, if you catch my meaning.
Then we'll just have to... how did you put it?
Keep our eyes on the prize.
You are the strangest lady I've ever met.

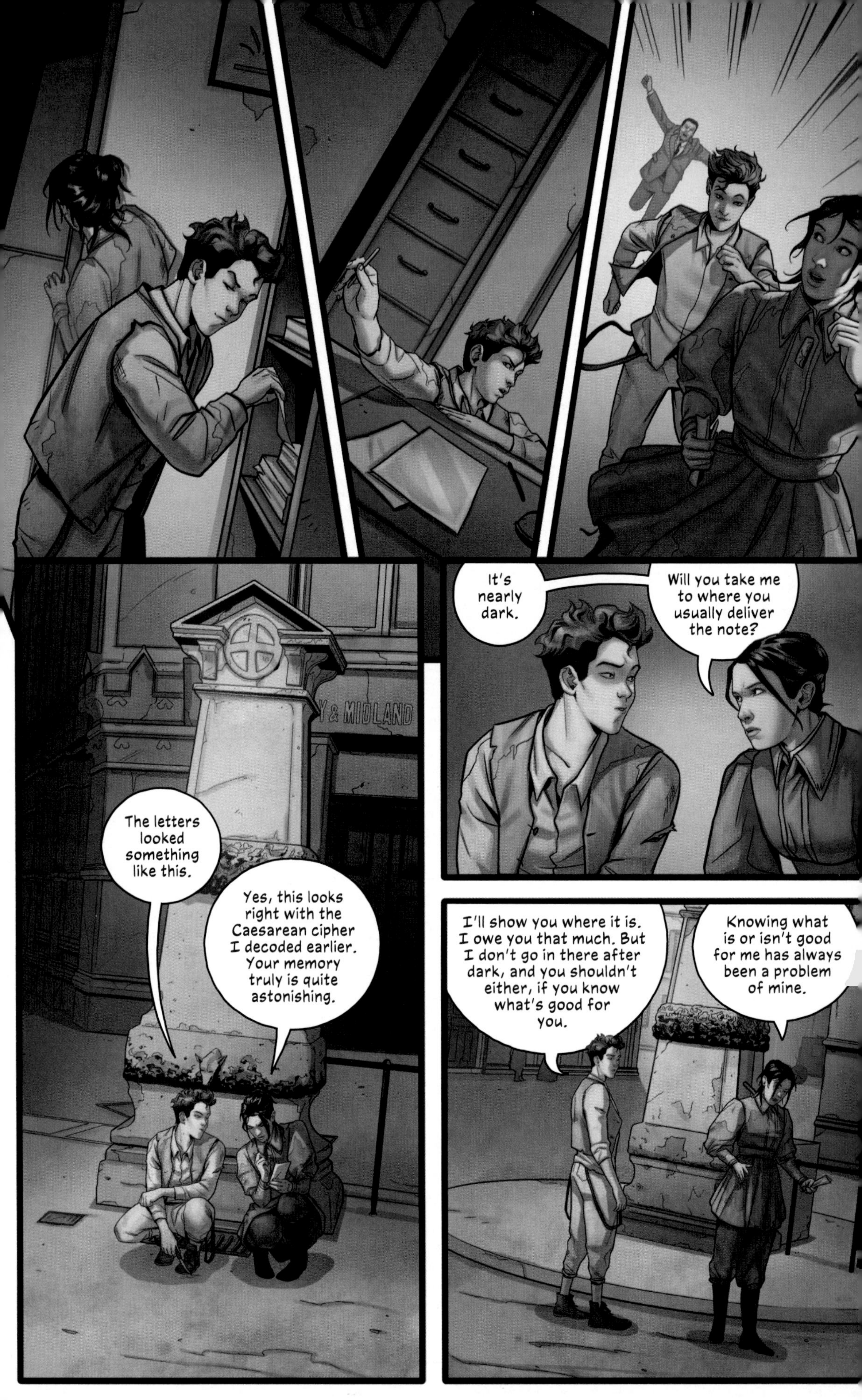
Y & MIDLAND
The letters looked something like this.
Yes, this looks right with the Caesarean cipher I decoded earlier. Your memory truly is quite astonishing.
It's nearly dark.
Will you take me to where you usually deliver the note?
I'll show you where it is. I owe you that much. But I don't go in there after dark, and you shouldn't either, if you know what's good for you.
Knowing what is or isn't good for me has always been a problem of mine.

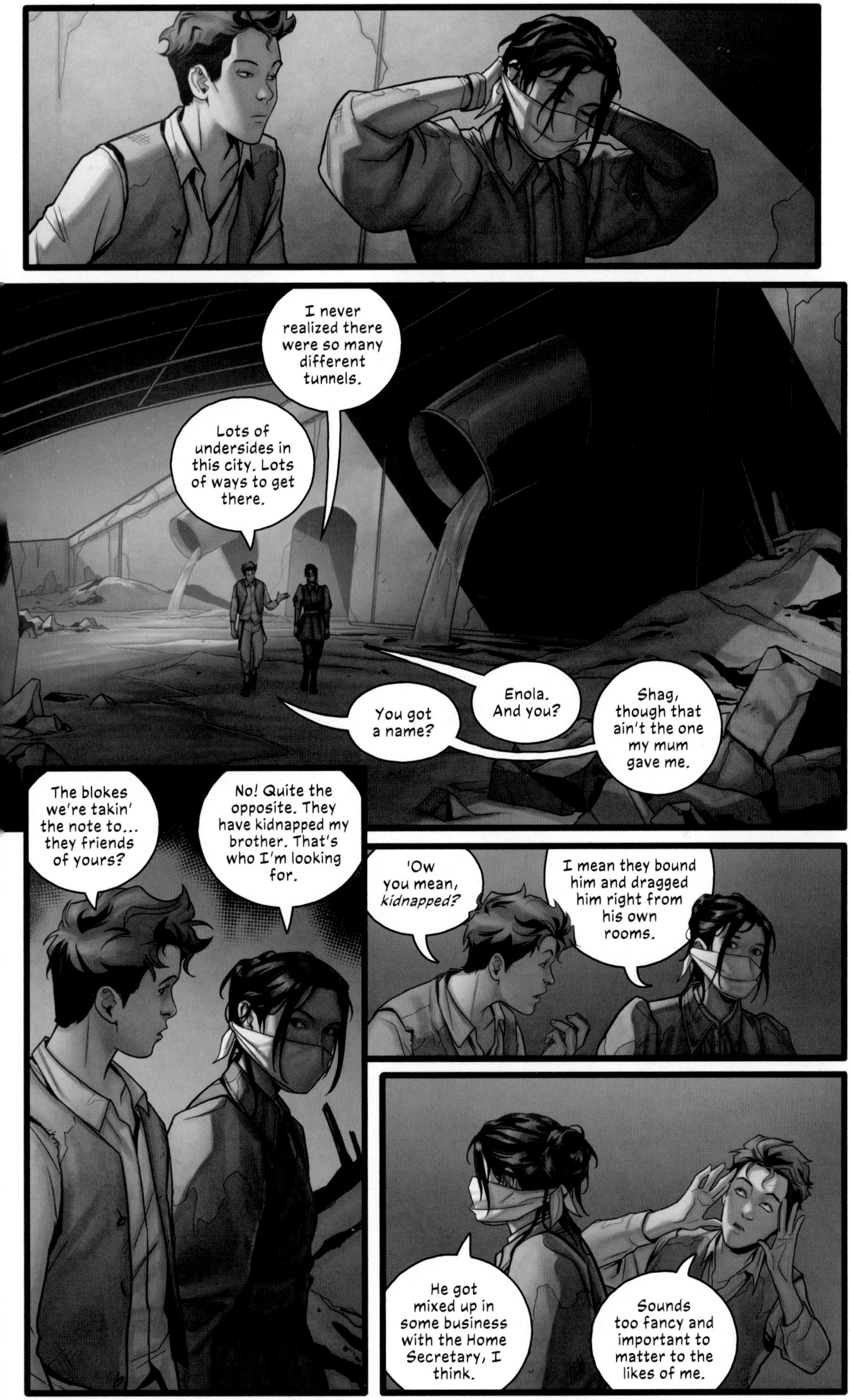
I never realized there were so many different tunnels.
Lots of undersides in this city. Lots of ways to get there.
You got a name?
Enola. And you?
Shag, though that ain't the one my mum gave me.
The blokes we're takin' the note to... they friends of yours?
No! Quite the opposite. They have kidnapped my brother. That's who I'm looking for.
'Ow you mean, *kidnapped?*
I mean they bound him and dragged him right from his own rooms.
He got mixed up in some business with the Home Secretary, I think.
Sounds too fancy and important to matter to the likes of me.

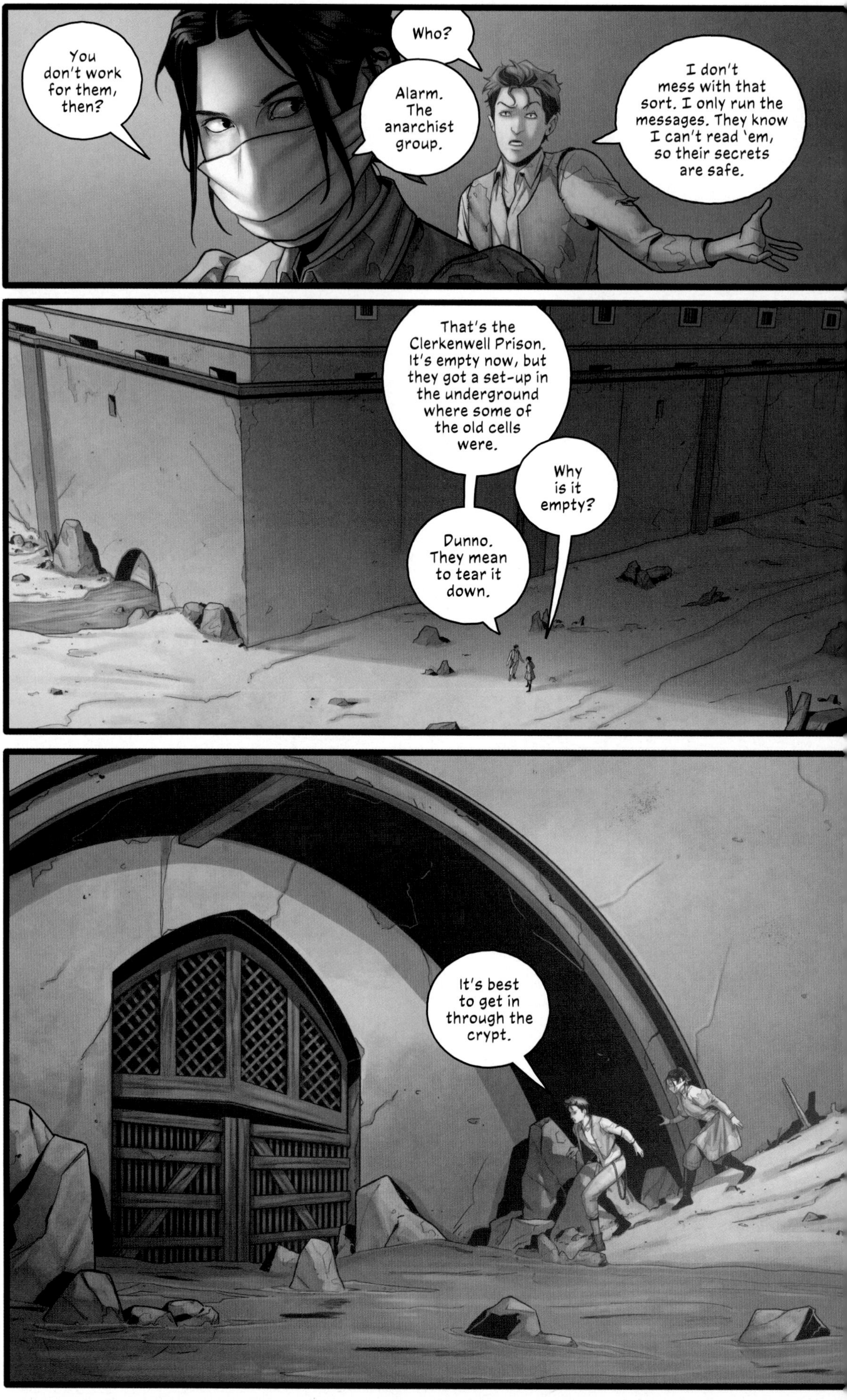
You don't work for them, then?
Who?
Alarm. The anarchist group.
I don't mess with that sort. I only run the messages. They know I can't read 'em, so their secrets are safe.
That's the Clerkenwell Prison. It's empty now, but they got a set-up in the underground where some of the old cells were.
Why is it empty?
Dunno. They mean to tear it down.
It's best to get in through the crypt.

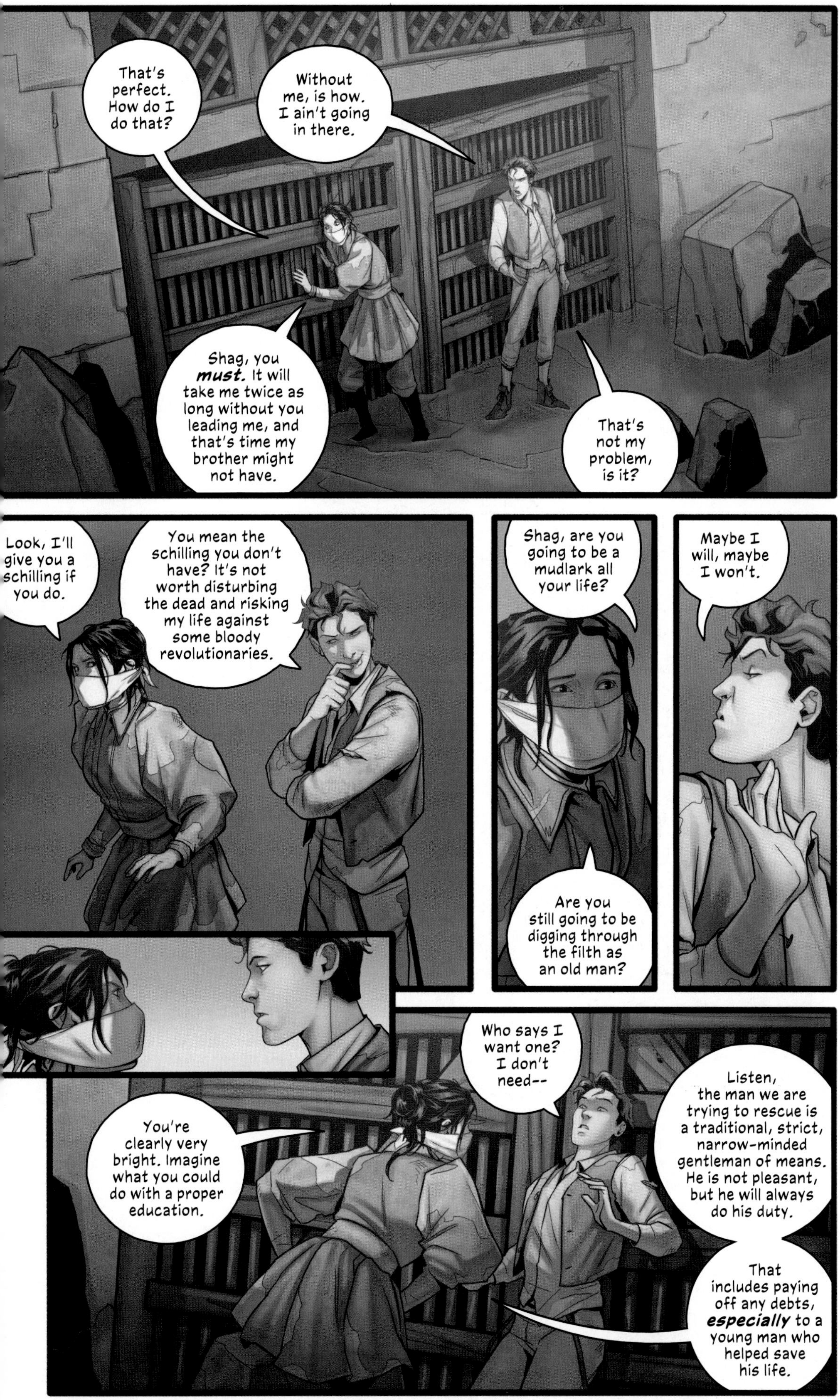
That's perfect. How do I do that?
Without me, is how. I ain't going in there.
Shag, you **must.** It will take me twice as long without you leading me, and that's time my brother might not have.
That's not my problem, is it?
Look, I'll give you a schilling if you do.
You mean the schilling you don't have? It's not worth disturbing the dead and risking my life against some bloody revolutionaries.
Shag, are you going to be a mudlark all your life?
Are you still going to be digging through the filth as an old man?
Maybe I will, maybe I won't.
You're clearly very bright. Imagine what you could do with a proper education.
Who says I want one? I don't need--
Listen, the man we are trying to rescue is a traditional, strict, narrow-minded gentleman of means. He is not pleasant, but he will always do his duty.
That includes paying off any debts, ***especially*** to a young man who helped save his life.

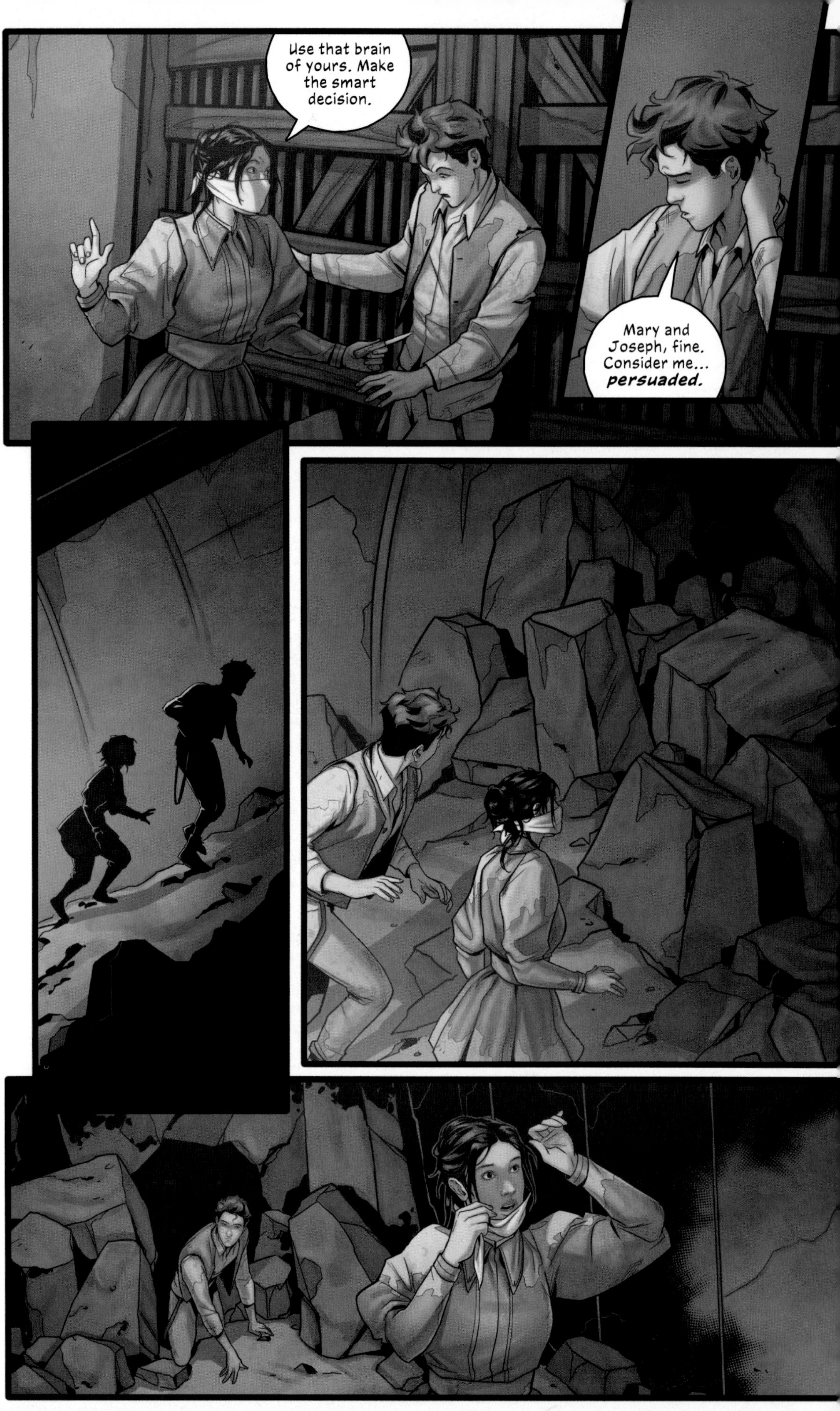
Use that brain of yours. Make the smart decision.
Mary and Joseph, fine. Consider me... *persuaded.*

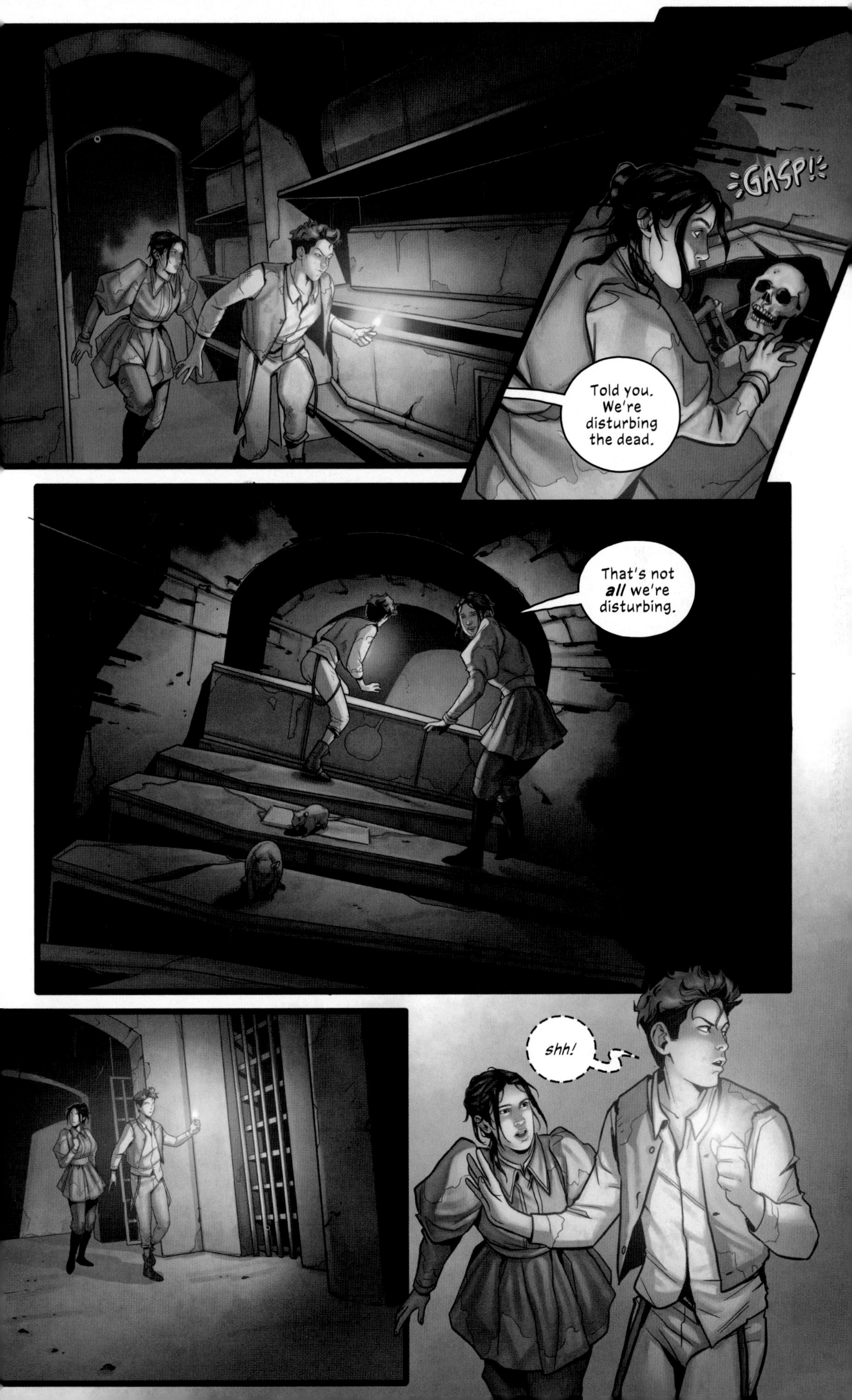
GASP!
Told you. We're disturbing the dead.
That's not all we're disturbing.
shh!

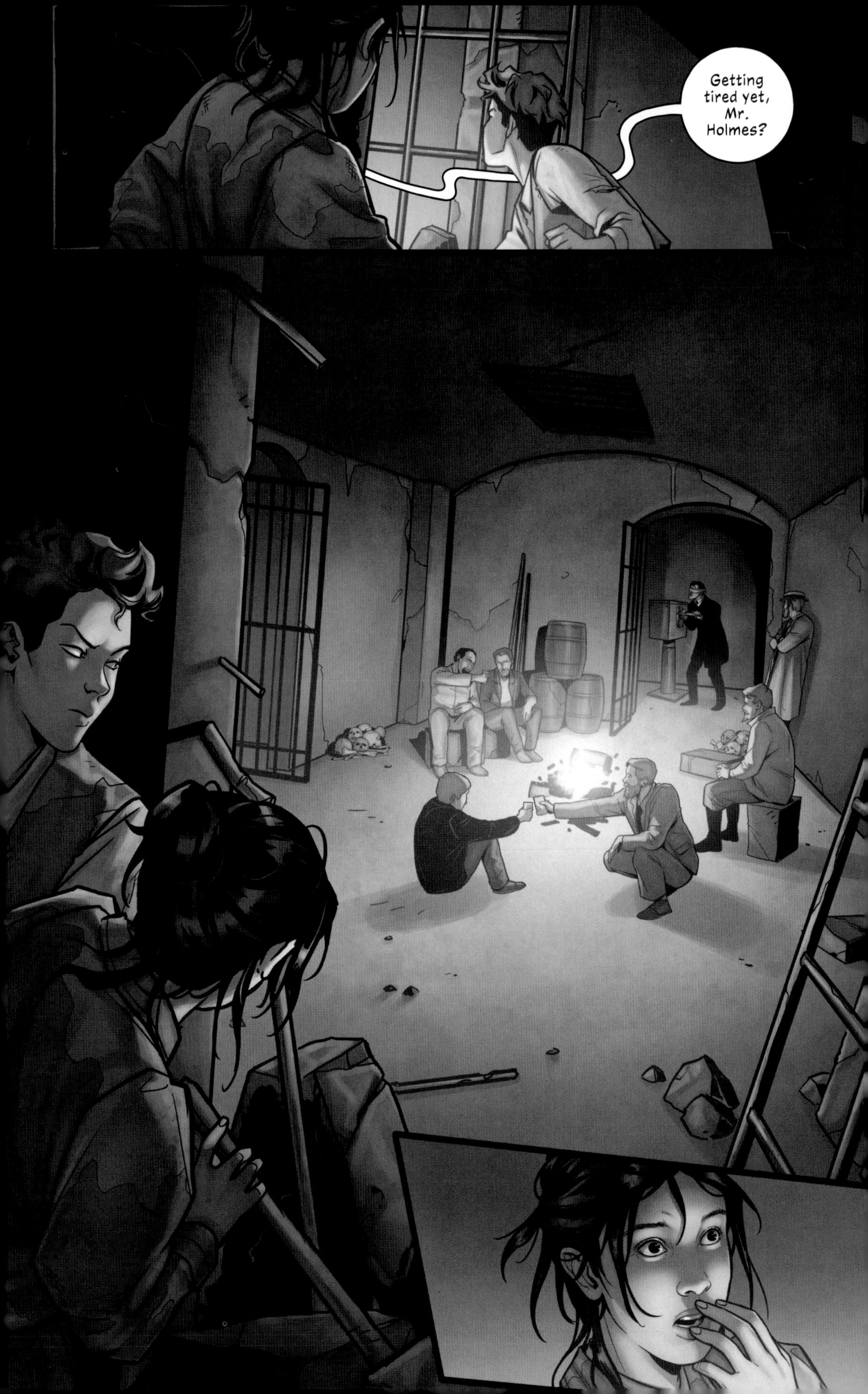
Getting tired yet, Mr. Holmes?

CASE FOUR:

FIRE

[Chapter Five]

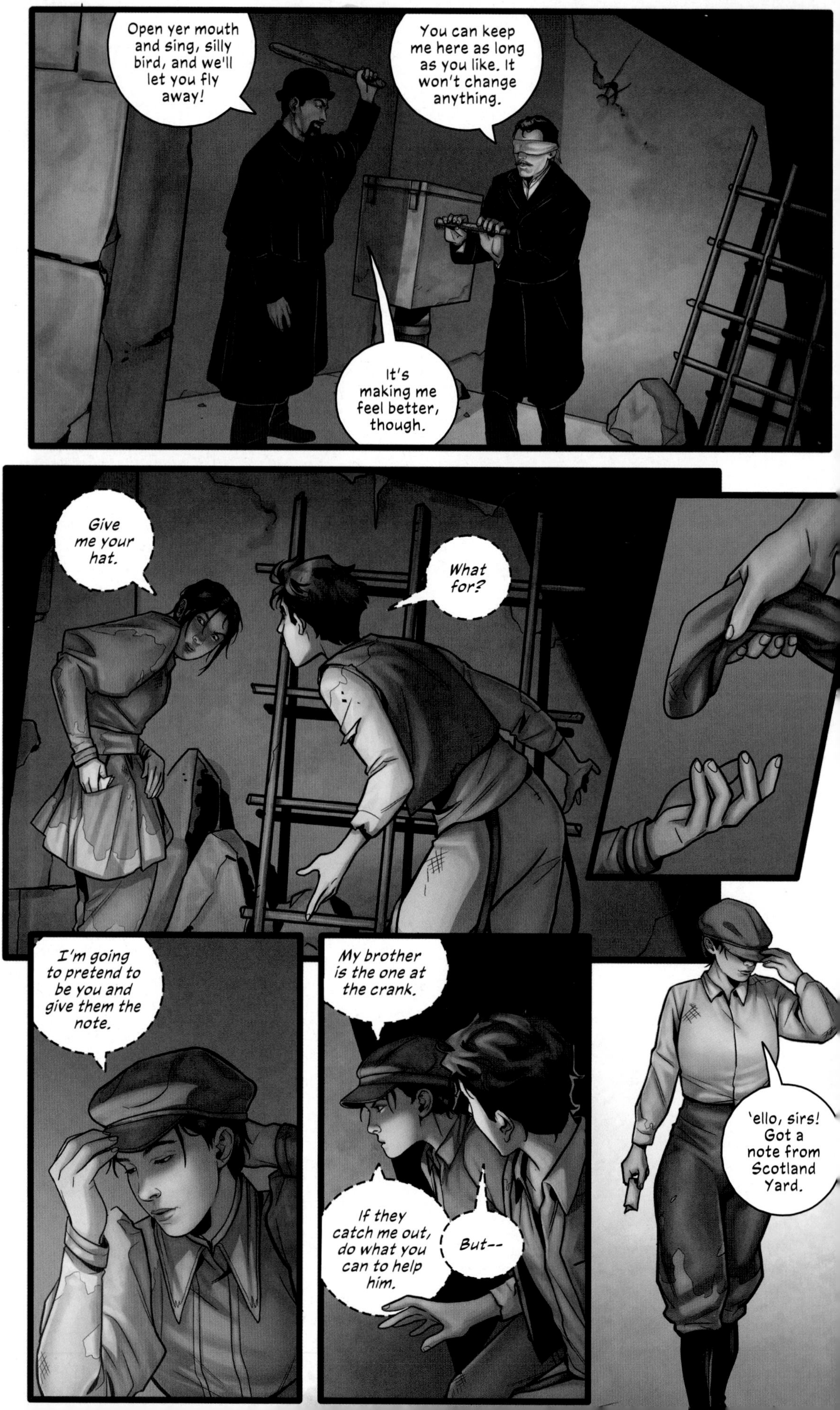
Open yer mouth and sing, silly bird, and we'll let you fly away!
You can keep me here as long as you like. It won't change anything.
It's making me feel better, though.
Give me your hat.
What for?
I'm going to pretend to be you and give them the note.
My brother is the one at the crank.
If they catch me out, do what you can to help him.
But--
'ello, sirs! Got a note from Scotland Yard.

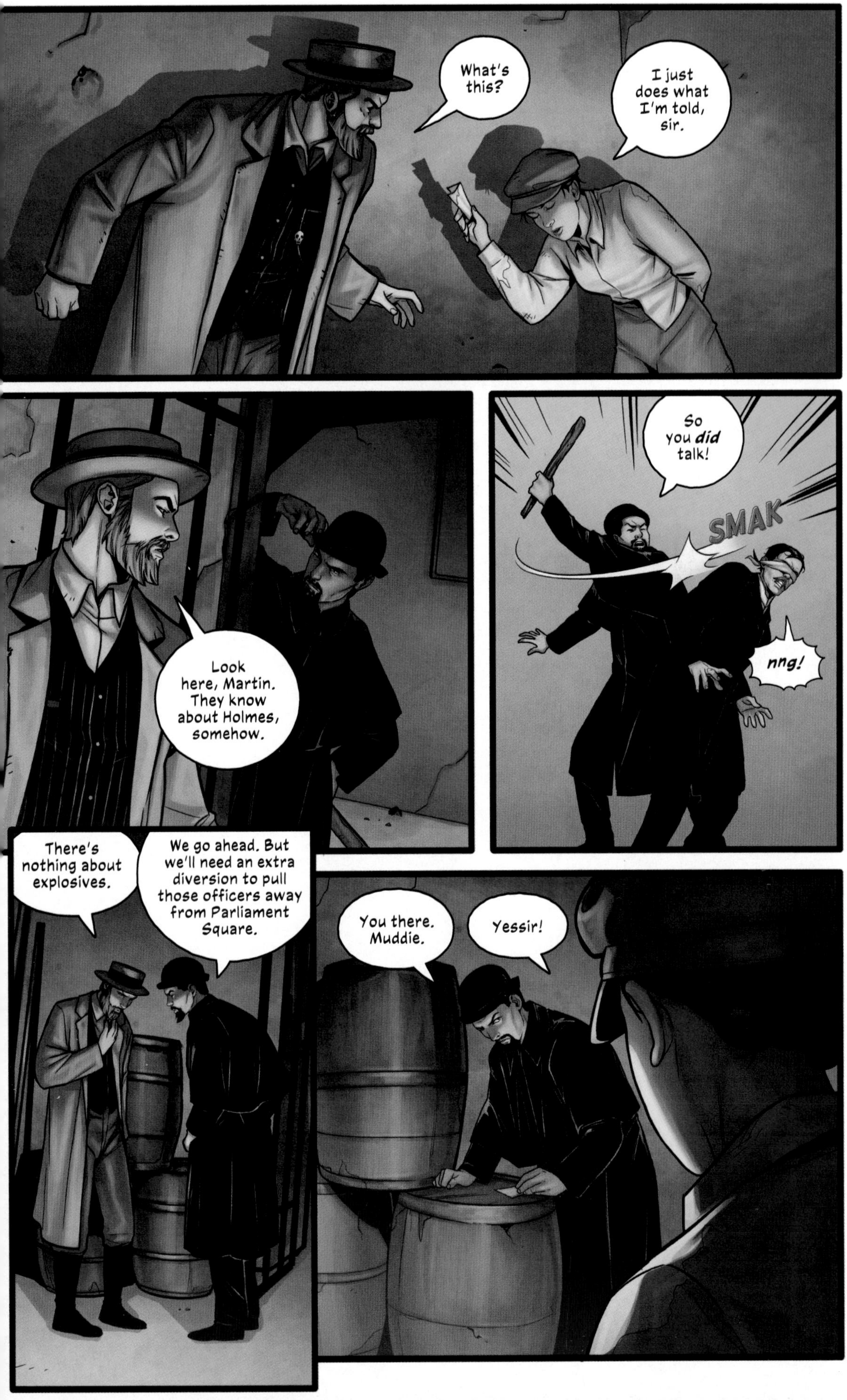
What's this?
I just does what I'm told, sir.
Look here, Martin. They know about Holmes, somehow.
So you *did* talk!
SMAK
nng!
There's nothing about explosives.
We go ahead. But we'll need an extra diversion to pull those officers away from Parliament Square.
You there. Muddie.
Yessir!

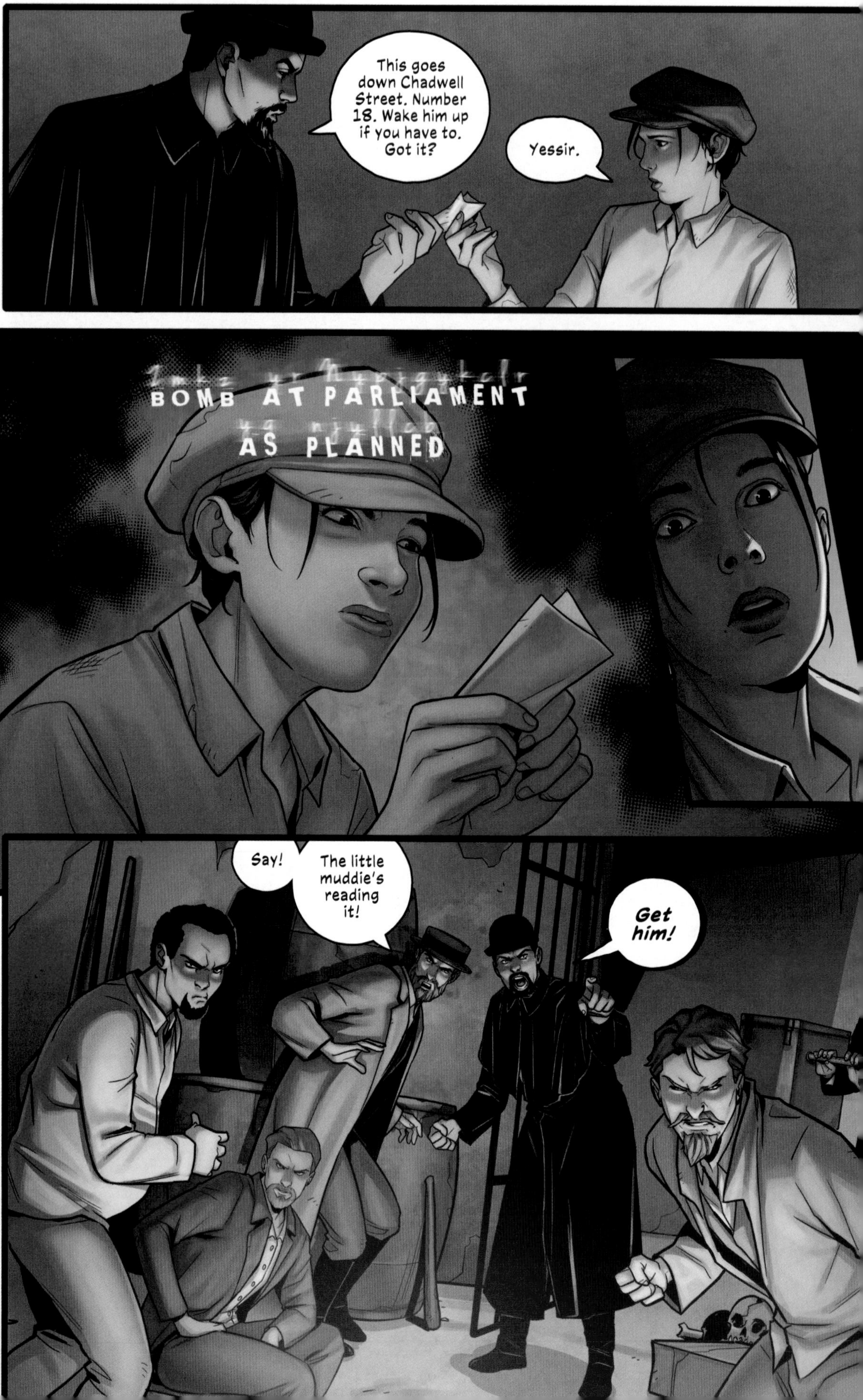
This goes down Chadwell Street. Number 18. Wake him up if you have to. Got it?
Yessir.
BOMB AT PARLIAMENT
AS PLANNED
Say!
The little muddie's reading it!
Get him!

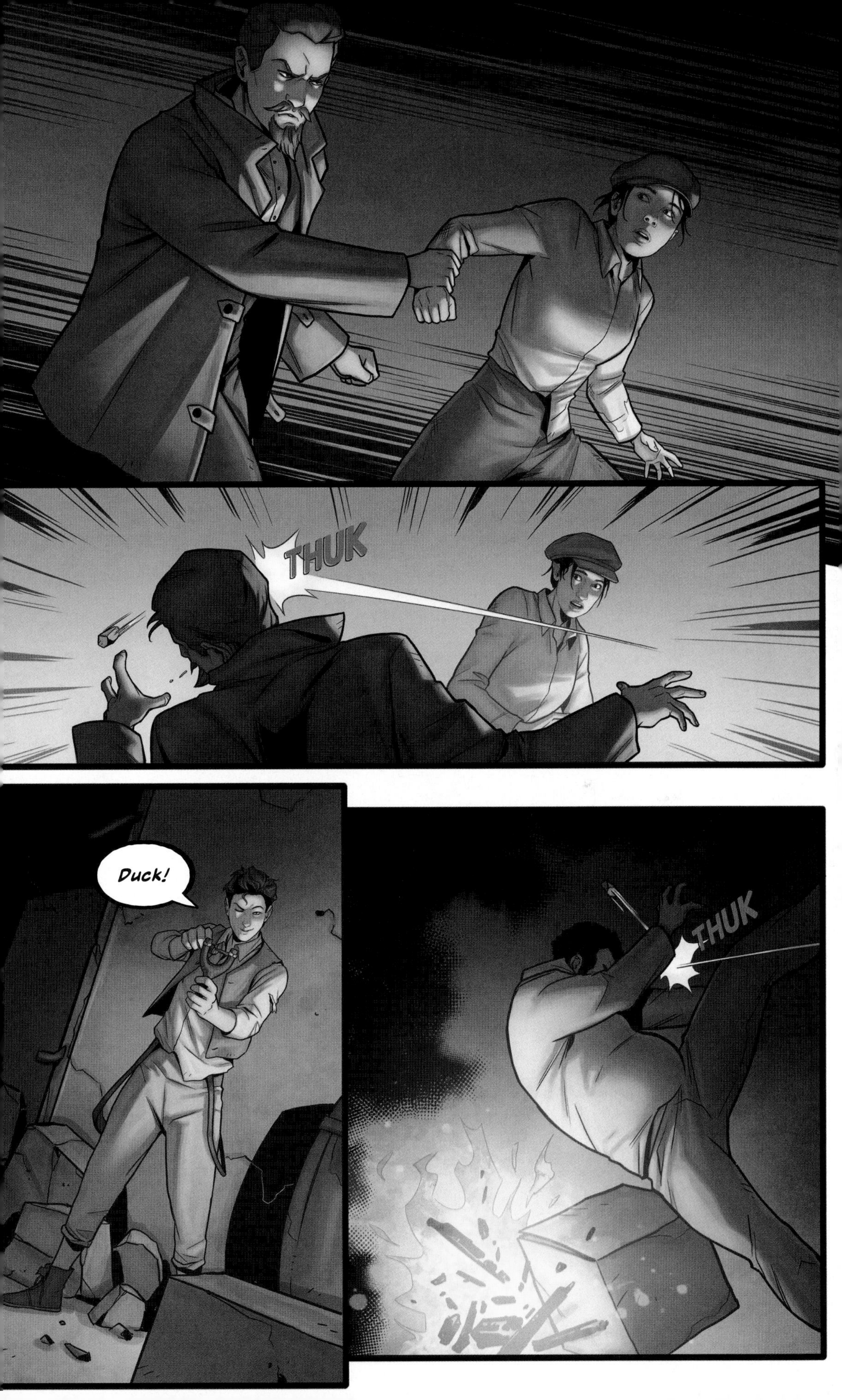
THUK
Duck!
THUK

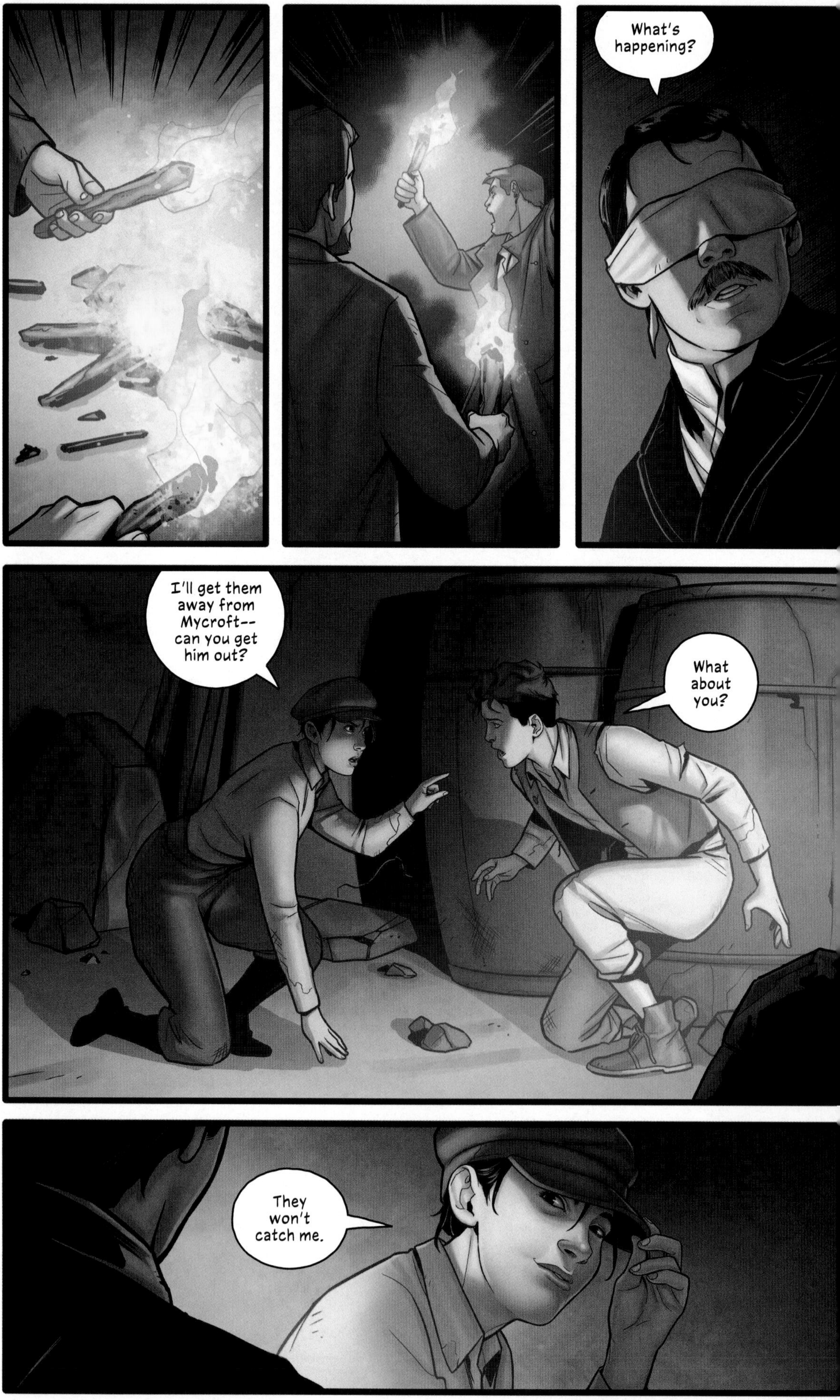
What's happening?
I'll get them away from Mycroft-- can you get him out?
What about you?
They won't catch me.

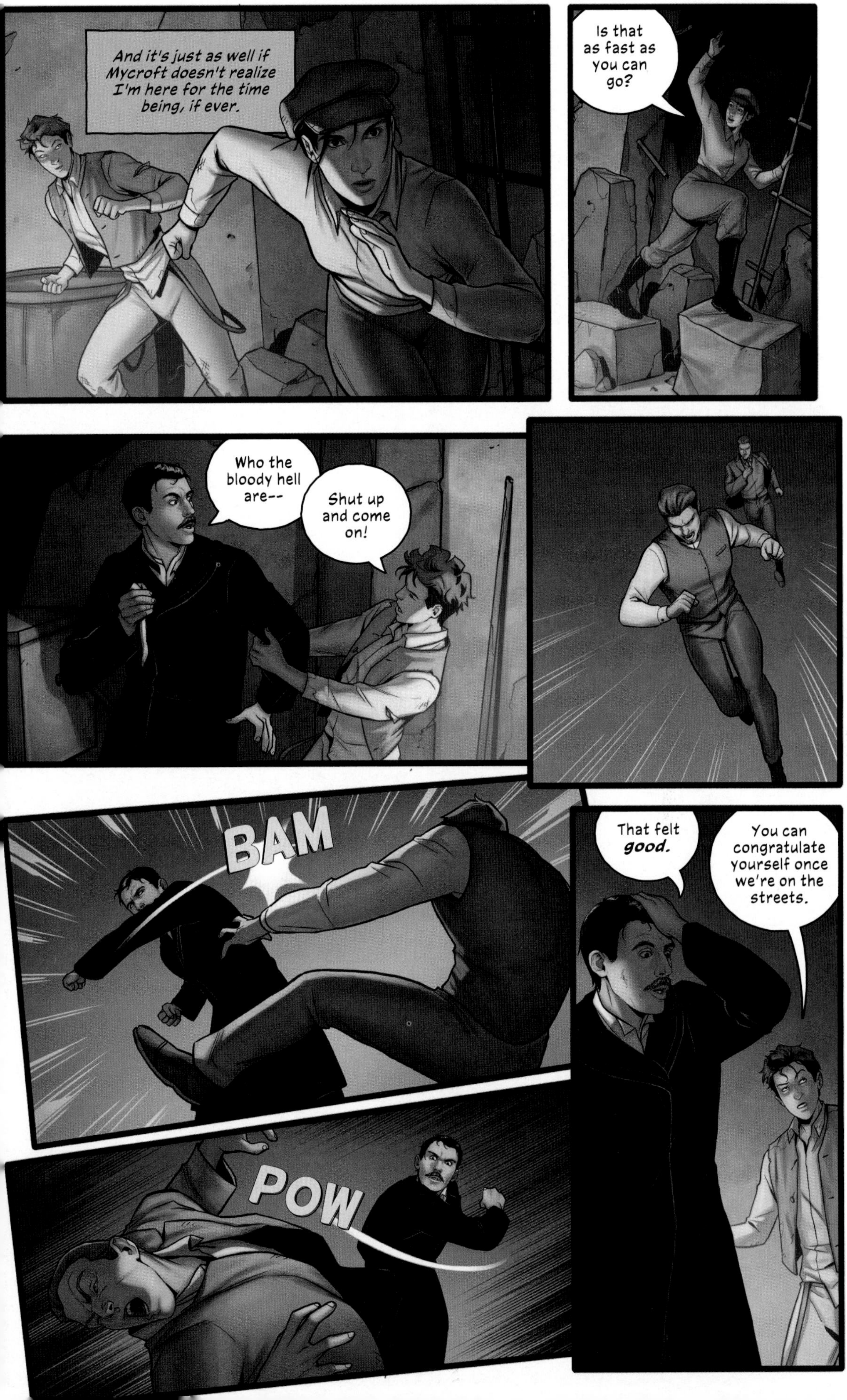
And it's just as well if Mycroft doesn't realize I'm here for the time being, if ever.
Is that as fast as you can go?
Who the bloody hell are--
Shut up and come on!
BAM
POW
That felt *good.*
You can congratulate yourself once we're on the streets.

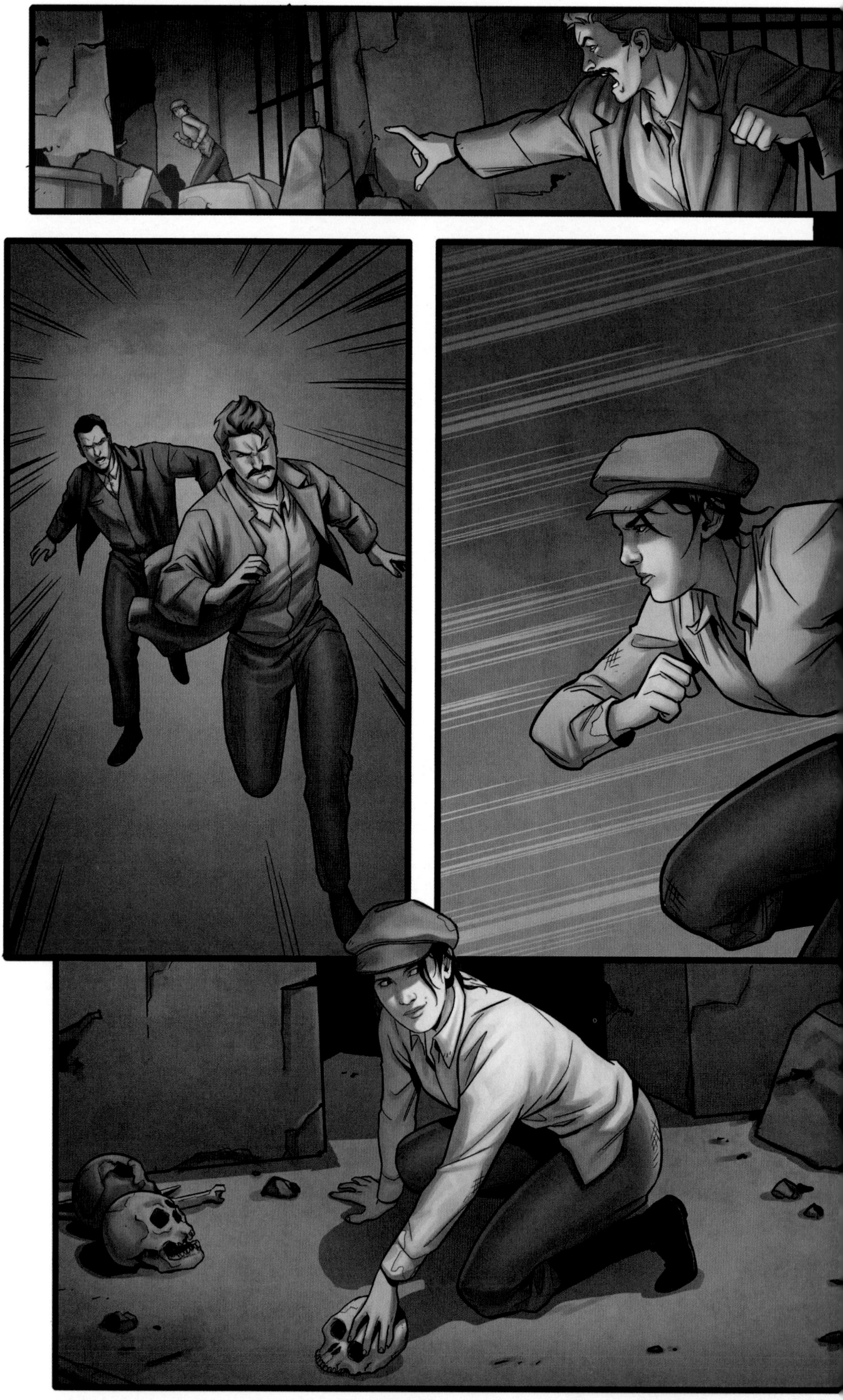

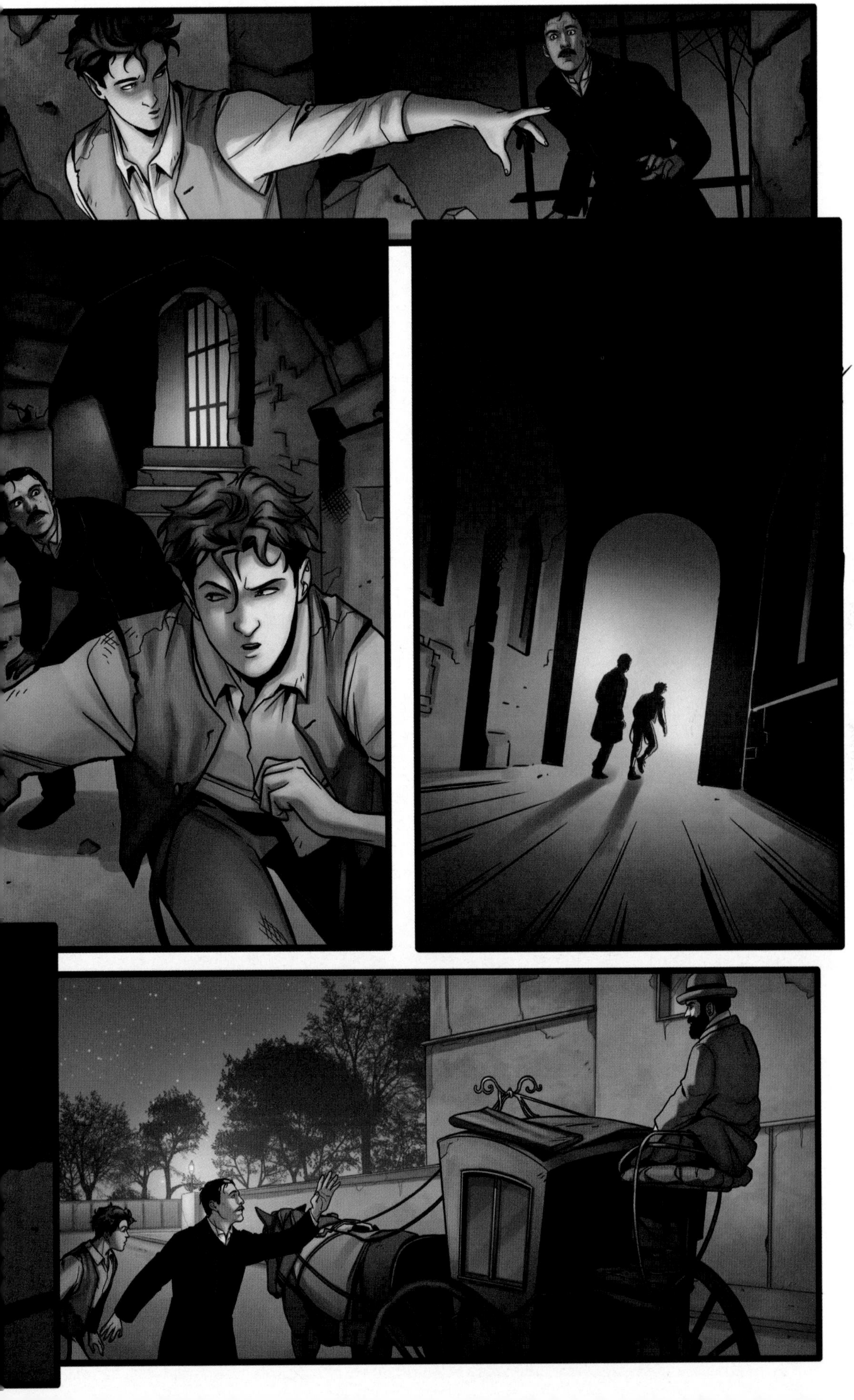

KLACK

THUNK

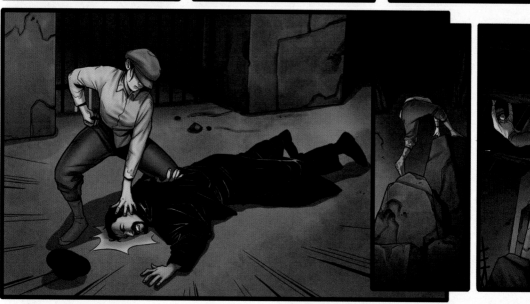

Where's he gone?!

Dammit all to hell.

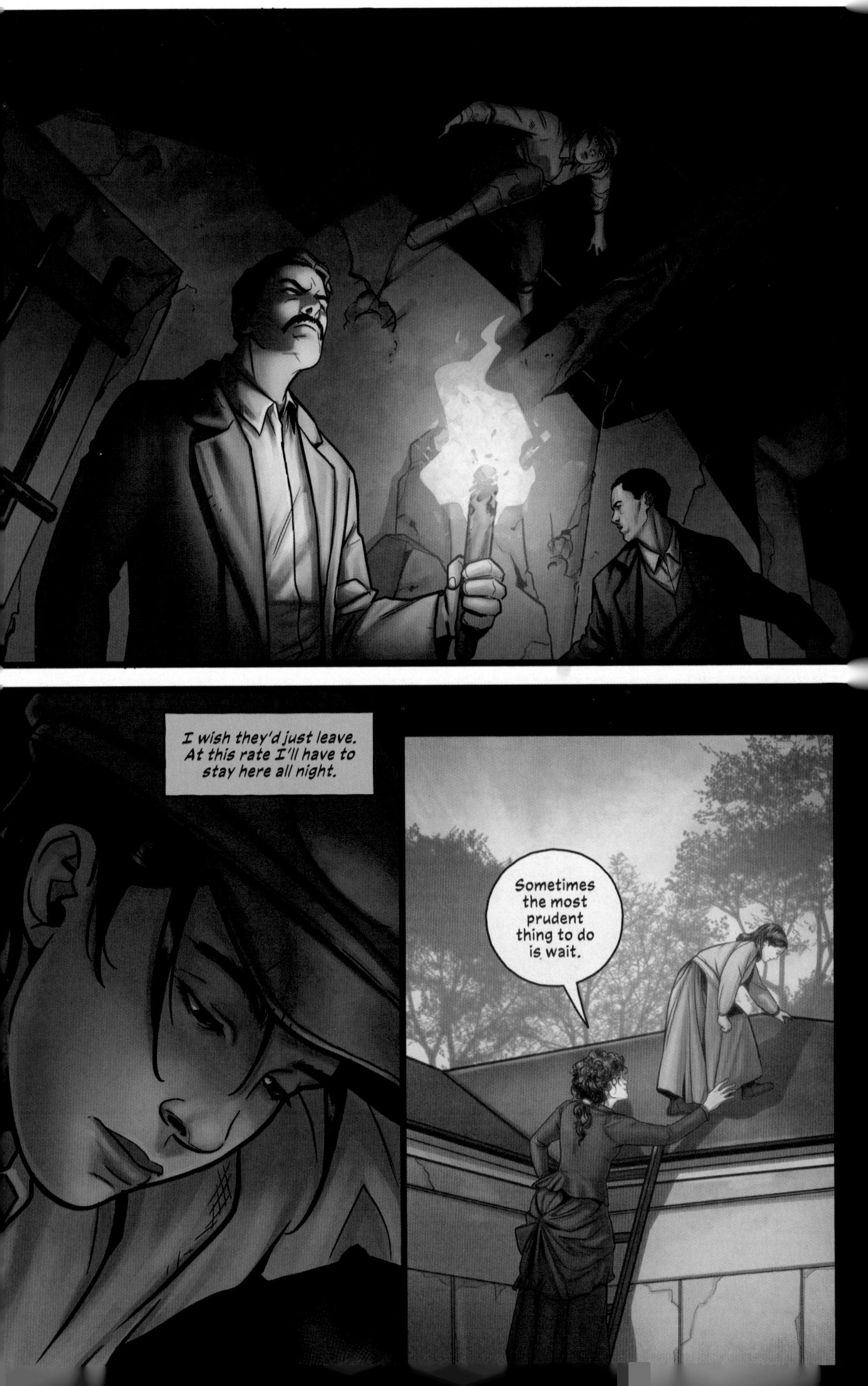
I wish they'd just leave. At this rate I'll have to stay here all night.
Sometimes the most prudent thing to do is wait.

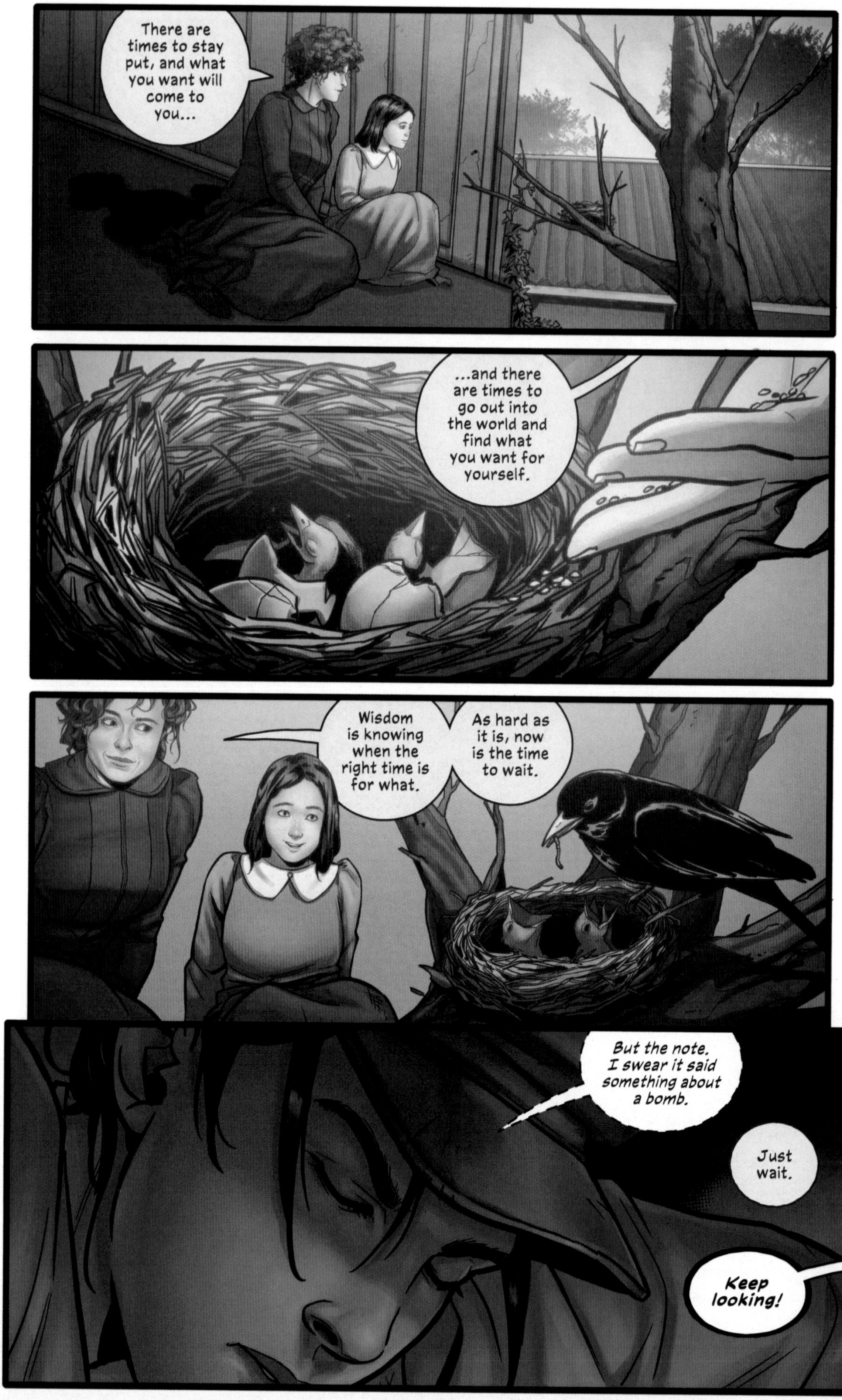
There are times to stay put, and what you want will come to you...
...and there are times to go out into the world and find what you want for yourself.
Wisdom is knowing when the right time is for what.
As hard as it is, now is the time to wait.
But the note. I swear it said something about a bomb.
Just wait.
Keep looking!

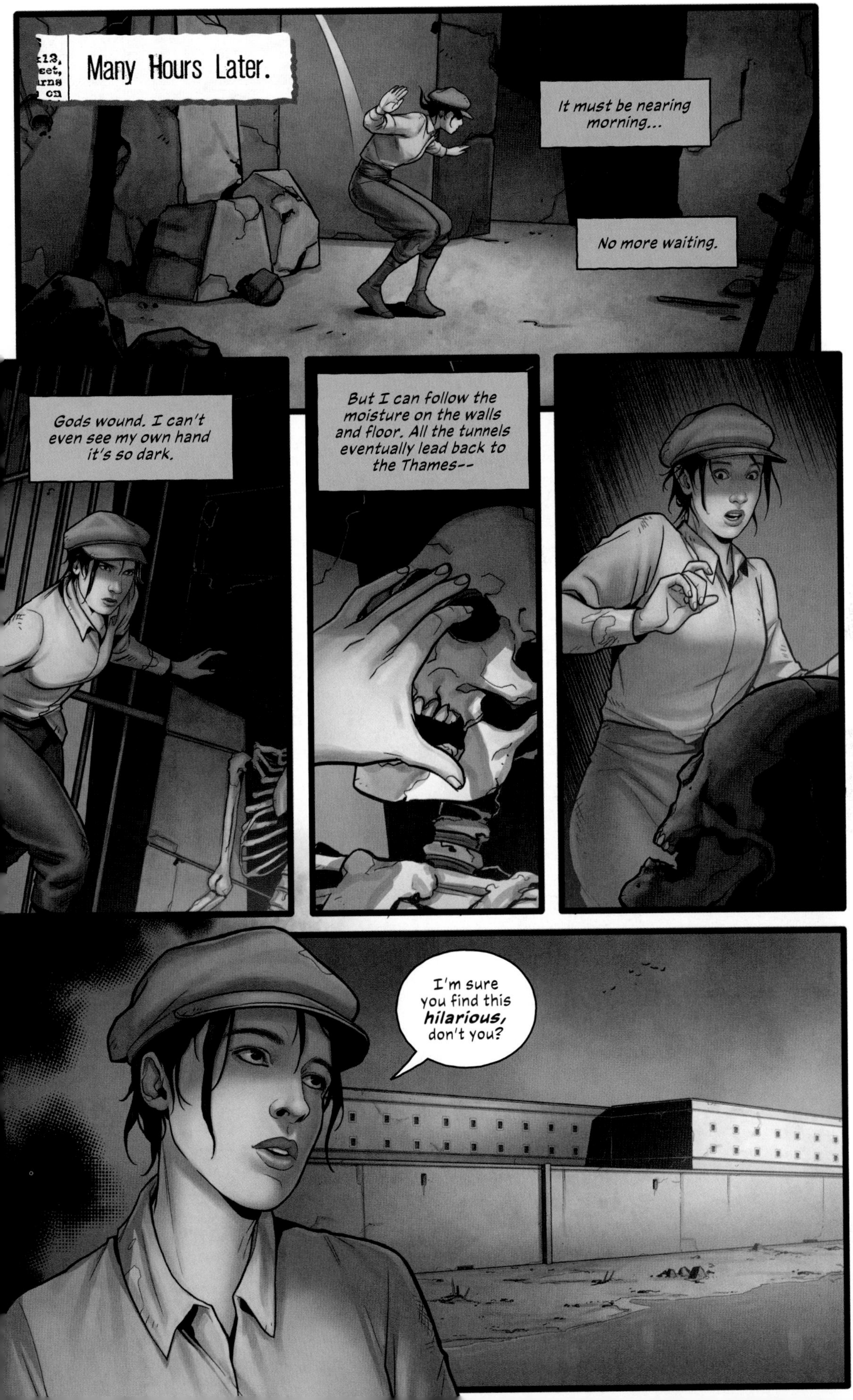
Many Hours Later.
It must be nearing morning...
No more waiting.
Gods wound. I can't even see my own hand it's so dark.
But I can follow the moisture on the walls and floor. All the tunnels eventually lead back to the Thames--
I'm sure you find this *hilarious,* don't you?

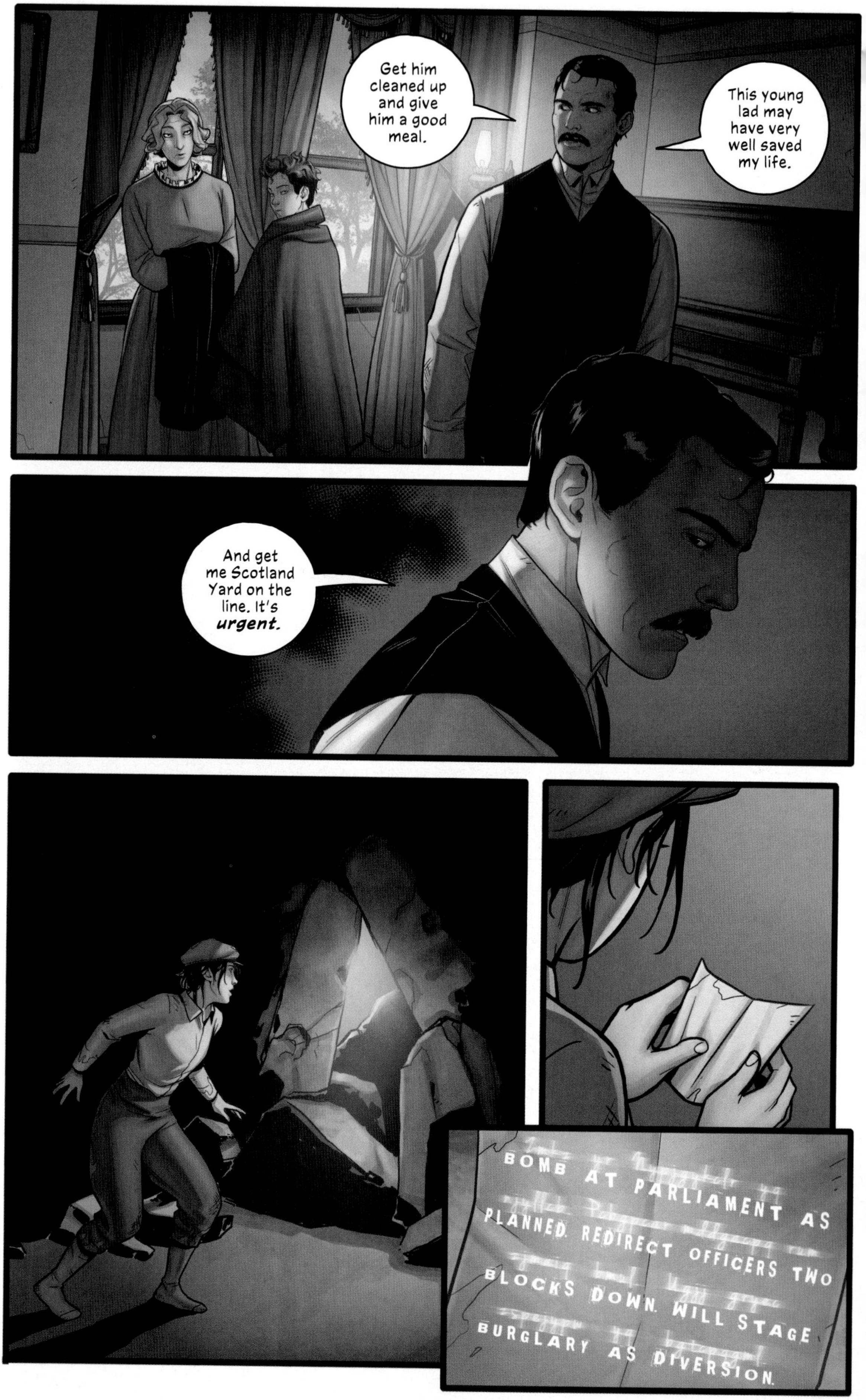
Get him cleaned up and give him a good meal.
This young lad may have very well saved my life.
And get me Scotland Yard on the line. It's *urgent.*
BOMB AT PARLIAMENT AS PLANNED. REDIRECT OFFICERS TWO BLOCKS DOWN. WILL STAGE BURGLARY AS DIVERSION.

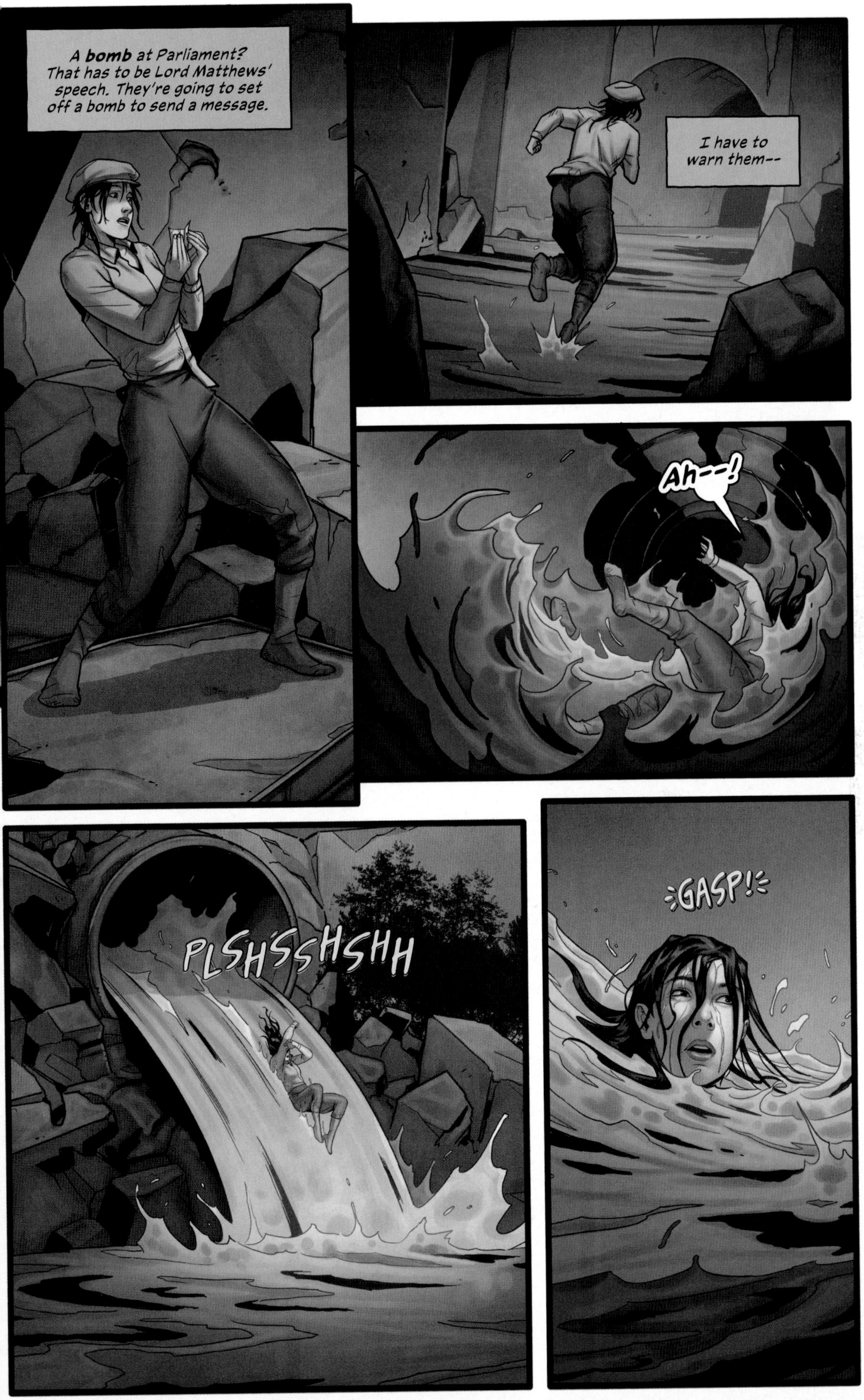
A **bomb** at Parliament? That has to be Lord Matthews' speech. They're going to set off a bomb to send a message.
I have to warn them--
Ah--!
PLSHSSHSHH
GASP!

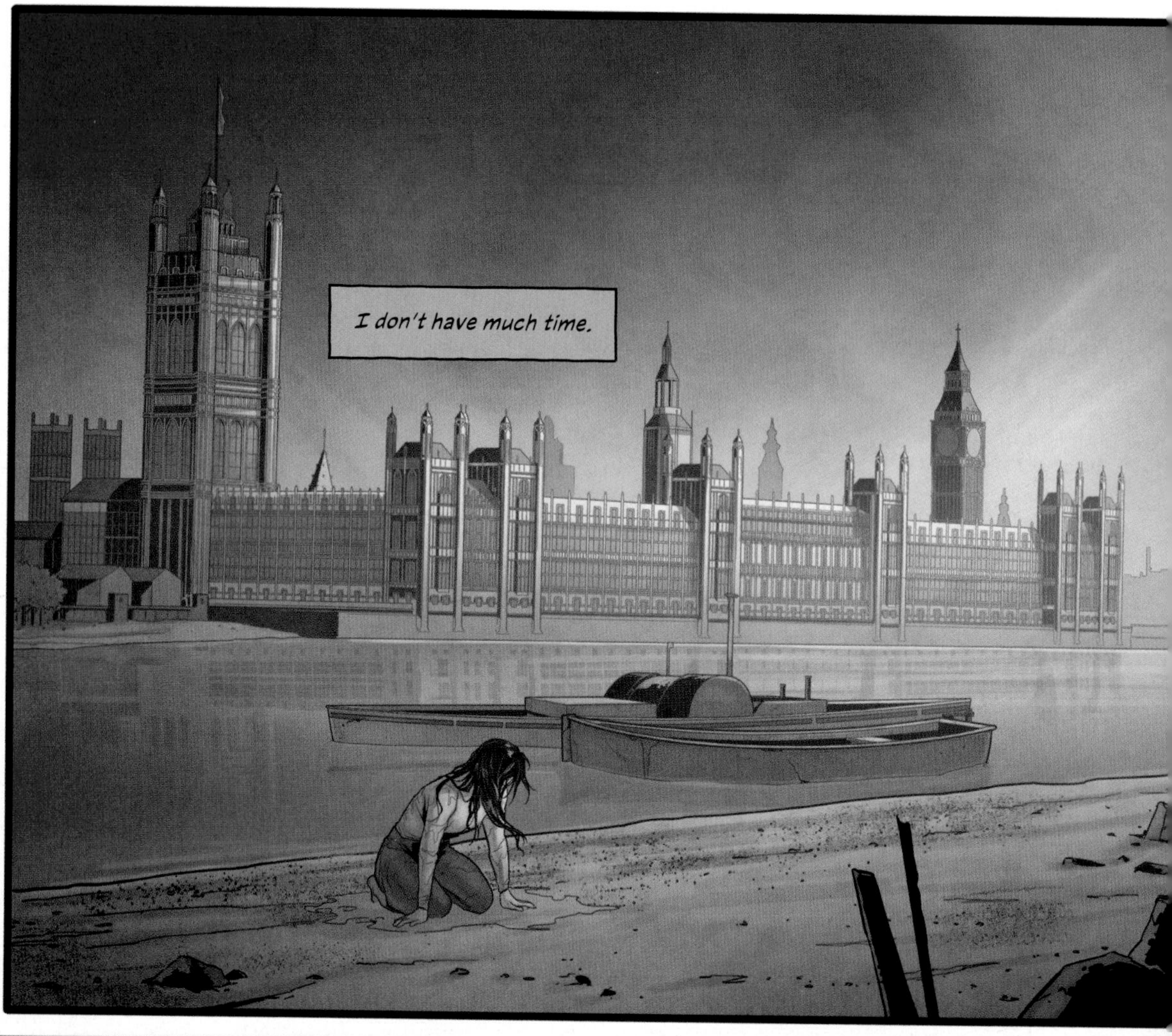
I don't have much time.

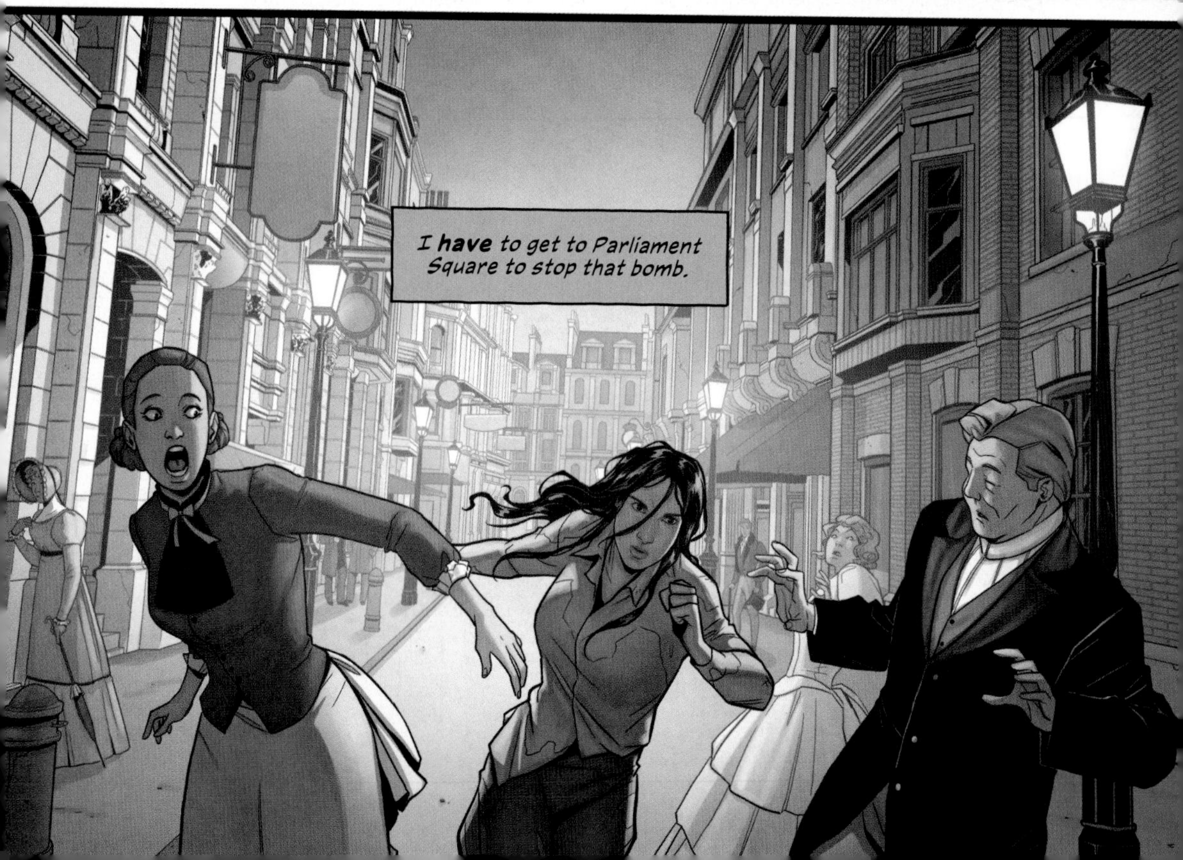
I **have** to get to Parliament Square to stop that bomb.

[Chapter Six]

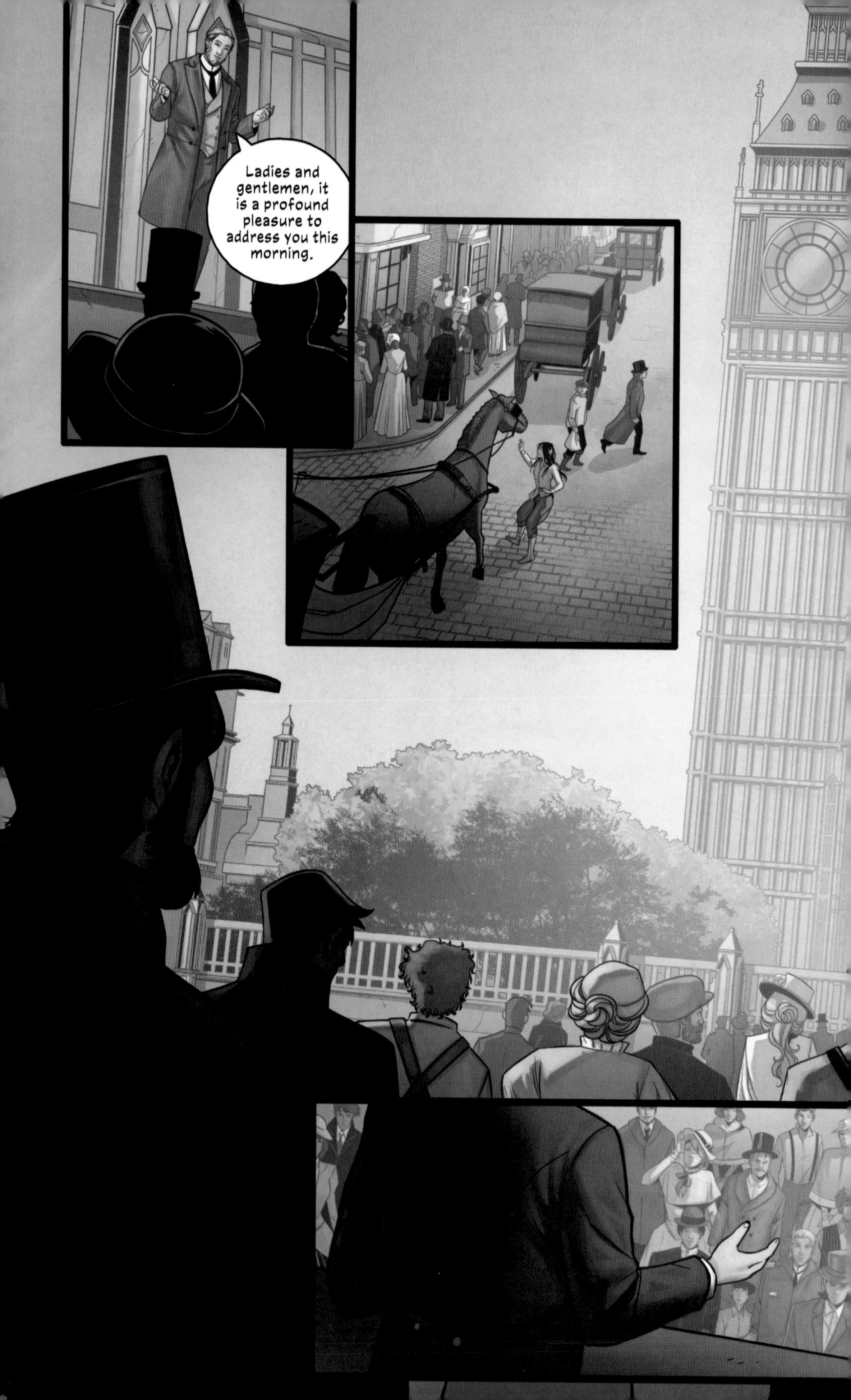
Ladies and gentlemen, it is a profound pleasure to address you this morning.

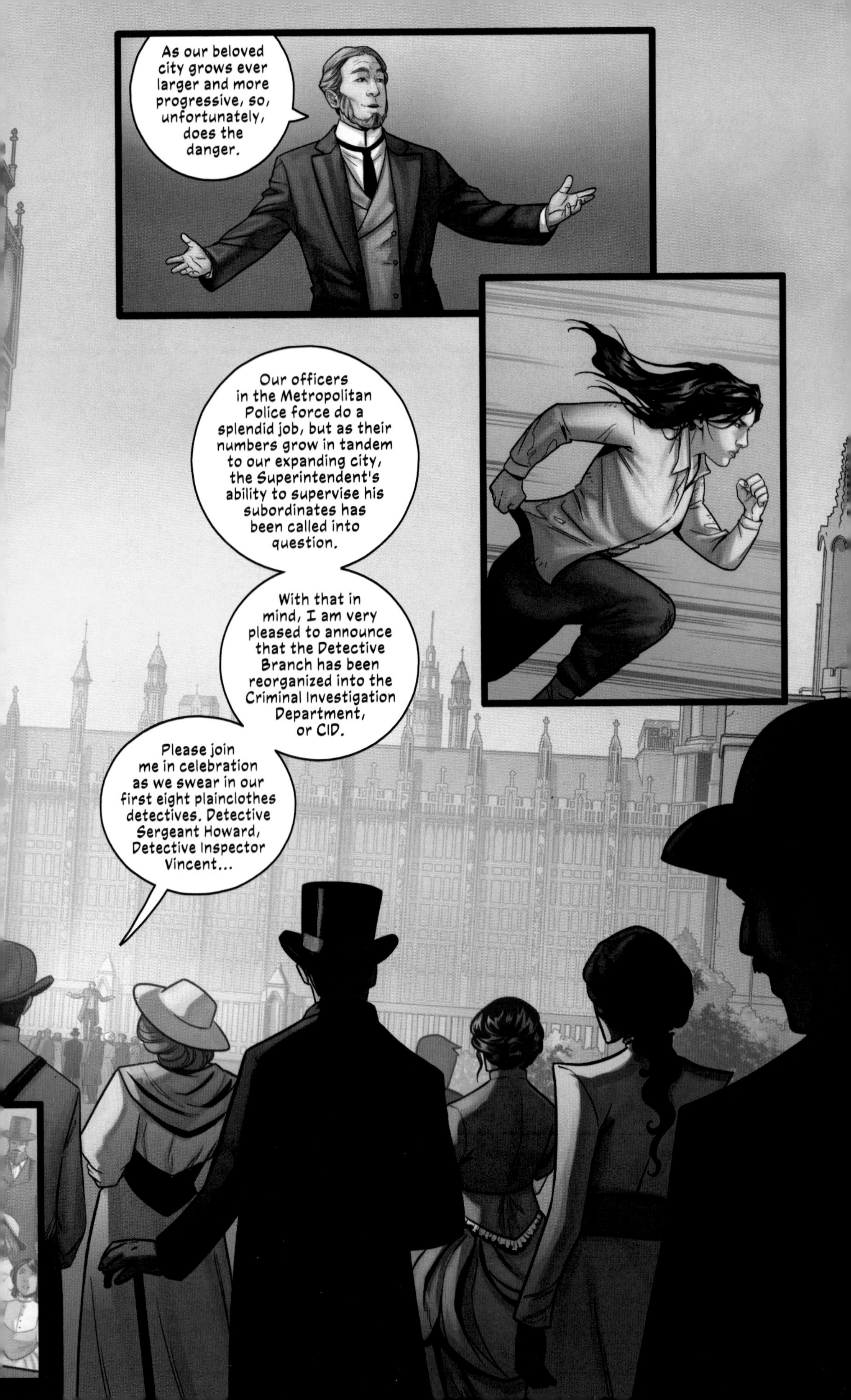
As our beloved city grows ever larger and more progressive, so, unfortunately, does the danger.
Our officers in the Metropolitan Police force do a splendid job, but as their numbers grow in tandem to our expanding city, the Superintendent's ability to supervise his subordinates has been called into question.
With that in mind, I am very pleased to announce that the Detective Branch has been reorganized into the Criminal Investigation Department, or CID.
Please join me in celebration as we swear in our first eight plainclothes detectives. Detective Sergeant Howard, Detective Inspector Vincent...

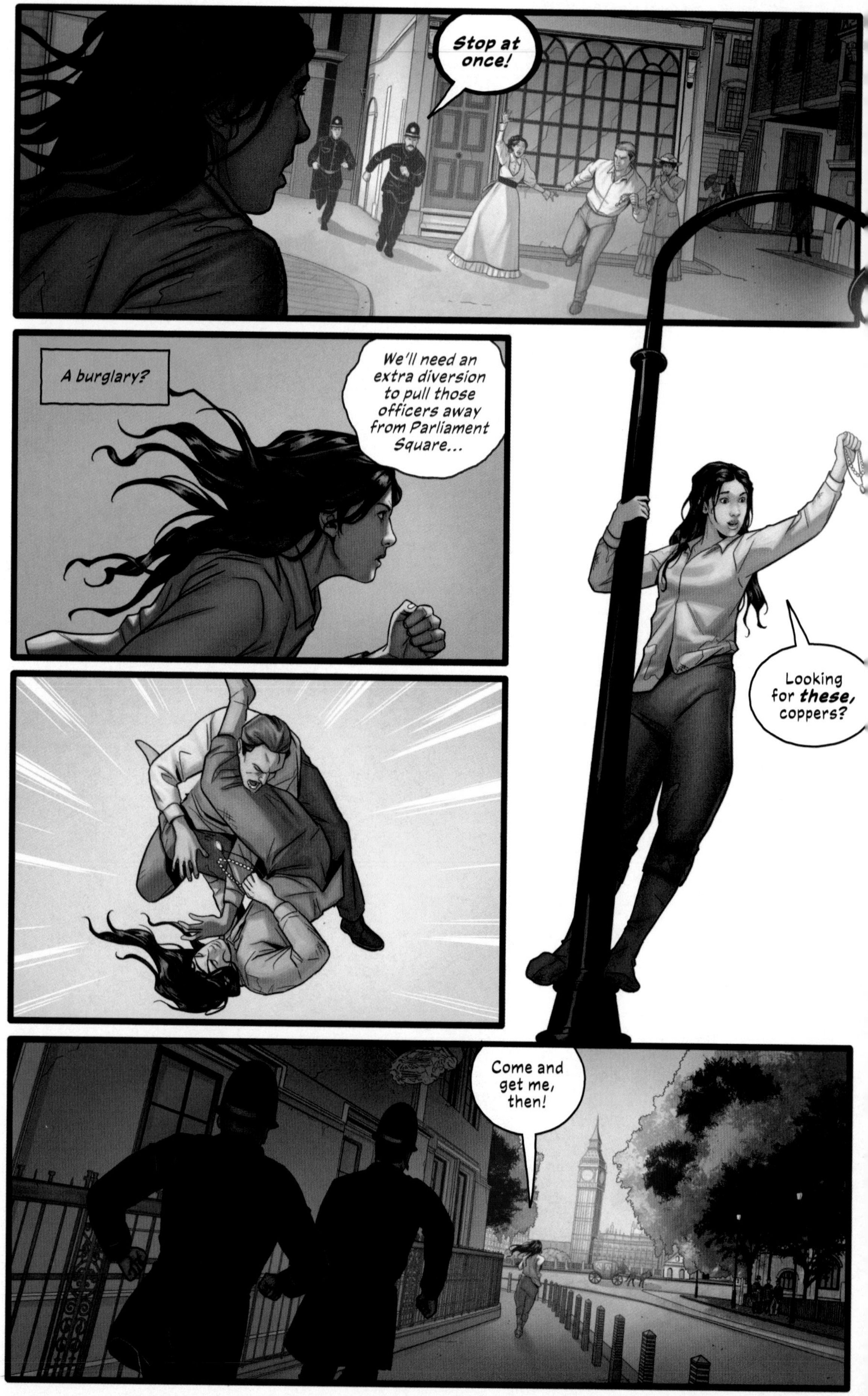
Stop at once!
A burglary?
We'll need an extra diversion to pull those officers away from Parliament Square...
Looking for *these,* coppers?
Come and get me, then!

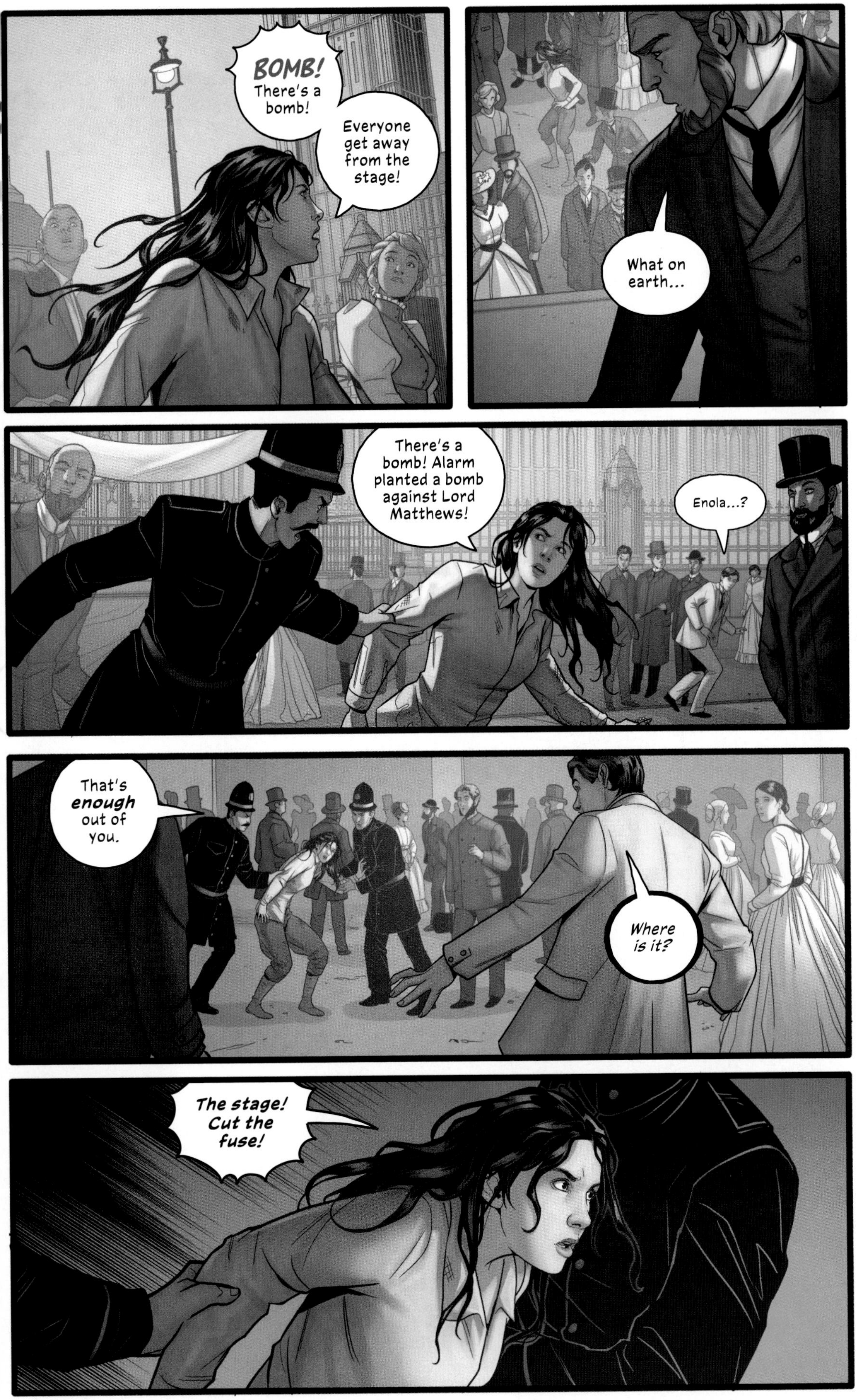
BOMB! There's a bomb!
Everyone get away from the stage!
What on earth...
There's a bomb! Alarm planted a bomb against Lord Matthews!
Enola...?
That's enough out of you.
Where is it?
The stage! Cut the fuse!

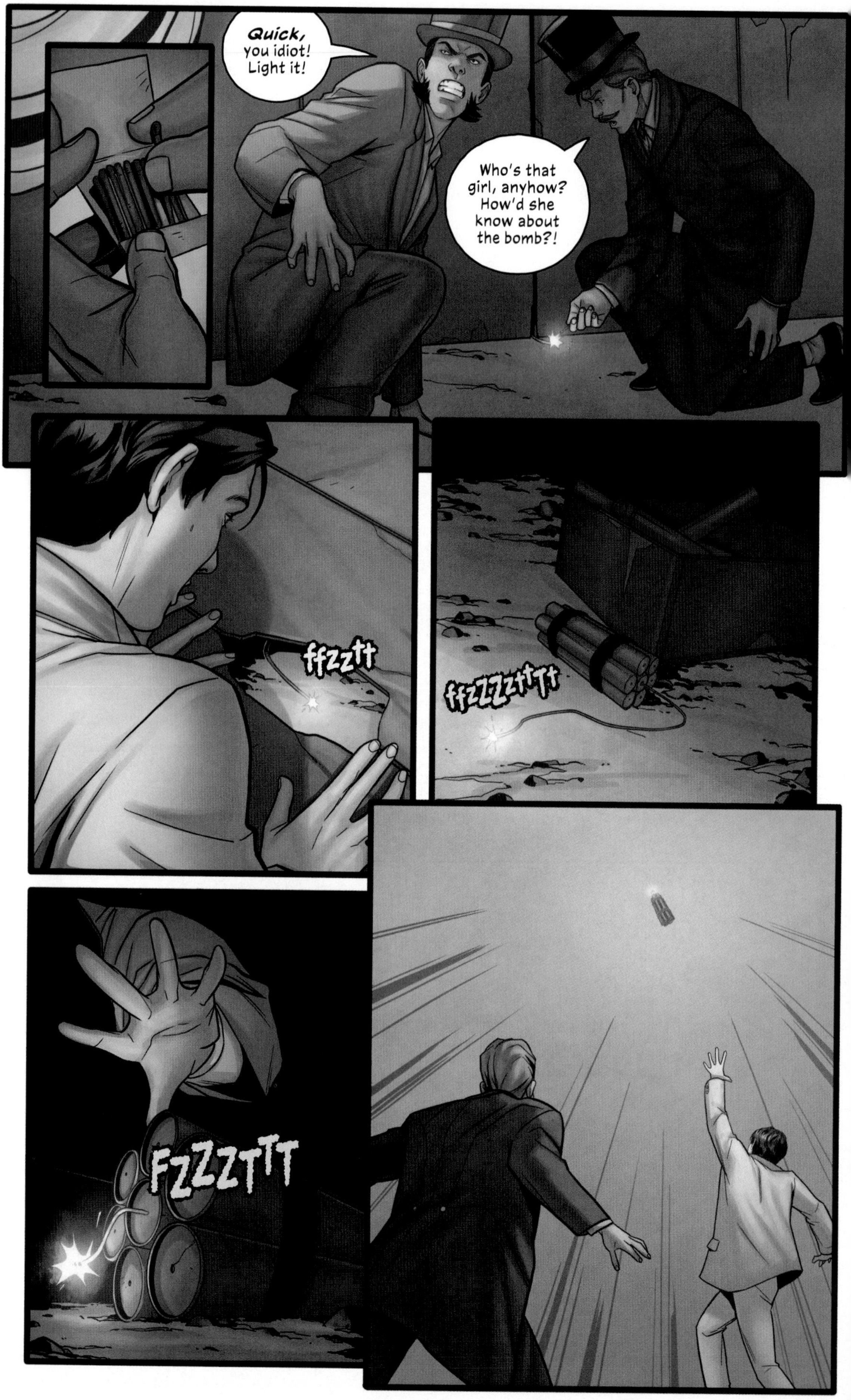
Quick, you idiot! Light it!
Who's that girl, anyhow? How'd she know about the bomb?!
ffzztt
ffzzzzttt
FZZZTTT

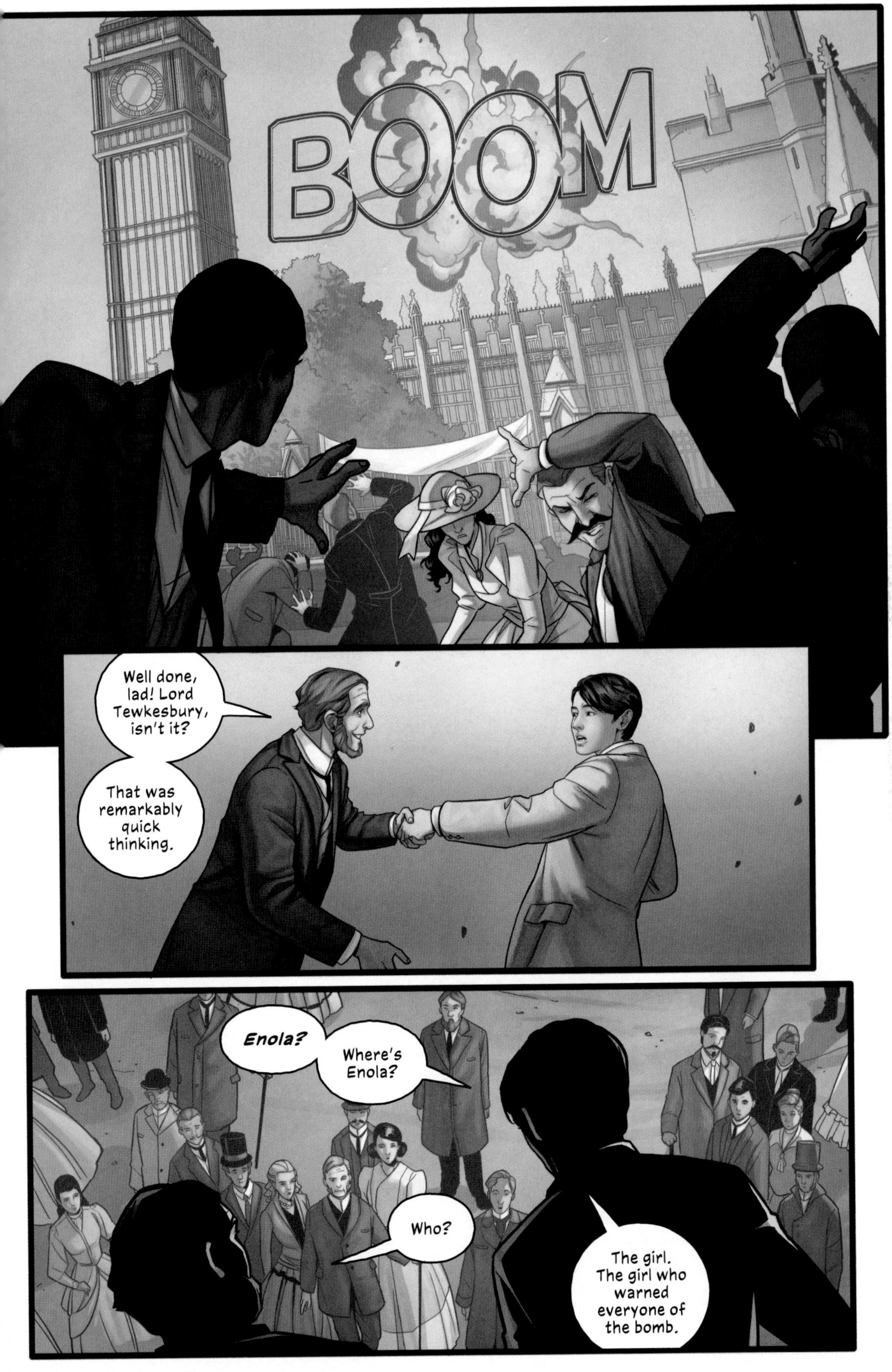
BOOM
Well done, lad! Lord Tewkesbury, isn't it?
That was remarkably quick thinking.
Enola?
Where's Enola?
Who?
The girl. The girl who warned everyone of the bomb.

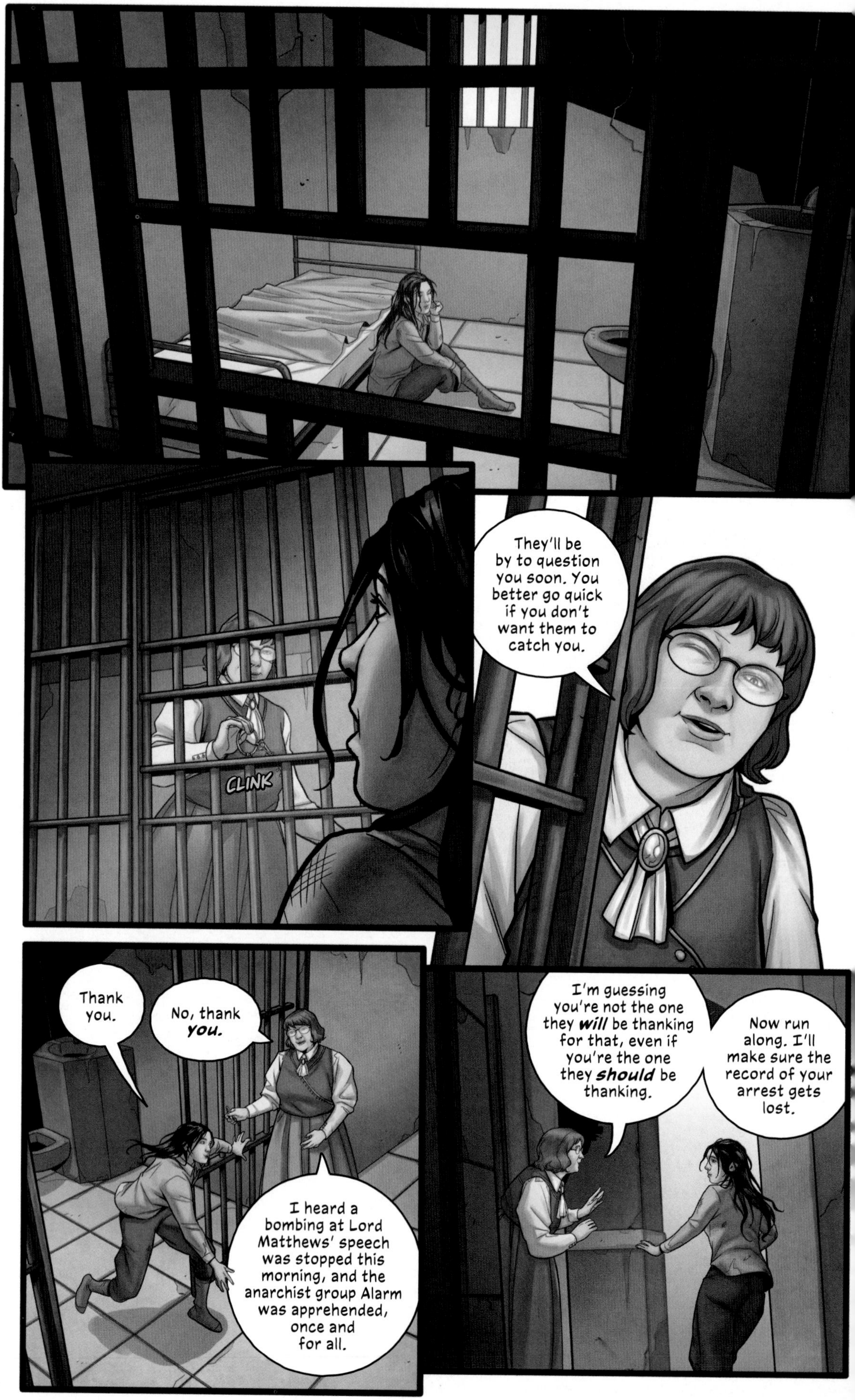

CLINK
They'll be by to question you soon. You better go quick if you don't want them to catch you.
Thank you.
No, thank *you.*
I heard a bombing at Lord Matthews' speech was stopped this morning, and the anarchist group Alarm was apprehended, once and for all.
I'm guessing you're not the one they *will* be thanking for that, even if you're the one they *should* be thanking.
Now run along. I'll make sure the record of your arrest gets lost.

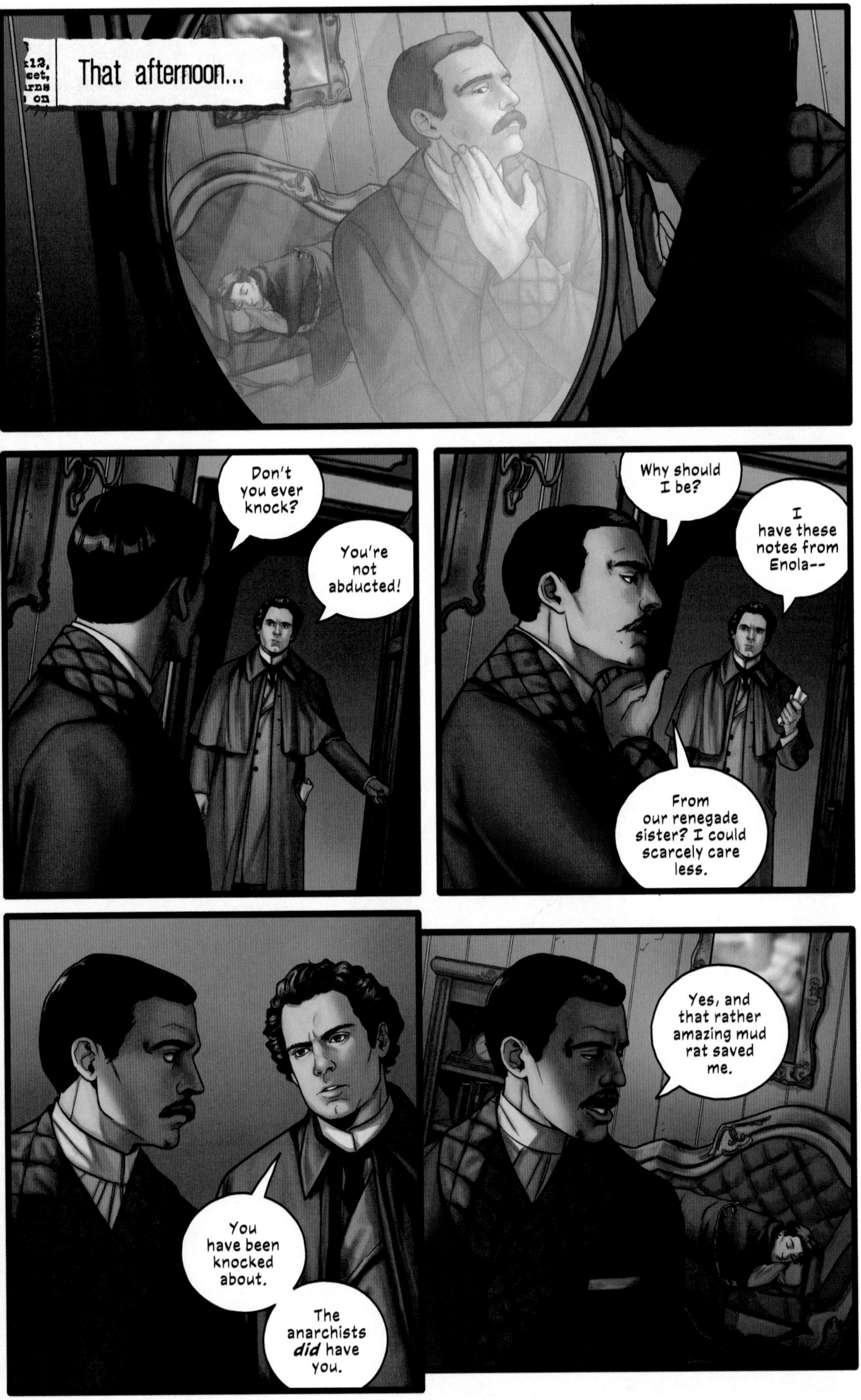
That afternoon...
Don't you ever knock?
You're not abducted!
Why should I be?
I have these notes from Enola--
From our renegade sister? I could scarcely care less.
You have been knocked about.
The anarchists *did* have you.
Yes, and that rather amazing mud rat saved me.

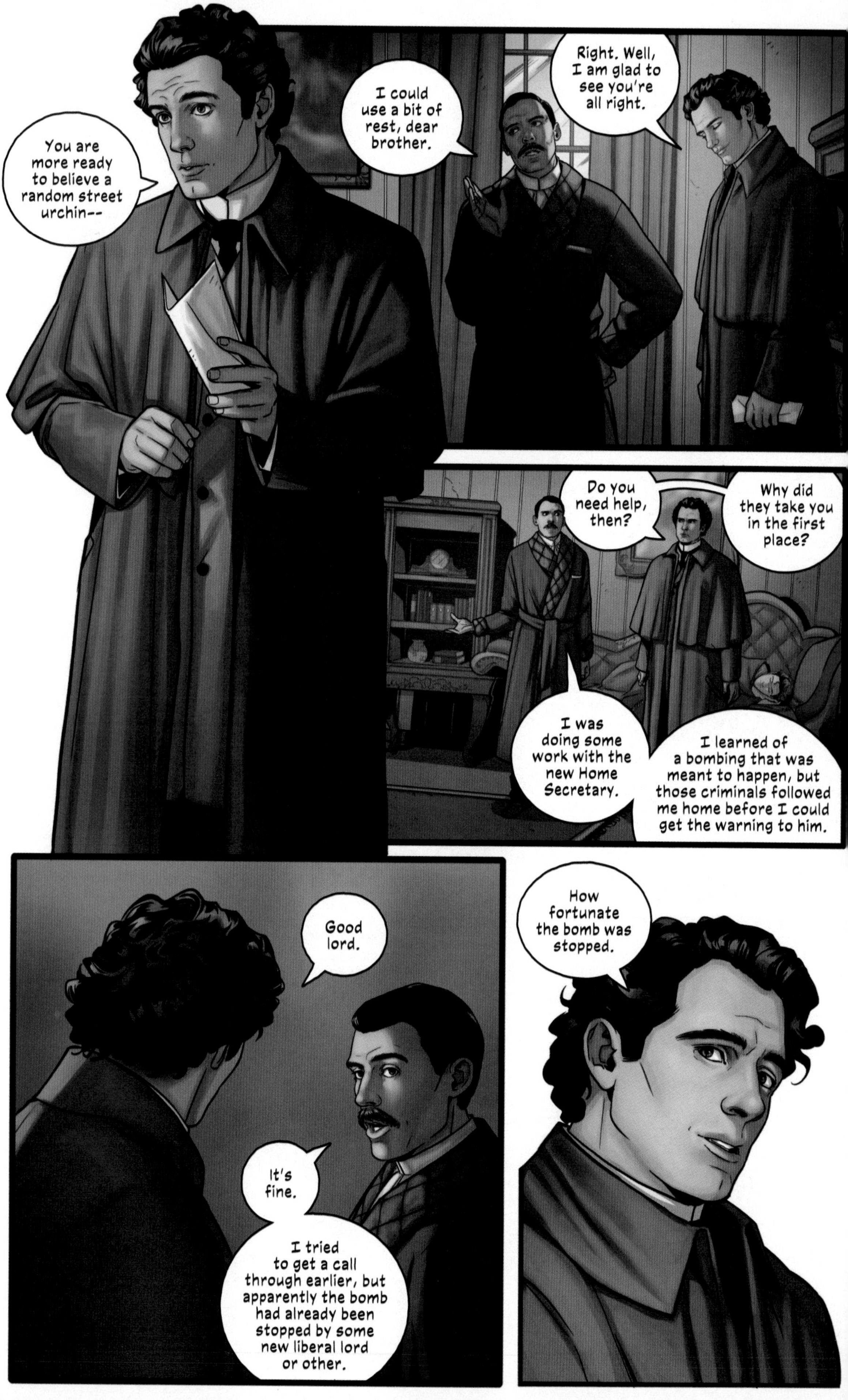
You are more ready to believe a random street urchin--
I could use a bit of rest, dear brother.
Right. Well, I am glad to see you're all right.
Do you need help, then?
Why did they take you in the first place?
I was doing some work with the new Home Secretary.
I learned of a bombing that was meant to happen, but those criminals followed me home before I could get the warning to him.
Good lord.
It's fine.
I tried to get a call through earlier, but apparently the bomb had already been stopped by some new liberal lord or other.
How fortunate the bomb was stopped.

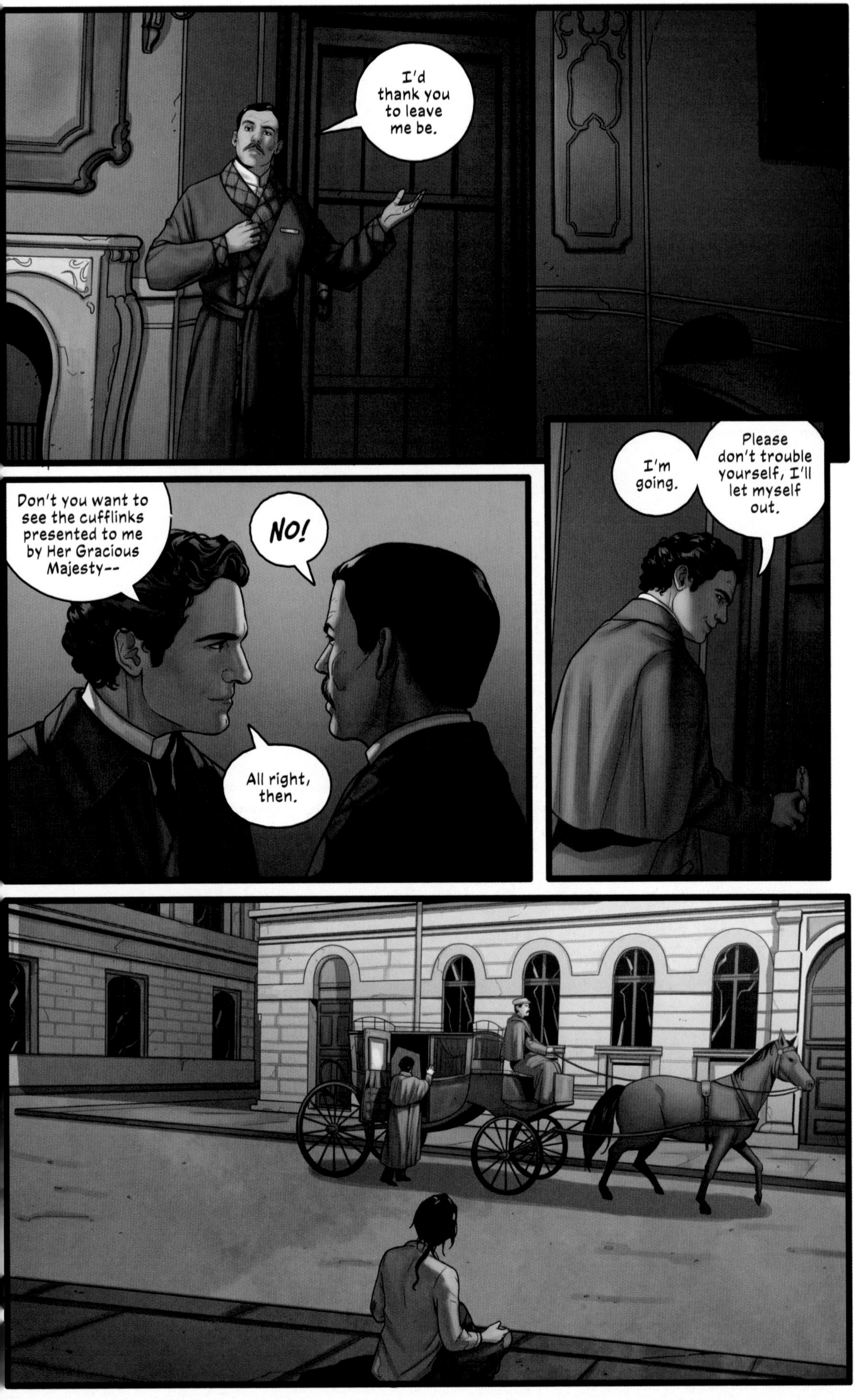
I'd thank you to leave me be.
Don't you want to see the cufflinks presented to me by Her Gracious Majesty--
NO!
All right, then.
I'm going.
Please don't trouble yourself, I'll let myself out.

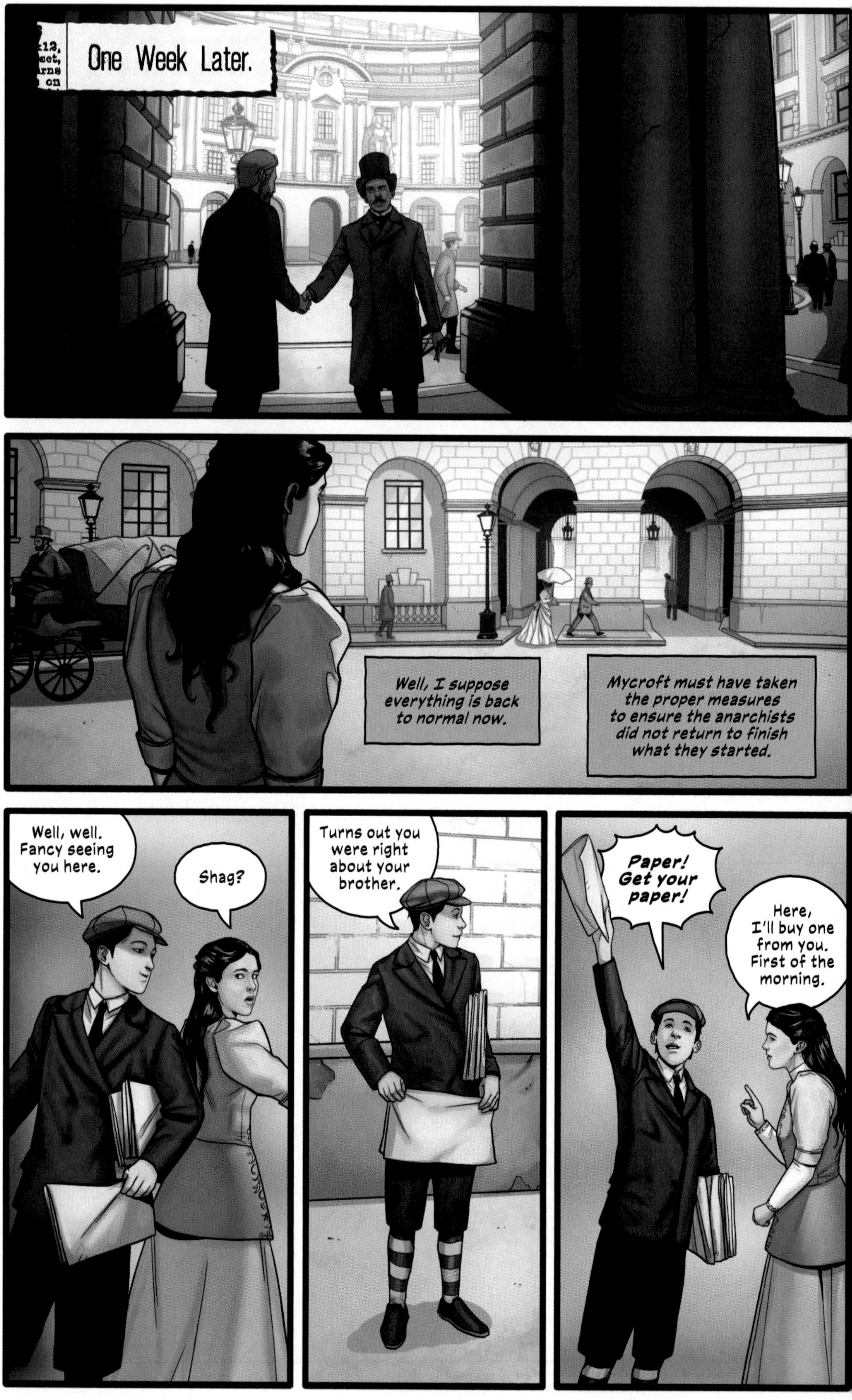
One Week Later.
Well, I suppose everything is back to normal now.
Mycroft must have taken the proper measures to ensure the anarchists did not return to finish what they started.
Well, well. Fancy seeing you here.
Shag?
Turns out you were right about your brother.
Paper! Get your paper!
Here, I'll buy one from you. First of the morning.

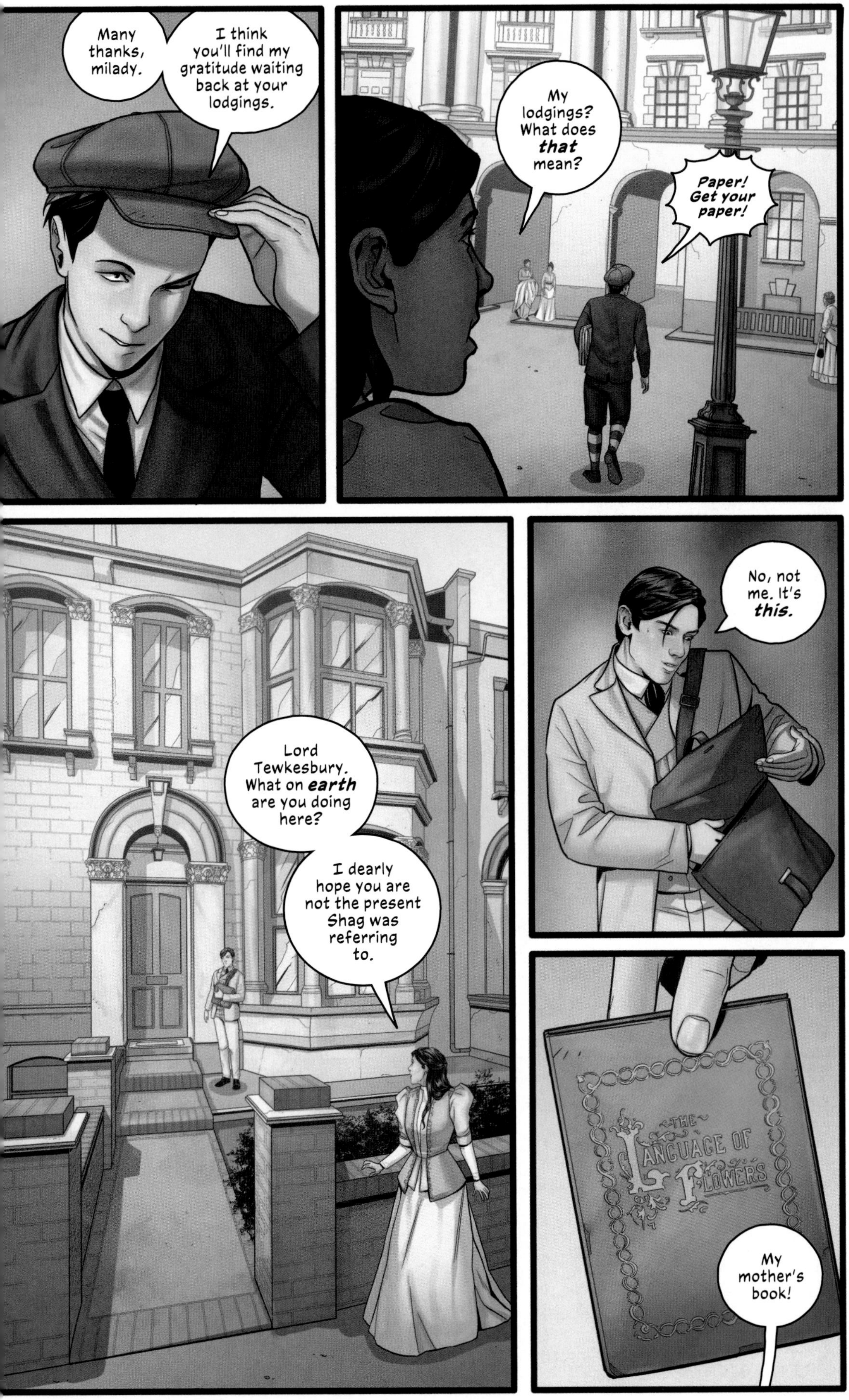
Many thanks, milady.
I think you'll find my gratitude waiting back at your lodgings.
My lodgings? What does *that* mean?
Paper! Get your paper!
Lord Tewkesbury. What on *earth* are you doing here?
I dearly hope you are not the present Shag was referring to.
No, not me. It's *this.*
THE LANGUAGE OF FLOWERS
My mother's book!

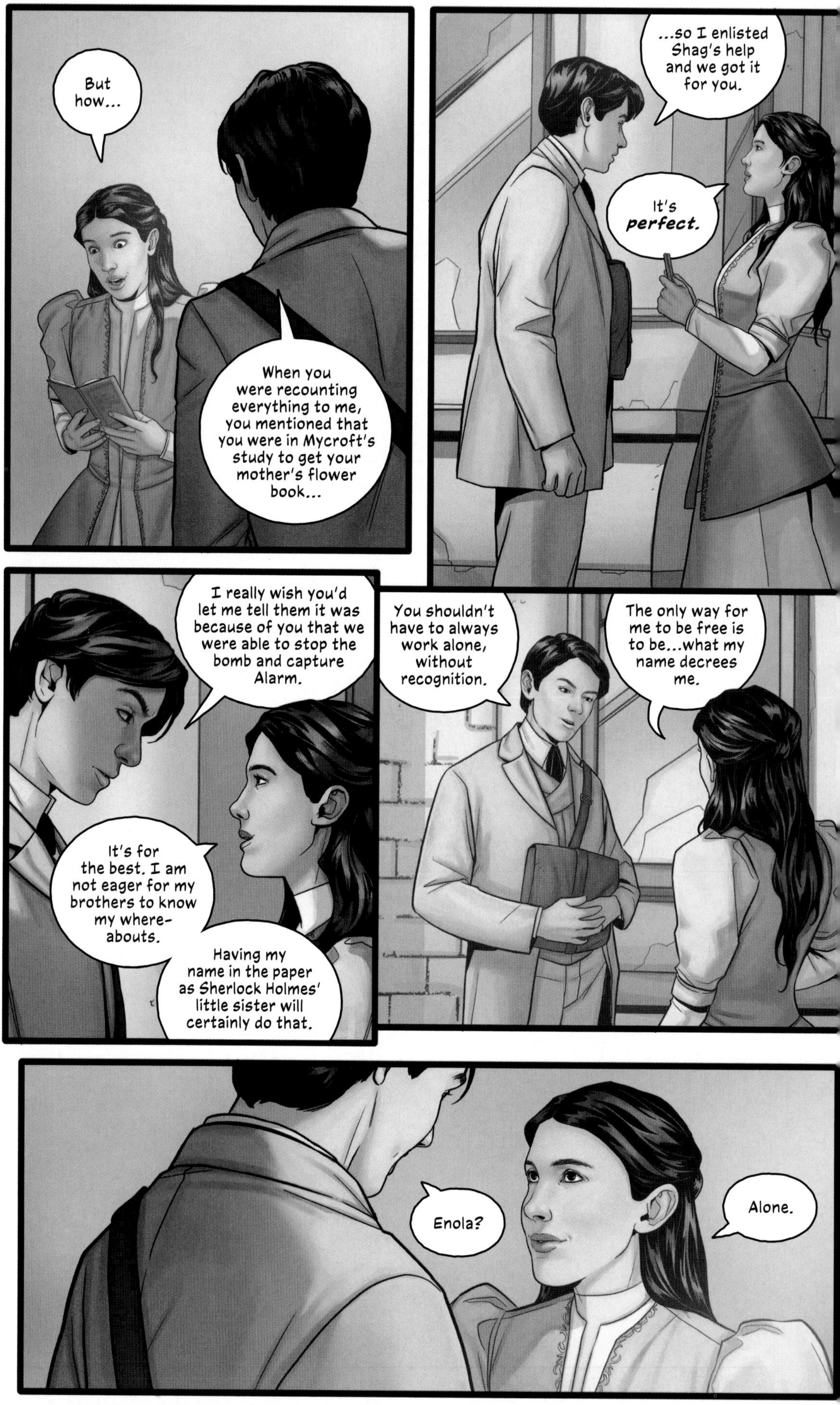
But how...
When you were recounting everything to me, you mentioned that you were in Mycroft's study to get your mother's flower book...
...so I enlisted Shag's help and we got it for you.
It's *perfect.*
I really wish you'd let me tell them it was because of you that we were able to stop the bomb and capture Alarm.
It's for the best. I am not eager for my brothers to know my where-abouts.
Having my name in the paper as Sherlock Holmes' little sister will certainly do that.
You shouldn't have to always work alone, without recognition.
The only way for me to be free is to be...what my name decrees me.
Enola?
Alone.

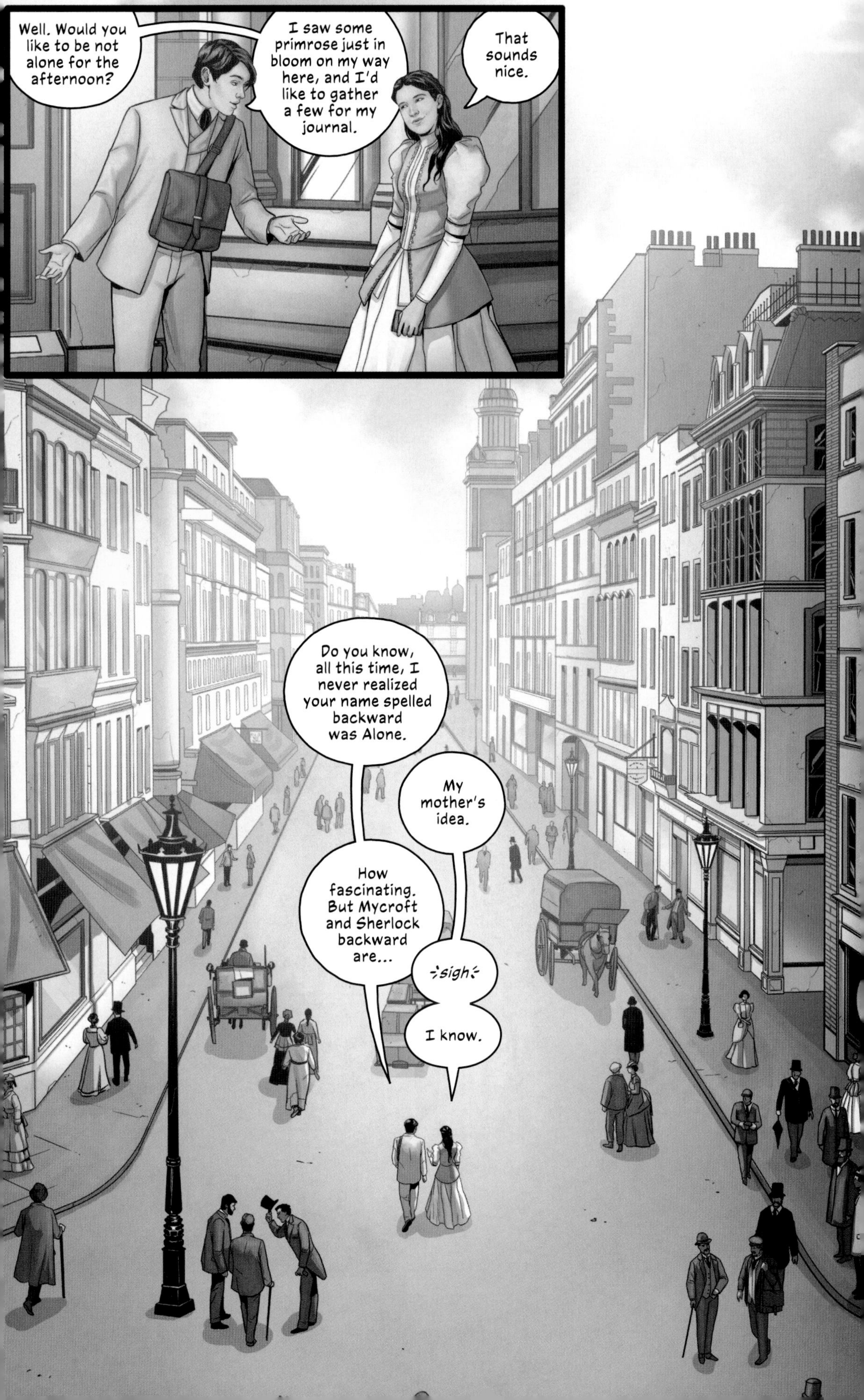
Well. Would you like to be not alone for the afternoon?
I saw some primrose just in bloom on my way here, and I'd like to gather a few for my journal.
That sounds nice.
Do you know, all this time, I never realized your name spelled backward was Alone.
My mother's idea.
How fascinating. But Mycroft and Sherlock backward are...
sigh
I know.

Script

Panel 1:

ENOLA: So you won't tell me where she is?
EDITH: I don't know where she is—but no, I wouldn't, even if I did.

Panel 2:

EDITH: Do you know who took your brother?
ENOLA: An anarchist group called Alarm.
EDITH: What do those villains want with Mycroft Holmes?

Panel 3:

Enola, interested; Edith shrugs and moves away from Enola (to get into fighting position), her smirk a bit smug.

ENOLA: You know Alarm?
EDITH: They are one kind of revolutionary, and I am another. So, yes, I know of them.
ENOLA: Would you know where to find them, or where I might—

MICKEY:

"This scene was a great way to include Edith in a story that might not otherwise include her. From a narrative standpoint, it makes sense for Enola to come to her for advice—if anyone knows how to fight against odds and subvert authority, it's Edith. She's living in a way that Enola wants to emulate, but unlike Enola, she's learned a thing or two about when to fight and when to mind her business. Just like Enola is going to bat for her family, Edith is holding her council to protect hers. It was also a fun way to showcase both of their martial arts skills—but I left that in Giorgia and Eren's capable hands."

Sketches

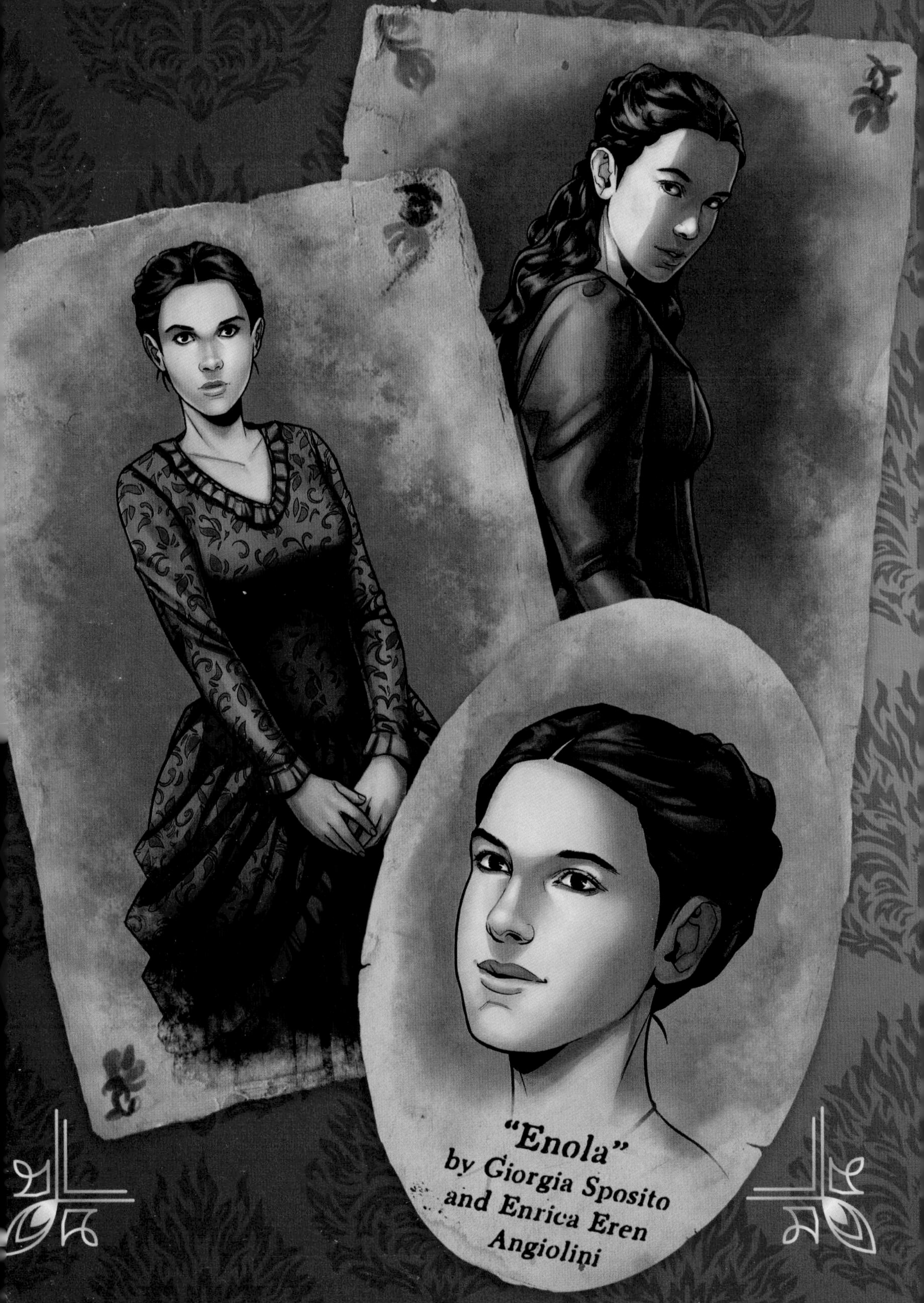

"Enola"
by Giorgia Sposito
and Enrica Eren
Angiolini

to Art

Panel 4:

Edith knocks Enola back a bit and gets into a fighting stance in clear invitation/challenge.

EDITH: You want information? You're going to earn it.

Panel 5:

They fight (whatever you want to do here is fine). The two women engage in jujitsu combat. They are evenly matched; they exhaust each other.

EDITH: If I were you, I'd be asking not where your brother is, but why they want him.

GIORGIA:

"When I read the script, one of the scenes I was looking forward to drawing was this one, set in the training room with its brick walls, the floor mattresses, the blackboard and the glass wall. I especially had fun studying the various jujitsu fight scenes and drawing them. Regarding the characters, I loved the interaction between Enola and Edith in the film and I tried to focus on this and bring it back into the graphic novel, working a lot on their expressions and gestures. The creative team loves Enola's character and her adventures and it all shines through on every page. I'm sure all of this will reach the readers."

EREN:

"When coloring these pages I referenced the scene from the movie in which we get to see Edith's training hall. I loved how the light filtered through the windows in the movie, so I wanted to replicate that in my colors. That also allowed me to play with the sunlight and how it creates shadows on Enola and Edith's faces, enhancing the brilliant expressions Giorgia drew and the likeness of the characters. The general palette of the scene is pretty muted, so Enola's lilac dress stands out in a lovely contrast. This was definitely one of my favorite scenes to color!"